For my wife, always

• A Personal Note from A.G. Mock •

WHAT WOULD IT take for one to kill, I find myself wondering. I think most would find it reasonable if it were an act of self-defense or protecting one you loved. But consider this: what if you were assured everything you could ever want for your life, as well as the lives of those around you? Perhaps you one day discover that you are terminally ill, but by taking another's life you can live their remaining years? What if you were permanently disabled and were assured your body or mind would be made pristine again if you would only kill another...perhaps one who was deemed vile or evil by civilized societal standards.

Could you really be so sure you wouldn't...?

This novel is the second in the *Gothic Horror* series, the continuation of the story which began in *The Little Woods*. Borne from a troubling concern as to why so many tragedies befell what by outward appearances seemed the paradisiacal place to grow up, this disturbing and gothic series explores the darkness that preys upon our world. Always there...lingering in our periphery.

I hope you will not only enjoy this novel but find it food for thought after its pages have been closed. Because you never truly know what you'd be prepared to do until you find the Devil himself has come knocking on *your* door...in your hour of greatest need.

So now it's time!

Come with me, and we'll head into the darkness together.

After all, you're not afraid to meet the Disciple, are you...?

Spookily Yours,

AG Mock

DISCIPLE

American Fiction Awards Winner

a.g. mock

EPOCH

EpochThrillers.com
AGMock.com

First paperback edition, Epoch Thrillers, December 2022.

Library of Congress PCN: 2022919769
ISBN: 978-1-7362919-3-1 | paperback
ISBN: 978-1-7362919-4-8 | hardcover

Published by Epoch Thrillers in Aiken, SC, United States
Epoch Thrillers and its raven imprint are trademarks of Epoch Thrillers

EPOCH THRILLERS
EpochThrillers.com
AGMock.com

ET 10 9 8 7 6 5 4 3

FIRST
DISCIPLE

The boundaries which divide

life from death

are at best shadowy and vague.

Who shall say where the one ends

and where the other begins?

—Edgar Allan Poe, *The Premature Burial*

The White Shadow

1:1

HER HEART HAMMERED in her chest, her pulse a runaway metronome. Sizzling in a veil of static, her mind froze as white-hot pokers of adrenaline sucked away her breath, only to return it at twice the tempo.

Between these labored gasps the woman fought away her tears. Cursing herself. Cursing the brothers. Cursing God most of all. She had always believed in the Universal Balance and the purpose Darkness served within it. For even shadows were borne of Light.

But that was before the Little Woods.

And the truth about Bryan.

Now a lifetime of conviction had been wrested inside-out, her faith, her life, perhaps her very soul falling prey to a thing so ancient and vile it was beyond our understanding.

And it all happened in just four days.

Well, actually four days plus eighteen years, one of her inner voices mocked. *You know, since that fateful summer when the boys played their game in the woods. Oh, plus a couple millennia before that. If we're going to be pedantic about it.*

A defense mechanism from more tragic years than were the woman's fair share, this voice served one singular purpose: to cut through the incapacitating mental static before her freight train of panic became a deadly, unstoppable juggernaut.

She wrung her hands together, twisting and kneading them so fiercely that her fingers had reddened.

C'mon now, sugar. You gotta pull yourself together, a different, more pragmatic voice coaxed. *Now's no time to be chicken-shit.*

Because there were footsteps.

Coming up the stairs.

At first her unconscious mind had dismissed them, so foreign was their sound at such an early hour that it must surely be another one of her dreams.

Those dark and dreadful dreams.

But when the old wooden treads of that empty stairwell groaned and scraped again, DeLaCroix Laveau started from thin and restless sleep. Bolting upright on the loveseat she sucked in breath, releasing it in a shriek when the forgotten bottle she'd wedged between the cushions dropped to the floor. Against the backdrop of night the sound was nothing short of a car crash. The bottle spun across the hardwood floor, humming an eerie tune which steadily lowered in pitch until it rolled to a stop against her treasured technicolor rag rug.

Della cocked her head to one side, staring at the tiny reflection of the moonlit window glinting off the bottle's curved glass.

She listened.

A snare drum patter of rain upon the metal roof; summer storm winds blowing—*no, whistling*, Della felt—through the trees as it danced across their branches, moving them in enchanting rhythms. Soft bellows of thunder resonating far, far across the hills.

But beneath this atmospheric score Della was certain there hid a different sound, and she quieted her breaths to find it.

For a moment there was nothing more, even the wind and rain subsiding as if submitting to her will. But then…faintly…she found it. A noise unlike the others. Coming from inside the building. Holding her breath she angled an ear toward the stairwell door.

There….

Buried within the others: a hollow thud, like a heavy weight upon the stairs. Followed by an unusual scraping sound she could only equate to fingernails dragging across each step.

She listened harder, focusing.

Silence.

Not allowing a single breath.

Silence.

Only the sound of her heart pounding in her chest.

Silence.

Then a harrowing *crack* that echoed like a gunshot through the stairwell and vacuumed the breath from Della's chest. She leapt to her feet, choking as she stumbled backward through the dark, her grasping hands clutching nothing but empty air until her palms found the cool, reassuring firmness of the kitchenette wall. She pressed the small of her back against it, steadying herself and her nerves as she stared unblinking at the stairwell door.

Her heart in her throat, this moment lasted an eternity. But eventually it came: another series of scrapes, another groan of tired wood. But this time, far from hiding within the storm's natural soundtrack, the pairings resonated throughout the stairwell as something climbed each step. Slowly. Unhurried. Deliberate. No longer concerned if it were heard.

The skin across Della's back prickled.

Is this part of your intimidation tactic? she asked only in her mind, not daring to give voice to the question. Her quickened pulse throbbed in her neck by way of reply. *If so, it's working. Okay? You win. Whatever you are. Please just go away now.*

Two more heavy thumps. Then a long, scrabbled raking across the landing halfway up, and her chest tightened with realization. Because it wasn't footsteps and fingernails, as Della first imagined. No, that wasn't it.

It sounded like something with hooves.

But impossibly…also claws.

Her head grew light, the synapses in her mind shorting. She started to wheeze, the threat of hyperventilation hot on the heels of those thin, gravelly wisps.

If you black out, you're done for. Got it? Dead.

She bent forward, clasping her hands behind her knees, and gave life to the scream which had been so desperate to loose. The air emptied from her lungs, expelling the excess carbon dioxide with it, and the crippling static cleared just enough to conjure the mental muscle memory of a grounding exercise she'd employed thousands of times before. Inhaling through her nose and out her mouth, she envisioned an igloo of light—a dome of impenetrable protection blazing all around her—and started counting and praying at once.

One.

Saint Michael, be with me.

Two!

... Breathing out.

Three.

Saint Michael, be with me!

Four.

Breathing in ....

Five!

Saint Mic—

—She was extracted from the incantation by a stench so intense it became metallic upon her tongue, an acrid mix of iron and sickening rot. She gagged as her eyes opened to the bottle at her feet, its contents seeping into the rug. Stale vodka had darkened and amplified the colors so that reds were deep burgundy; maroons, muddy brown. Creams, the color of pus. To Della they were congealing pools of blood and decay and she fell to her knees, retching... oblivious of the thing which now loomed over her.

Its face swollen and charred, one eye empty, the thing that had once been a child moved closer, reaching for the woman as she heaved. Three of the dead boy's digits were snapped from his hands. Splintered and blackened bones protruded from the tips of those that remained. Clicking as they fingered the air about Della's head, they were the flitting tongues of a seven-headed serpent savoring her revulsion.

She continued to gag in violent spasms as he pulled her to him unawares, his flayed and blistered hands palming the crown of her head as it bobbed up and down—over and over again.

A prurient grin twisted the demon's contorted mask.

"Hoc est corpus meum, pro vobis datum," he broadcast in low, grating vibrations as if to a servile priestess kneeling before her worm-riddled king. *"Comede in honore meo. Comede!"*

The corpse tossed its head back in laughter and it lolled upon its elongated neck, a piercing falsetto bubbling up from the torn throat and expanding until it was the screeching caterwaul of a thousand disharmonic flutes. Soon the sound became the screaming of the very wind itself as the storm danced through the trees.

And the clawing in the stairwell climbed closer.

Faster....

II

Della rose to her feet, shaking and confused. She wept silently as she emerged from the nightmare, wiping spit and gelatinous bile from her mouth.

Every cell of her being tremored.

It had felt so real. The clawing in the stairwell; the sensation of something holding her head as she gagged, cradling—even bidding—its up-and-down motion. And yet her mind was otherwise blank, recalling nothing of the night and very little of the past few days. She certainly had no idea why she'd awakened to find herself kneeling on the floor, sweat pouring from her body; no recollection of why she'd felt the need to down so much vodka that she was now encircled by pools of vomit across the rug.

All she knew was that she was filled with the dread of a thing so unholy and violating it was impossible to comprehend.

She scanned the small apartment, eyes darting. Projected across the room, sheets of moonlit rain upon the windowpanes caused every surface to slither; every shadow to move. Every corner to harbor a lurking ghoul.

The overhead light dispelled them all with a click, the tube flickering to life as Della shielded her face from its blistering fluorescence. She blinked to protect her pale, smoke-green eyes until the inverted bursts behind them faded.

When she reopened them she was no longer in her apartment.

Instead, a bright, sterile hallway stretched before her, the air crisp with the aroma of cleansers.

Is this a vision? A dream inside a dream, maybe? Such internal dialog was routine as DeLaCroix Laveau's rationale and extra-sensory processes sifted truth from fiction, reality from fantasy. Present from past or future. *Perhaps it's a tangible Rememory.*

The latter had begun to occur more regularly as Della's intuitive abilities honed. She would find herself at times immersed in what seemed a physical reality ... but was, in fact, an artificial event created from the recall of her subconscious energy. Such is the human condition that none of us receives any moment in time with pure, impartial objectivity, for each is viewed through a lens of our past experiences and perspectives. This is even more prevalent during times of recall, and the reason why police detectives are faced with the unlikely task of establishing the facts of a crime when no two witness statements will ever match ... or even recall the event in remotely the same way.

For Della, the spiritual ability to push this innate, natural subjectivity of memory to a supernatural extreme would often result in the creation of a new reality altogether where specific features would be accentuated, sometimes to the point of being caricatured. Other aspects might be lessened, or even withdrawn entirely if deemed redundant. And in some cases several events might be blended together as one, including events she did not experience firsthand, allowing her to easily extract their emotions and commonality by making them a single, new encounter.

Hence not reality. And not a memory, as such.

But a Rememory.

She began walking slowly down the hospital corridor as the tube lights overhead stuttered and sizzled—with every step the stroboscopic effect worsening—and the hairs on the back of her neck stiffened. Goosebumps gathered between her shoulder blades and began marching down her back like a line of ants.

This was supposed to be a place of safety and healing. But in this new interpretation Della felt only deep vibrations of menace. For a moment she considered pulling herself out of the Rememory, only to castigate and reassure herself at once.

Now, sugar. You know by now you're supposed to be here.

Which was true. For though she hadn't seen her, Della knew there was a woman she sought in this bleak and soulless place.

A woman called . . . *Rebecca*?

She began choking as the memory of the name came to her, as if the air itself had become thick with exhaust fumes. The brilliance of the corridor extinguished in turn and she was now on a floor, gasping for air in a dark and windowless place. Above her, three small beacons shone weakly, each reflecting a whimsical design that looked like two letter 'J's entwined by some thread.

No, not letters, she realized as they hovered over her head. *It's a stylized boat anchor. Designed on something metallic.*

BRASS BUTTONS.

The image was fleeting, lasting only a moment before the shimmering buttons morphed into three flickering candles which burned upon the dais of a chapel. Though the only light, they projected warm brilliance and safety. Yet there was an underlying current here too, Della felt. A brooding energy all too eager to pervert the temple's vibrations of faith and succor to dark, weary abandon. Given the chapel's diminutive size, the crucifix above the altar was disproportionately large. Perhaps even life-size. And bound to it was not the Christ Savior ... but a girl, shrieking in pain.

Oh my God, Rebecca's daughter. That's ... Diane!

Now the cross was no longer wood, but thick rope wrapped around Diane's neck, the girl's delicate fingers scrabbling and clawing but the cord was too tight. Legs kicking and unable to scream, her mouth was a silent oval as the walls of the chapel expanded then blew apart, the child hanging like a grotesque marionette—

in those woods

—so young and all alone—

those repulsive woods

—as her father stood helpless—

oh my God, Bryan

—before killing himself there?

And then there was his brother, Ian ....

With a sharp intake of breath Della was jolted from the Rememory. Fragments of recall assaulted her senses as she ran to the rear window and pressed her face to the glass, its condensation cool and grounding upon her flushed cheek. There, in the gravel parking lot, sat her beloved VW Thing.

Right next to it was a blue Chevy Blazer.

Rebecca Cockerton's Blazer.

She squinted as the dial of her watch swam in and out of focus, the hands finally settling on three-forty-two a.m.

This doesn't—I don't know—God, help me, what's happening?

A wooden stair tread groaned and fresh panic rose in her throat.

It hadn't been a nightmare.

C'mon, girl, remember!

She paced the living room in tight, concentric circles.

I know there was ... something ... about Ian. At his brother's house. I was angry—no, I was hurt—by an argument we'd had. Something he didn't like me saying about... about his sister-in-law? I came home. Late. I started to drink, and Ian kept calling. Wouldn't stop until I picked up. He was going to collect Rebecca from the hospital. Later this morning?

She then remembered the promise she insisted Ian make, that he would bring Rebecca by the tavern to see her on their way home from the hospital.

But why?

Something thumped on the last stair tread. Followed by a scrabbling on the landing.

Della flinched then hurried to the door. Running her hands over its rough surface in the dark, her icy fingers found the dead bolt, checked it, then checked it again. Her mouth was dry, her pulse becoming a noticeable rhythm in her throat. Still she pressed her train of thought forward.

Why did I need to see Rebecca so badly?

Waves of confusion ebbed in and out, tendrils of stubborn denial still clinging to her thoughts. Tamping down the fear and forcing aside the confusion, she implored her spirit guide to allow her to reconnect with the past four days and reclaim her purpose in whatever brutal reality they presented.

The response was instant.

Word-for-word, that night's phone call with Ian replayed in her mind, the one immediately before choosing oblivious detachment at the bottom of a vodka bottle:

"Bryan said that seven childhood friends died," she'd asked as the line clicked and buzzed, a sure sign that a summer storm was beginning to brew. "But are you sure? What I mean is, was Jack Raker's death ever confirmed?"

"No," Ian answered honestly and without hesitation. He audibly swallowed as if realizing a moment too late what such an admission might lead Della to discover. Recovering quickly, he switched tack. "Listen, I want to clarify something with you, okay? Rebecca can't be

pregnant. However you choose to interpret—or misinterpret—what Dr. Fieldhouse was saying. In fact, Rebecca can never be pregnant again. Not after Diane. That's why they adopted Andr—"

The stairwell door shuddered, a percussive bang that squeezed Della's chest like a vice. Her heart mirrored the pounding as it was hammered upon again, over and over, in fast, intense strikes.

"Della! Open up!" The voice was urgent, commanding. "I know you're in there! Open the door!"

Behind the door Ian Cockerton smirked at the red dust which had been spread in a haphazard line across the landing, nothing more than a visual barrier between where he stood and the entry to Della's apartment.

"Brick dust, Della? Really?" he spoke loudly from behind the heavy wood door, his voice echoing down the stairs. "I really thought you were more sophisticated than that."

He shook his head, appearing almost disappointed.

Della had no words, offering only silence in reply as she crept back from the door, her chest constricting.

Ian watched with curiosity as her shadow shrank from the gap beneath to allow cold, fluorescent light to stream into the stairwell, illuminating his feet. "If you believe this stuff, why are you moving away, Della? Isn't brick dust supposed to keep you safe 'cause your enemies can't cross it, or some Voodoo bullshit like that?"

Della ran her tongue over moistureless lips, achieving nothing in her attempt to wet them. She swallowed hard, her voice wavering though she tried hard for it not to. "G-Get out of here, Ian! I have a g-g—"

"—G-Gun?" Ian finished for her, the tone of the single word soaked in derision. "No, Della. You don't. Remember?"

He paused, allowing the reality of her situation to sink in, and on the other side of the door Della's eyes fell upon the handbag she'd tossed on the floor hours earlier, its contents raked through.

"The police have your pretty little gun. Tucked away somewhere in an evidence locker. You know, seeing as my brother used it to blow out the back of his skull 'n all yesterday. But something tells me that you've just figured that out for yourself, haven't you ...."

For good measure he added a snarky, "...Sugar."

Della recoiled, the low vibrations Ian broadcast coming at her like the bass from a speaker stack at a rock concert. Waves of destructive energy spooled around her, stifling her aura and twisting into her gut like a snake. How had she not felt this before? Given everything they'd been through; the rare intuition they both shared? And yet she'd felt nothing of this dark energy from him.

Oh, the Great Deceiver, she was sure Ian answered in telepathic vibrations, and a strangled cry escaped her lips as she withdrew further from the door to the protective cocoon of the tiny kitchen.

She steadied herself behind the breakfast bar, her fingers brushing the handle of a bread knife. It had been more than two years since she'd bought the tavern, which included the apartment above it, and still the knife hadn't found a permanent home. Too wide for the knife block; too long for the silverware drawer. And so it laid there, upon the counter, day-in and day-out. Until it had simply become invisible.

It wasn't invisible now.

Dozens of sharp, serrated edges glinted in the light and Della swiped it from the counter with a soft, metallic *clang*. Would she really find it in her to use it? And against Ian, of all people?

If I have to, I will. I swear to God I will, she affirmed in bullish vibrations, the message intended for her own benefit as much as it was for the man on the landing. Because it couldn't possibly be Ian behind that door.

Could it?

"You killed your own brother! Jesus, help me. You killed Bryan. Right in front of his own daughter!"

Ian scuffed his foot through the brick dust, casually brushing it this way and that. It feathered out with a subdued, almost soothing sound like the raking of sand patterns in a Japanese *karesansui* zen garden. Layered atop the pattering of rain on the tin roof, it was almost entrancing.

"No, I didn't. You got that part wrong." Head down, spoken softly, it was a statement but seemed perforated with uncertainty. "Hey. You know this stuff only works if you believe in it, right?"

Della said nothing, her nails digging into the knife's mahogany handle.

"The brick dust, I mean," he clarified. "It only works if the other person believes in its Magick, too. Kinda like those old-world Hoodoo curses . . . or Catholic absolution."

"Why, Ian?"

"Well. We had this conversation in the car that day, didn't we? And unless I'm mistaken, it was you who referred to Catholicism as being filled with—wait, let me get it right—'bizarre ceremonial ritual, mystical ideology and superstition.'"

"WHY, IAN?" Della's voice cracked, on the verge of tears.

"Oh . . . . You mean Bryan." He cleared his throat, the smugness gone from his expression. "Like I said, that didn't happen the way you think it did. Let me in. And we'll talk."

Della steeled her nerves. "If you don't believe, then why don't you just cross that line and open the door yourself? Even though she knew it was locked, she took a deep breath and braced her left hand with her right, steadying the knife. Her body stiffened, her eyes unblinking and fixated on the door.

"They're coming, Della. You've been marked."

The door burst open without warning.

Wood splinters exploded like shrapnel as it slammed against the wall. Catching in the jamb at an angle, it twisted, teetering as plaster showered down like volcanic ash.

Ian Cockerton walked in, stepping across the red line with barely noticeable hesitation. A cursory scan of the apartment found Della in the farthest corner of the kitchenette, rigidly holding the gleaming knife as far in front of her as her arms would reach.

He took a breath as he studied her face, a mix of regret and captivation upon his own. "I could have loved you, you know," he admitted, the affection in his voice sincere, almost playful.

It was the last thing she expected, and the knife unconsciously loosened in Della's grip, its point dipping toward the floor.

His tone instantly sobered. "I don't want to hurt you. I don't. But they're coming. And if you're still here, I won't stop them. They'll do worse than kill you. Do you understand?"

He moved closer, the distance between them swiftly cut in half.

"They'll devour you, desecrate all that you are, have been, or ever could be."

Della didn't flinch. Instead, the knife sprung back up, its tip resolutely angled in the direction of his throat.

"Not another step, Ian!"

"It's a blunt-tipped bread knife, Della. Do you really think it's gonna stop anything? As easily—or as quickly—as you need it to?"

"I-I think," she momentarily stuttered before adrenaline-fueled confidence began to bubble up from a place deep inside. "I think it's enough to make it a fair fight."

She inched toward him, squaring her shoulders, their distance reduced to a mere handful of feet. The knife became more comfortable in her grip, and she brandished it with a single hand.

"So, what say you just call it a night and turn back around, before we have to find out."

"See? That spirit right there. That's exactly what I'm talking about. I love that about you. God, I really do!" He was beaming, shaking his head while taking a small, gliding step closer.

Reflecting inward in that moment, Della hadn't noticed. "How can you even *say* that?"

"What ... that I'm into your spirit?"

"No. LOVE. You've got no right to even use that word. You sick, treacherous psychofuck."

Psychofuck? Where did that come from? She'd never used that word in her life, but it had slid across her lips as smoothly as a Delta oyster. Something about her aura was shifting, exposing vibrations unfamiliar to her. Becoming…murky.

Ian cocked his head slowly to one side. Evaluating. "There's more to what's happening than you realize. When we were in the chapel? I experienced something, Della. A spiritual download. Universal insight so profound I can't begin to describe it."

"I know. I was there!"

"No, it was so much more than what you saw. I wish I could tell you in a way to make you understand. And I'll try, I promise. But right now we just have to get you out of here. They're coming, Della. For *you*. And I don't have the time to explain."

"Who's coming, Ian? You're the only one threatening me!" She gestured toward the door hanging cockeyed behind him, but Ian's gaze upon her remained resolute.

Skirting along the counter, Della pressed the small of her back against the breakfast bar, using it as a guide so she could keep her eyes on Ian. He rotated in place, following along but not moving any closer as she edged toward the bookshelf.

"It's all here," she said as her foot nudged a book lying face down and spreadeagle on the floor, its spine buckling. It was the book she'd rediscovered—or more accurately, had rediscovered her—earlier that night: Dr. R. Bartholomew's, *The New Apocrypha*. She kicked it and the hardcover skirted past the rug, pages wafting. It came to a spinning stop at Ian's feet. "Pick it up."

Ian lowered his gaze but not his head.

"Pick up the fucking book, Ian!"

He held up his hands in mock surrender. "Okay, but I won't move from this spot. So don't freak out and come at me with that thing."

"This blunt ol' thing, sugar?" She twisted the blade in the light, drawn to its shimmer. "I thought this wouldn't stop you."

He smirked, a visible profession of admiration rather than scorn as he retrieved the oversized volume at his feet. "I said it couldn't stop any*thing*. It wasn't a reference to me."

Della waggled the knife. "Just read it. I want us both to hear the words in your own voice." She didn't concern herself with a specific page or passage, as she knew the one they were meant to hear would find its way to this moment.

She must have also projected this notion in an unintended telepathic wave, for Ian lifted an eyebrow in Della's direction. Without question he started reciting from the top of the random page to which the book opened:

"... Finally unleashed from the wilderness where it had been cast, the archdemon Azazel, leader of the Watchers, shall mock the seven archangels. It shall feed in this place upon the innocence of seven sacrificial scapegoats, one for each of its blasphemous heads. Then, and—'"

"STOP."

Della stared unblinking as Bartholomew's words hung in the air from Ian's tongue, blending into the trance-like rhythm of the rain and a faraway, rolling rumble that was felt more than heard.

Ian's eyes met hers and he allowed this final shared moment to wash over him; to etch upon his memory. Though it would pass in an instant, an eternity of regret flooded his thoughts.

How he wished he could rewind every ill-fated event which had led to this moment and return to the blissful ignorance of not realizing how tenuous his happiness had been, how fragile its course that everything could turn on a dime.

So easily and without his consent.

Skipping work for a beer and some baseball down at the 'Major League' with Felipe was now a lifetime ago—an utter impossibility that it was all but a matter of weeks.

And then there was Anonymous, the violent stranger who had been the catalyst of everything.

After the shooting Ian had become consumed by the realization that any given moment in our lives could spin from our control and mutate to become an indelible choice at an ominous crossroads.

But he knew now that Della was right: there was no such thing as coincidence. Anonymous and he had not been a fluke, but rather, their meeting ordained by an instrument of darkness. An entity with interminable patience, hell-bent on finishing what it had begun so very long ago.

Had the shooting in the bar never happened, Ian would not have succumbed to his long-suppressed psychic vulnerabilities. He would not have reopened the spiritual doorway which allowed the revenant of his dead childhood friend, Matt Chauncey, to return. That same aberration of his meek young friend would not have been in the middle of the road on Hamburger Hill, and Ian's parents might still be alive. He would not have then returned to that childhood home and his brother would not be dead . . . because Bryan and he would never have gone back into those fucking woods. Ever again.

"Seven, Ian!" The authority in Della's voice plucked him from the retrospect. "It shall feed on seven innocents! You and Bryan—*both of you*—had me believe that seven of your childhood friends had already died in the Little Woods, all those years ago. But that isn't true, is it. Jack Raker's still alive, isn't he, Ian. *Isn't he!*"

"I told you when we spoke last night that his death was never confirmed. I don't know if Jack's still aliv—"

"Can you not stop the lies, Ian, even now? Only six friends were desecrated, so it needed one more. And it got it. Your brother was about to sacrifice his own life to save his little girl. It was an act of love and would have ended the cycle. Do you not get that? It may have taken eighteen years, but Bryan . . . is the seventh innocent."

Breathless, Della visibly wilted before him, everything about her stature shrinking. She lowered the knife, clutching her sides as tears welled in her eyes, the light behind them dimming. Drained of all but the primal will to survive, she could only cast in vibration the words she could not say.

You shot him, Ian. YOU. You killed your own brother.

"NO. That's not what happened!" He reached for her.

Della sprang back to life like a cornered animal.

"Get away! I swear I'll fucking run this across your throat!" Slicing crisscrosses in the air between them, she forced him a half-step back. "I *know* that's what happened!"

She thrust the knife at the book in his hands, driving the casebound cover up towards his face.

"Keep reading!"

Ian assented without dispute, returning to *The New Apocrypha* where he'd left off: "'. . . seven sacrificial scapegoats, one for each of its blasphemous heads. Then, and only then, can the archdemon Azazel, right hand of Satan, fulfill its destiny to propagate the most heinous Nephala of all—the unholy 'virgin' birth of the Dragon Lamb. A blaspheme of both the Sacred Virgin Birth and the Holy Trinity, the Dragon Lamb shall be the Satanic inverse of Jesus, our Holy Christ. Being the great deceiver, this Dragon Lamb will possess the power to lead the world into Darkness as it ultimately extinguishes all Light.'"

The silence as he finished was so powerful it was almost a sound in itself. It took everything Della had left in her to break it.

"I know that Rebecca's pregnant, Ian," she spoke so weakly it was barely audible. "Is it yours?"

Ian stared unspeaking, his face devoid of emotion.

"No," he eventually answered.

"Did that—*thing*—inside her come from this demonic entity? Is Rebecca somehow carrying this sick corruption Bartholomew calls the 'Dragon Lamb?'"

Ian didn't have to answer.

Intense repulsion had already twisted Della's face, appearing as if she, herself, were possessed. She began trembling beyond her control, knees buckling as the room started to spin; Ian's features wavering before her.

Wild-eyed and sobbing she fell to the ground as a flash of the nightmare from which she'd awakened once again skewered through her mind, its tentacles piercing her aura, wrapping around her spiritual energy like black barbed wire.

... The dead boy pulls her to him as she continues to gag in violent spasms, his blistered hands palming the crown of her head which bobs up and down, over and over ....

Ian clapped the book closed and swung it, swatting the knife from Della's hands. In hindsight he'd realize it was barely necessary, for the psychic had already begun to convulse. Recoiling in terror, her entire body had tensed. Her eyes had dilated until barely a hint of iris remained. Black and transfixed, they pleaded for help.

In the faraway distance, something screeched.

"*Shhhh*, it's okay, babygirl," he reassured indifferently as he stroked her hair, lifting her jittery face to look upon him. "This is all so much more than you understand. But you will soon—it's inside you now—and there's a reason for what's happening. There are no coincidences, remember? *You* taught me that, Della."

Choking and unable to focus, DeLaCroix Laveau discerned only Ian's shape as he knelt beside her and placed his hand in hers. She did not feel his fingers as they laced between hers; did not witness his remorseful smile as his features morphed to little more than a vague, dusky form.

Outside, the screeches grew louder.

While Ian's senses perceived them clearly, he was grateful Della seemed deaf to the shrill, whistling cries of the Shadows as they stormed the night sky, swooping ever nearer.

There must be at least three of them, he thought and hastily lifted her off the floor, carrying her to the top of the stairwell.

"You fought the good fight, Della. Lord knows you were its biggest threat." His words were becoming garbled; faraway. A tuning fork under water. "But it's time for you to let go now ...."

The venomous black ribbons had now multiplied and spread inside her like a web, enshrouding her energy, her light, her very life force.

Though she could no longer see him, Della sought Ian's eyes as he half-carried, half-dragged her down the steep wooden steps.

Her breathing reduced to wisps, she was powerless to speak, the thing inside her taking full dominion and rendering even her telepathy impotent. As her last moments ticked down, she channeled all that she had into one terminal effort. Not into her tortured breathing, or her labored heartbeat, but into the psychic projection of just one single word:

WHY...?

"Not *why*," he replied out loud as he deposited her brusquely upon the bottom landing, catching his breath. "But...*who?*"

He paused with purpose, allowing her strained and expiring faculties the opportunity for this to sink in.

"You see, you've entirely overlooked the fact that my brother and I weren't alone in the woods that night. There was another person with us when Bryan was killed ... wasn't there?"

He kicked open the rear door to the parking lot and it caught in the wind, slamming against the outside wall of the tavern. Cool, night rain spritzed them both as he grabbed Della by the ankles and began dragging her body across the gravel.

It was the last physical sensation DeLaCroix Laveau would experience. It was not, however, the last thing she would see. For one final synapse fired off an image in Della's mind, bright as a star and crisp as flash paper.

Her eyes froze in horror as the infinite nothingness took her, the image of young Diane Cockerton imprinted upon her soul ....

SECOND DISCIPLE

Hell is empty,

and all the devils are here.

—William Shakespeare, *The Tempest*

The Black Shadow

2:2

MY DAD'S DEAD. I watched him put a gun to his head, back in the woods where we used to live. Or so they tell me, anyway…I don't really remember. And okay, you're right. Of course they don't say it exactly that way (oh, and by 'they,' I mean my mom and my uncle) 'cause they're über-sensitive about it 'n all. But that's what they mean.

He did it a couple years ago, back in ninety-five.

Took his own life in order to stop something unimaginable from happening to me. Sometimes the way they tell it changes. It might be a small detail here, a little fact there. And I pick up on these things even though they think I don't. But that's the word they use, every single time.

Unimaginable.

They never say what 'unimaginable' means, though. Because I'm only fourteen (fifteen next month!) and they think I wouldn't understand. Which kinda sucks because I'm actually pretty sharp. Especially for my age. I read a lot of books and pride myself on my vocabulary. My teachers tell me I'm way above my grade level, especially in English class, and put me in all the advanced classes. I know I'm going to grow up to be a famous writer someday. That's just gonna happen. When I was a lot younger, my dad used to listen—so intently—when I'd tell him all my elaborate stories. Then he'd ruffle my hair and kiss me on the forehead, smiling as he called me 'precocious.'

That made me happy, after I looked up what it meant.

My mom's always been more protective of me. And even though I keep pestering her to tell me what really happened to my dad that day in the woods, she still won't.

"One day," her softest voice coos soothingly from behind as she brushes my hair and I admire her features in the mirror. She does not see me watching. A gentle smile softens her face as she concentrates only on lifting and smoothing the thick blonde layers which waft slowly, tidily upon my back halfway to my waist. "One day you'll be ready, babygirl. And then you'll understand. I promise. But for now, just know that your father loved you. More than life itself.... And so do I."

She pauses a moment before adding: "Your Uncle Ian does, too."

The funny thing is, even though I was there when my father killed himself, I can't tell you if what they say is true. I mean, I know it mostly is, but something deep inside—this queer, scratchy little vibration I can never quite get a hold of—tells me that maybe it's not completely true. I wish I could just figure out which parts are legit and which are a big fat lie, but I haven't learned how to yet.

I know my father loved me; I know that for sure ... I can *feel* that. But I don't know what happened that day. I mean, I can tell you some bits of it—the parts I can see through the fog. Like, I can see Andrew, my annoying little brother, and my dad and my Uncle Ian and this lady I never met before called Della who was actually sorta cool. We were at the hospital in town because something was wrong with my mom. I do remember that the lights were super bright and mega harsh and made me feel all exposed. Oh, and that nasty chemical smell. *Blecch.* It still makes me gag. That sterile odor of cleaners they probably get by the five-gallon tub instead of by the bottle from the supermarket—you know, the normal-sized household cleaners with the pretty pastel pictures on the labels and names like Fresh Spring Linen or Gentle Autumn Breeze.

Then, all I remember is that I'm suddenly alone in these freaky woods. It's super dark and I can't breathe. My neck was hurting really bad, like someone was trying to twist it. Kinda the same way my arm felt back in the third grade when Mack, that jerk of a kid, gave me an Indian burn. Just like that, except this was in my neck. And then that hot, stinging feeling wrapped around my whole body. It felt like ribbons of fire. I still see them in my mind—these fingers of blue flame trying to burn me alive. But they never actually existed. I was scared and screaming though, I know that much.

But then it all just goes blank and I don't remember anything else about it. I don't remember hearing the gunshot, even though they tell me that my dad and Uncle Ian were right there with me; I don't remember how I got out of the woods; I don't remember the ambulances or the sirens or any of those things my friends would tell me they heard from their parents or saw for themselves on TV. Because, yeah, that stuff was plastered on every local news station and paper for miles around.

In fact, I don't remember anything at all for a pretty long time after that. I'm not even sure how we ended up moving to Manhattan from Pee Aay. (That's short for Pennsylvania—no one who's from there actually says the full name. Guess we're all just too lazy or somethin'.)

I know there was an airplane trip, and a moving van that met us at my uncle's apartment building on West 93rd Street, across from Central Park. But that's only because it's what my mom and uncle have told me. Oh, and the fact that I live here now. I'd have to be pretty much of a spaz to not know where I live.

So, you see, there's this big gap I don't remember at all.

Basically, from the day my dad died in the middle of June '95 all the way to August '96 is a big blank. It's only been the last year or so that I've started to feel a little more like my old self again. And I think I'm pretty okay now.

I still get the nightmares though.

II

Simon Peter was born in September 1995, three months after my dad died. Which is weird, because my mom didn't even know she was pregnant until a couple weeks after my dad was already gone. But she must have been at least a good six months along by then. Maybe even more.

So, ummm, I'm still trying to figure out how that's even possible?

Of course, I was a mental vegetable at the time so, like I said, I don't remember much about any of that. Plus, I'm something of a late bloomer when it comes to the whole sex thing. I've only just had my tenth period even though most of the girls at school have been having them for a couple years. Some of them even call me Delayin' instead of Diane because it took me so long to 'become a woman,' as my mom says.

So, what do I know?

Well, I know you can't have a baby in three months.

Duh.

I guess it makes sense why my Uncle Ian calls Simon Peter a miracle, not just because the whole pregnancy thing seemed to happen so fast but because my mom couldn't have kids anymore. One day at the end of last year, when I started to feel more like my old self again, I asked Uncle Ian what he meant by that. He just turned a little red in the cheeks, stammered, and left the room with the excuse that he had to go check on Simon Peter, or something.

My mother came into the room a few moments later, smiling thinly and taking my hand as she sat cross-legged on my bed.

"Many years ago, sweetie, right around your first birthday, your father and I found out I was pregnant again. It would have been your first baby brother or sister. But that pregnancy went wrong." Mom paused. I could tell she was trying her best to keep her emotions from carrying her off the way they must have done so many times before. "I know you're a smart girl, so I'm going to tell you everything, okay?"

I nodded, a little nervously, suddenly feeling sad and less sure about the world again, realizing how quickly your legs can be swept out from underneath you.

"That pregnancy was ectopic. That means the baby was forming outside of my uterus. They had to perform surgery because the baby had ruptured my fallopian tube. You were far too young to remember, but I'm afraid we lost it. And, well . . . I almost died too."

You could hear a pin drop. I don't think I was even blinking.

My mother cleared her throat. "Despite everything, we still tried again a few more times after that, your dad and me. But I just couldn't carry a baby to full term anymore."

The silence just laid there, like wet on a dog.

Then Andrew bounded into the room. Realizing he'd stumbled into something weird but not understanding what, my then seven-year-old brother screeched to an awkward stop, sliding on the round, pink rug in the center of my room and unintentionally doing a perfect impression of Tom Cruise in *Risky Business*. It was actually kinda funny.

Mom's face brightened, opening her arms and beckoning him into her embrace. "And that's when we decided to bring this awesome guy into our lives. And isn't that just wonderful!"

"Yeah!" Andrew said, beaming that awesome Andrew smile but also pulling away as she smothered him with mom kisses and nose nuzzles. "That's when I came! Alright! Uggh, enough, mom!"

We've never been one of those families that tiptoe around the fact that my brother Andrew is adopted. He was only three when he came to live with us, which is just a little older than Simon Peter is now. We were still in Pee Aay in those days. I was nine, and that I remember for sure because I was in the middle of my first crush. Valentine's Day was coming and all I could think about was Robbie Hanson, the cutest guy in our homeroom. And of course, how much I wanted to get a card from him. All the girls called him Robbie

'Handsome' and would stare when he walked by their desks before burying their heads in their books and giggling.

Not me. I couldn't stare. Robbie was just too cute.

You ever get like that? Like it's too hard to look at someone 'cause they're just so darn gorgeous? That's how I was with Robbie. And even though it wasn't on purpose, me not gawping and fawning all over him must've worked somehow because, guess what? Yep! Not only did I get a Valentine, but it was one of those really fancy big ones. You know, the kind that are as big as your homework folder. It had this cute cartoon lion on it and when you opened it up, its mouth opened and lots of hearts and really big letters popped out that read, "I'd be 'lion' if I said I didn't like you."

I couldn't believe it! Me…getting such an elegant Valentine. And from Robbie Hanson! I was over the moon. After school, I ran straight home from the bus and just stared at it, lying on my bed and wondering what my name would sound like when we got married.

Diane Hanson. Mrs. Robbie Hanson. Mrs. Diane Louise Hanson.

I couldn't wait to show it to Crystal Riley, my best friend, as soon as she came home from her clarinet lesson. She was gonna just die, right there in my bedroom. I knew she was.

Even though I was hungry I couldn't eat my dinner that evening. I was too excited. But Dad wouldn't let me leave the table until I finished everything. It was torture. "We're a family, and time together like this is important," he said as he looked at me and Andrew.

So, I sat there and moved limp asparagus spears around my plate as my dad told my mom about his day and Andrew chomped greedily on the dinosaur-shaped chicken nuggets she'd cut in half for him. It was sort of weird. I mean, this strange kid's sitting next to my mom like he belonged with us. But I wasn't really thinking about that at the time because all I could think about was getting back to my room so I could invite Crystal over to rub her face in what I got from Robbie.

"She can come over—for just a little bit—as soon as you finish," Mom promised as she lifted Andrew from his booster seat. Like some kind of kid sized wind-up toy, he was off and running the moment his feet hit the floor, stumbling across the kitchen in this awkward toddler way that always looked like he was about to face plant. "Just for a short visit though, Diane Louise. It is a school night, after all."

Uggh. She used both names. Which was her way of letting me know that she meant business. Crystal said when adults talk that way they're being 'passive aggressive.' I didn't completely under-stand, but got the gist.

I forced another cold, wet asparagus spear in my mouth and swallowed with a dramatic, audible gulp. My stomach protested with a rumble that was almost as loud. I couldn't stand this. All I wanted to do was call Crystal and go to my room to practice the perfect pose for when she'd walk in. I imagined lying on my bed, my chin in my hand as I swooned over that great big card. Yeah, that was the pose. It was gonna kill her. I mean, she was literally just gonna die right there on that pink rug.

I scarfed down the rest of the cold asparagus, forcing myself to ignore how much it felt like fat, dead worms on my tongue—or maybe tiny little eels—rinsed off my plate and took the steps two at a time before hopscotching down the hall to my bedroom all the way at the end. I threw open my door...and that's when I saw it.

Andrew was in my room.

On the floor.

With marker pens.

Scribbling all over Handsome Robbie Hanson's card.

"NOOOO!" I threw myself at him and plucked the pen out of his grimy little fist, but it was too late. He'd already scrawled great big sloppy circles all over it in green and black. I could barely make out the lion's puckered lips, or his great big gentle paws he held over his heart. And I definitely couldn't make out Robbie's signature anymore. "You little bastard! How could you do this?! I hate you, Andrew. I wish you never came. I hate you, I hate you, I HATE YOU!"

Yep. I actually said that.

Oh boy, did I get in trouble. Not only for screaming like some crazy person and swearing, but for saying such awful things. I still don't know where it came from, to be honest. I didn't think I had it in me, but there you go. In a way though, it's sorta funny when I look back on it. Remember, I was only nine at the time. I wasn't near as mature as I am now, now that I'm almost fifteen. Because me and Andrew became a lot closer after that ... once I got over the whole Valentine incident. And we've been really tight since my dad died. Even though we're almost six years apart I have to admit that Andrew's actually pretty cool. For an eight-year-old.

But what I actually want to share with you is what's been happening more and more around Simon Peter. Because I think my uncle's right: Simon Peter might be some kind of miracle. And I don't just mean his birth. He's two years old now which means he's almost the same age Andrew was when we adopted him. The difference is, Andrew was just a normal toddler.

There's nothing normal about Simon Peter.

He has this unnatural way about him that you can *feel*, y'know? This energy that sorta draws you in. I haven't decided if it's a feeling I like, or if it completely skeeves me out.

And then there are these things I've been seeing.

Strange things.

Things I can't explain.

Things that only happen around Simon Peter....

2:3

TODAY IS SIMON Peter's birthday. For the record, they say I was at the hospital when my mom delivered him two years ago, but that's all a fog for me. Deep inside, I can somehow *feel* that day, even though I don't remember anything about it. The same way I sometimes feel other things I don't understand either. Things that come to me out of nowhere. I can't explain it, and I don't know how to control it. I wish I did.

"Deedee, come and help me with the cake?" I hear my mom shouting from the kitchen. She says it like a question, like she's giving me options. But there's really only one right answer.

See? Passive-aggressive, Crystal's little demon on my shoulder whispers in my ear and I mentally swat her away, realizing how much I miss her.

Oh, and by the way, my mom calls me Deedee.

It started way back when my dad used to shorten my name to Di, which my mom always hated. "It sounds like you're saying, 'die,'" she used to tell him, and would give him a playful little slap. But she was right because it did. I didn't mind though. "How about something like, 'Deedee'?"

And so, it stuck.

The thing is, Deedee isn't any quicker to say than Diane. I mean, they're both two syllables. It's even longer to write. I'm not sure what the point is.

But whatever.

"Okay Mom," I shout back to her and close my notebook where I've been journaling my thoughts and other stuff. I don't do it every day, just when the mood strikes. It might not be state secrets I'm scribbling here, but believe you me, I still don't leave this thing lying around, no siree. The Handsome Robbie incident might have been a good five years ago, but I learned my lesson. After all, as cool as he is, Andrew's nine now and can still get on my nerves ... you know how little brothers are ... and now Simon Peter is about the same age that Andrew was when he almost ruined my life, and I'm not gonna let *that* happen again. So, I bury my journal in a special stash place I made in my underwear drawer, then go help.

I think Simon Peter's cake is supposed to look like Big Bird, but the bakery we go to on West Seventy-Second is probably afraid of getting sued for copyright infringement, so to me it just looks like a big yellow turd on two skinny orange twigs.

"Hey," my uncle exclaims as he passes. "Look at that awesome cake. What is that, a potato on pipe cleaners? If so, they nailed it." At which point my mom instantly deflates and I find myself needing to laugh so hard I can't hold it in, even though I know she's upset. Uncle Ian chuckles too, but pulls her close and apologizes, giving her a hug and a deep kiss.

There you go—that takes my laughing down about ten notches.

You see, I still haven't gotten used to seeing them like that yet. I mean, Ian *is* my uncle, after all. So, it's a bit weird seeing him and mom kiss. But here's the thing: Uncle Ian is my *dad's* brother, not my mom's. Plus, we hardly knew him before Dad died.

Sure, we were aware he existed 'n all. But it wasn't like we were close family. You know the kind, the ones you see most weekends, and always on holidays, and you never knock, you just walk right in and make yourself at home. Uncle Ian was never like that to us. He moved to New York before I was born, and pretty much steered clear of Pee Aay. In fact, I can count on one hand the number of times he came to visit and it's like three, tops, if you wanna include that last visit when my dad ended up blowing his brains out in the woods.

I guess what I'm trying to get across is that to my mom, Uncle Ian was never really family. He's just a good man she feels comfortable with ... and who also happens to share my dad's DNA. Which I have to admit feels pretty nice to be around. So, I get it. And my mom was never really family to Uncle Ian. She's just a beautiful woman called Rebecca that happened to be married to his brother.

Truth be told, I kinda feel bad for Uncle Ian because, deep down, I know my mom sees him as a kind of walking-talking substitute for my dad. And that's half the reason they're together.

Of course, Uncle Ian loves us and takes care of us. And we love him right back. We're family ... now. A new kind of family, maybe. But family all the same. I guess it's just gonna take me some more time—maybe a couple years—until I can see them together in that kind of way and not be a little creeped out by it.

I clear my throat. "Hey, um, guys? How 'bout you get a room."

Oooh, that sounded awkward. So, I force a chuckle. But that comes out even more clumsy. Which results in me just beaming a great big cheesy grin as I grab the cake knife and pretend to use it like a mirror, acting like I'm picking something out of my teeth.

Thankfully, Simon Peter saves the day by stumbling into the kitchen like the Pillsbury Dough Boy (the exact same way Andrew used to) and barely avoids a face plant even though I'm sure this is the time it's gonna happen. (Also, exactly like Andrew.) Uncle Ian snatches Simon up with hugs and a sloppy kiss on his infant duck lips before such an atrocity can happen. Simon giggles and pulls his head to the side, running his palms over his mouth to wipe away the kiss before spying his birthday cake.

"Bigbirrr!" he exclaims with unbridled joy in the way only toddlers can and points with equal enthusiasm, waving his arms so excitedly that he nearly bumps himself right out of my uncle's arms.

How in fuck's name Simon knows what that cake is supposed to be is beyond me. Because, well, I told you why.

And by the way, sorry about the swearing. Sometimes it just slips out. My teachers have threatened to tell my mom, but I have a feeling you're cooler than they are and won't tell on me.

"Yes, little man," my mom says and tweaks his nose. "He's come straight from the TV to celebrate your birthday! Come on everybody!"

She takes Simon Peter by the hand and walks him into the living room where a half dozen adults and four or five little kids are wearing paper party hats. When my uncle appears behind them with the cake and a big waxy number 2 burning on top, they all start singing *Happy Birthday.*

Now, I know I made fun of that cake, but it's actually pretty good. Like, go-back-for-another-slice good. Chocolate with chocolate fudge icing in the middle. Who doesn't mind a few extra calories for that? *And* I get the piece with the big yellow potato/turd/bird's face, which is a yummy bonus. I pig out on a second slice, realize my eyes are too big for my stomach, and now I'm about ready to melt into a sugar coma as I mold myself into the couch under our window overlooking Central Park.

I try to close my peepers for a moment, but Simon Peter is squealing with delight at the gift he just unwrapped, and Lina, the girl from a few blocks west, is crying and stomping because she wants to play with it, and he won't let her.

"Now, Simon," my mother's voice lilts as she pries the toy from his trembling fingers as though it's an IED that could go off with the slightest jar and kill us all. "Lina can play with it too. We share our toys, don't we?" Again, one of her questions that's really more of a statement. I gotta hand it to her, she's really quite masterful.

But I just need to mentally check out of this toddler time for a few. It's only 6:30, but it's already getting dark and I'm sleepy as heck. The streetlights have begun to fizzle on: briefly pink, then greenish, and finally a hazy, flickering yellow. They cast overlapping halos on the sidewalk as more and more shapes exit the woodland park, materializing from the tree line to reveal smiling groups of friends, romantic couples, and the occasional individual huddled beneath a hoodie as the night air begins to chill. I like watching them all from here, knowing they don't see me. Five stories up, I'm a god looking down upon her subjects. I create stories about them in my head.

This one's a famous rock star, on a break from touring.

That one's a wannabe actress. She works at the diner on the corner and doesn't know she's about to have the break of a lifetime when a bigshot director stops in for lunch tomorrow.

The couple snuggling against the phone pole are young lovers. Their parents have been grooming them for other companions, far better suited to each family's stature. They kiss one last time, a bittersweet goodbye, before making their way back home. "Parting is such sweet sorrow," *the young woman says as her fingers slowly slide from his, the last one lingering before it touches nothing but air.* "That I shall say goodnight till it be morrow...."

I can't take credit for that last part which is from Romeo and Juliet. We're reading it in my advanced English Lit class, and Mrs. Linebaugh says if we ace the test, she'll let us put on a shortened version of the play for the rest of the school. Which would rock, because I'm a shoo-in for Juliet.

When I check what's happening with Simon Peter's party, I realize I must've been daydreaming for some time because almost everyone has gone. Andrew is already in his room playing some racing game on his PlayStation, the volume up way too loud. My mom is tidying up. And Uncle Ian is on the sidewalk with Mr. and Mrs. Sonoro, five stories below. I can tell by my uncle's body language that he's thanking them for bringing Lina to the party, and probably apologizing again for Simon's behavior.

Speaking of the devil, the birthday boy has stumbled across the living room and is climbing up onto my lap. He likes to watch out the window with me sometimes and listen to my silly stories. Being only two, he doesn't understand them of course. But I don't care. We have fun and it's nice to have a little brother nuzzling up against me again. He smells like toddler, and it brings back warm and fuzzy memories of me and Andrew back in Pee Aay before . . . well . . . before you-know-what happened.

"Look, Simon," I say and point to the sidewalk below where his little friend Lina and her parents are saying their last goodbyes before retiring for the night in their building on Amsterdam Avenue. Simon Peter presses his face against the chilly glass and mumbles something that feels so forlorn it kind of breaks my heart for a second. "What's that, buddy?"

He points, stubbing his finger against the window so hard it turns pale around his little fingernail. Raising his voice in frustration, he repeats what sounds like 'no duy,' but must be trying to say: 'No toy.'

Now I'm pressing my face against the glass too. And yep, Lina has the toy they were both throwing a tantrum over. I don't know what the thing is, but even from this high up I can see its wobbly, bright purple silliness. I guess it's filled with some kind of gel, the way the old Stretch Armstrong dolls used to be.

"Hey Mom?" I shout over my shoulder so she can hear me over the clanking dishes and glasses she's washing in the sink. "I think Lina has one of the toys you gave Simon. Is she supposed to?"

Mom dries off her hands and comes to the window. She strokes Simon Peter's hair and gives me a reluctant smile, nodding.

"The Sonoros are going through a bit of a hard time at the moment," she half-whispers. I'm not sure why she does. We're five stories up. And inside. It's not like they can hear a word she's saying. Or likely even see her, for that matter. My little brother is so engrossed in the scene outside that he's not listening to us at all. That, and the fact that he's only two years old and couldn't give a crap about what we're saying. "We're blessed to have so much,

Deedee. Simon got *so many* presents today, he won't even know one's missing. And Lina was really drawn to that particular toy."

Mom returns to the kitchen without another word. She doesn't see how agitated Simon Peter's becoming as, fifty feet below, Mr. Sonoro attempts to pry the purple toy from his daughter's grip and return it to my uncle. It's obvious that both Lina and my uncle disagree with Mr. Sonoro's gesture. My uncle's body language is clear about the matter, reassuring that there's no need to give the toy back. While bawling, Lina tugs even harder on one end of the long, wiggly purple thing whose other end is firmly in her father's grip. He equally refuses to release it, so the toy is now stretched to at least twice its original length.

Watching this all play out, Simon Peter's breath becomes short and fast. His cheeks are rosy red. He's so upset he's almost quivering and begins bouncing up and down. "*Deeee*dee, look!" he tells me, drawing out the syllables of my name in that adorable way he does. "Look, Dee*deeeee!*"

I lean closer to the glass, but Simon stops me from peering out. Instead, he places both little hands over my eyes, covering them. They feel sticky with cheesy puff powder and smell of mouth. "Simon, silly boy!" I chuckle. "If you cover my eyes, I can't see what you're showi—"

My mouth hangs open mid-sentence, sucking in breath. There's a sudden, intense warmth from Simon's hands that feels somehow comfortable and invasive at the same time. If I didn't know better, I'd think he was reaching straight into my head and manipulating my mind. Because I am no longer in our apartment.

But somehow, down on the sidewalk.

"*Looook . . . Deeedeeeee . . .*" Simon Peter instructs so slowly he's nearly growling the words, the voice nothing like his own. Neither does the sound come from his mouth, but rather, somewhere inside my own head. I *feel* his words instead of hear them—a deep minor chord vibrating through me like a subwoofer. I'm reminded of what my dad used to tell me when he'd lower the bottom end of my bedroom stereo's equalizer: 'You should *feel* the bass more than hear it. The greatest power comes from a sensation, not a volume of sound.'

Now that driving bass in my memory has become the pounding of my own heart. Its beating is way too burdened; the rests between becoming dangerously short.

... thum thum...... thum-THUM ... thum-THUM ...

I'm sure it's going to punch right through my ribcage.

My blood feels so cold and thick that my hands tingle with frostbite. I can't breathe; my throat suddenly too small.

"No! Mine!" Lina shouts from only feet away, determined to free the purple wiggly toy from her father's grip. She's leaning back and putting the weight of her whole body into it as she tugs so hard that she's shaking,

The scene wavers like water on glass, my mind swimming in its impossibility.

... THUM ... thum-THUM–thum-THUM . . .

"Now, Lina," Mr. Sonoro insists as he holds fast to the toy, even tugging upon it himself a little. The words I hear don't seem to match his lips, and his voice is all warbly, as if we're under water. "This toy belongs to Simon Peter. It was a birthday gift, remember? So, let's be a good girl and give it back to Mr. Cockerton. Okay?"

"Really, there's no need—" my uncle insists once again and takes a half step back, holding out his open hand as he removes himself from the situation in hopes of defusing it. His stance reminds me of the way our school crossing guards look when they're getting ready to stop traffic.

"I appreciate your generosity," Mr. Sonoro claims. "But the toy is not Lina's to take." By his tone, it's obvious he does *not* appreciate my uncle's charity. He even sounds a bit peeved. (I'm really starting to recognize this adult way of verbal sparring, thanks to my friend Crystal.) "I don't know how she even ended up with it. Elaine? Did you say Lina could take this toy from young Simon here ... and on his birthday, no less?"

Elaine Sonoro flushes. Saying nothing in reply, she all but wilts on the curbside.

... thum-THUM-thum-THUM ...

Lina wails. It's a shrill, deafening scream as if the three-year-old is being beaten. Several pedestrians rubberneck but choose to keep walking when they can't quite place the source of the distress.

The little girl pulls on the toy again, this time as hard and fast as she can. The purple wiggly stretches ... way too long, way too thin. Almost translucent, it's at the point of splitting.

Aware that the toy is near its breaking point, Mr. Sonoro releases his grip. Still clutching it, however, Lina's hands rebound up and over her head as the elastic plaything snaps back to its original shape, the three-year-old's eyes alight in joyful achievement.

... thumTHUMthumTHUMthumTHUM ...

The victory is short-lived.

Stumbling backward in recoiling momentum, Lina's eyes darken to stark reality. Arms beginning to pinwheel for balance, her feet scrabble for center of gravity. They do not find it.

And so, Lina Sonoro reels backward off the curb.

Into the street.

Right in front of the metro bus.

I cry out a warning, but no sound will come. I try to run to the sidewalk's edge, but my feet are anchored in concrete. I reach to pull her from danger, but my arms are impossibly slow in air as thick as glue.

The ticking of time slows. Then slows again.

I see the MTA driver's eyes so clearly, it's as if I am in the cockpit next to her. An expanse of white appears all the way around them. Her mouth a gigantic, twisted oval. And for a brief moment, the driver has become that famous painting of an egg-headed person clasping their cheeks as they scream soundlessly on a bridge.

Stomping both feet, she slams the brake pedal as far to the floor as it will go. Her effort makes no difference.

On the oily city street, the bus tires only shudder and bounce.

With a sickening thud, Lina Sonoro folds in two and disappears beneath the giant wheels. A geyser of blood paints the bus's chassis as the little girl's curtailed scream shreds the calm of the night, everyone within a hundred yards wincing and jerking 'round with a worried frown.

Now the rear wheels of the bus bounce up over the hump of Lina's body. They do not pass over her but instead grind to a halt atop her, pinning Lina down. The driver has slammed on the brakes. She does not know that those massive rear tires are now dragging and grinding little Lina down the street.

A long sausage trail of intestines squeeze from the little girl's mangled body like a blood-covered worm forcibly expelled from a tube of cinnamon gel toothpaste.

I inhale so sharply my lungs burn before the air explodes from my chest in a single, piercing scream.

Then Simon Peter removes his hands from my eyes.

And I am back on the couch, in our home on the fifth floor.

My howl has shattered the silence of our apartment, causing a plate to slide through my mother's nimble fingers. Exploding against the tile floor, it becomes nothing but a thousand useless shards, the sound of its destruction buried inside my scream.

Oblivious, Simon Peter presses his face to the window.

Against every instinct, trembling all over, I force myself to do the same. There is no bus. There are no screaming people. There is no blood, or little girl's mangled body. There is just Lina and her parents on the sidewalk, engulfed in verbal debate with my uncle about that stupid, purple toy.

"Jesus H!" my mom exclaims once she catches her breath, jump-stepping back from the array of shards as if she were about to tread upon a landmine. "Deedee! My God! What's happened?"

She doesn't wait for my answer before skirting the broken pieces to rush to the window and peer down upon the street.

At the edge of the sidewalk, Lina pulls hard on the purple wiggly toy. "No! Mine!" She's leaning back and putting the weight of her whole body into it, determined to free it from her father's grip.

"Now, Lina," Mr. Sonoro insists in as calm a voice as he can muster. He holds fast to the toy. "This belongs to Simon Peter. It was a birthday gift, remember? So, let's be a good girl and give it back to nice Mr. Cockerton here, okay?"

"Really, there's no need—" my uncle pleads.

Again.

Haven't we just been here?

Watching this replay with his palms to the glass, Simon Peter now squeezes his eyes closed. His hands are eerily steady, the window misting around them in a growing halo of heat. His level of focus is far beyond the capacity of a toddler and much closer to that I've seen in adults at very intense moments.

… Moments like that terrible day in the Little Woods….

My mom does not notice this in her two-year-old son, her attention occupied only by the interaction on the street below where, yet again, Mr. Sonoro is asking his wife about the purple toy in exactly the same way a father might ask a child, even though he already knows the answer: "Elaine? Did you say Lina could take this toy from little Simon …?"

Lina starts to wail.

Onlookers turn, annoyed at the interruption but barely breaking stride when they realize it's only a toddler's tantrum.

Lina yanks on the toy. Again, as hard and fast as she can.

The purple wiggly stretches long and thin.

And I know I am breathing too fast, close to hyperventilating. I don't know what to do. What to say.

How do I tell my mom that Simon Peter has just shown me this? That I know how this is about to play out. How do I stop it? Do I explain or just run down there?

Either way, Lina is dead within seconds.

As I'm paralyzed by confusion.

Now, once again, the purple wiggly is at the point of breaking. When Mr. Sonoro lets go of his end ....

"Mom!" I cry but can say nothing more.

"Darling, what on *earth* is *wrong*?" She holds my face in her hands, her soft blue eyes searching deep into mine. She senses that something in this moment is very wrong but doesn't understand what it could be.

I want to let it all spill out. But like a stroke victim who knows what they want to say, the words refuse to reach my tongue.

Tears start to pour down my cheeks and my mother pulls me tight. In her embrace, I see only Simon Peter. His hands pressed firmly to the window, he's frozen in statuesque concentration.

Then my baby brother shoots open his eyes.

He's about to scream, like *really* scream. He sucks in his breath, and I can feel he is about to let loose like I've never heard him do before. But instead, Simon Peter whispers two simple words. The same he spoke earlier: "NO DUY—"

He says this in a commanding manner, so at odds with what we both know is about to happen that it makes my skin crawl. And in that same moment, unlike the dress rehearsal of this scene, my uncle spins around and looks up. Five stories apart and a quarter inch of safety glass between us, it's impossible he could have heard his whisper. Yet Uncle Ian appears almost spellbound, held in Simon Peter's gaze—man and boy connected as if the only two people on earth.

The most powerful music is a sensation, not a volume of sound. You feel it, my father's stereo wisdom plays again in my mind. And like a rush of understanding, I realize it is not 'no toy' that Simon Peter has been saying.

It is ... 'NO DIE.'

Before I know what's happening, Uncle Ian breaks Simon's stare and lunges for Lina. He clamps onto the lapels of the toddler's jacket and yanks her to him with all his might. The purple wiggly shoots from Lina's grip as she is jerked forward, slamming into the sidewalk. Too shocked to even cry, she just lies there at the feet of my uncle and her father.

"HEY! WHAT THE—" Springing forward, Mr. Sonoro cocks back his arm, ready to spread my uncle's nose wide across his face. He freezes mid-punch as the bus blows past, so fast and so near that everyone's coattails lift in the gust. The purple wiggly embeds in the bus's grill as the MTA barrels on, the driver oblivious.

It's forever before anyone moves.

From our vantage point high above, my mother and I realize we have been holding our collective breaths.

Simon Peter gurgles quietly and claps.

And little Lina, now over her stunned silence, begins to shriek as she lies at the adults' feet on the cold, dirty sidewalk. This time, every pedestrian within earshot stops on a dime as Mrs. Sonoro, snapped to the present moment by her daughter's cry, sweeps Lina into her arms. A few small scratches, she notes as she alternates between protectively cuddling her baby girl then examining Lina with detached objectivity. Maybe a bruised chin for a day or two. But nothing serious. What Mrs. Sonoro simply will not allow herself to acknowledge—not just yet—is how different her life was about to be, had my uncle not acted so quickly.

What she will never know is that it was Simon Peter who was the catalyst. Or that I'm the premonition's only witness.

My head spinning, I can't even begin to imagine what would have ... what could have ... *what should have?* ... happened. I know that sounds terrible. I can't believe I'm even thinking it instead of being grateful I didn't have to see my brother's little friend spread like fresh strawberry preserves across the intersection of West 93rd and Central Park. But I can't stop thinking how every circumstance in each one of those lives—my uncle's, the Sonoros', the MTA driver's—had to be positioned *just so* for all of them to be here, at this exact spot ... out of all the spots in our gigantic world. At this precise moment ... out of all the moments in a sea of time.

Every single thing—every choice, every step, every action, no matter how big or small across decades—led each of them to this specific place and time, to play out this unique scene in the Universe's Grand Drama.

But in one tiny, if incredible, moment my two-year-old brother altered the storyline forever. For better or for worse, Simon Peter rewrote the script.

Somehow, he possessed the power to change it all.

Because if she had died, as was about to happen, Lina Sonoro would never grow up to go attend college in New Jersey where she would study to become a teacher. She would never meet the man she would later marry in a private, quarantined ceremony in 2020. She would never have three beautiful and intelligent children, the middle one, in turn, giving birth to Lina's granddaughter. As that bright young girl would never exist, she would never grow up to be part of the research team responsible for discovering the prevention of cell mutations in humans, effectively killing cancer in the year 2081 (though Lina herself would never live to see that day). A middle-aged Lina would not be at the local flea market, just two days before her sixteenth wedding anniversary, where she would meet Darren, a handsome musician much younger than she. They would never begin their short but intense love affair, and Lina would never possess the guilt to soon break off that relationship. Darren would not feel he had a reason to then come to the school where Lina taught in 2036 and set off the explosion that would not only kill Lina but six other teachers, twenty-nine children, and a bunny that was widely accepted as the school mascot.

If Lina had been hit by that bus, as had been seemingly orchestrated to happen, none of this would one day come to fruition. What we don't know is if that research team would still have discovered their cancer breakthrough, even without Lina's granddaughter. Or if Darren would simply have found another reason to do the terrible thing he would one day do at that school.

We never know any of these answers.

Because, instead of sobbing uncontrollably over the mangled and lifeless body of his daughter, Mr. Sonoro is gushing over my uncle, vigorously pumping his hand while patting him repeatedly on the shoulder. I think his eyes are even beginning to moisten, though it's hard to tell from all the way up here. You don't have to hear him though to know the two words he keeps repeating. Over and over. A moment later he grabs my uncle and pulls him close, enveloping Uncle Ian in a huge bear hug.

My uncle does not return Mr. Sonoro's affection.

He only looks up to our window, eyes glazed and dark.

Staring at Simon Peter . . . .

2:4

I'M OFFICIALLY FIFTEEN, though I've been saying I was for a while now. My birthday was yesterday. Yep, only a week after Simon Peter's. Sort of a bummer, right? I used to have October all to myself. Well, me and Halloween of course— *I just loooove Halloween, don't you?*—but then along comes Simon and now mine's just diluted. I mean, who cares about throwing a party for an emo fifteen-year-old when toddler parties are so much more fun? So, mine was pretty anticlimactic. Nothing like my baby brother's.

At least no one was nearly roadkill at mine.

As yummy as Simon's cake was, I'm too old for something that might look like a weird potato or big yellow turd, or whatever, so Uncle Ian got me an ice cream cake from Carvel. I really like those little crunchy chocolate bits that taste like cookie crumbs.

After I blew out the candles and we all ate, I opened my presents. I got a couple gift cards, some clothes from my favorite store, Saks Off 5TH, and the new U2 CD. Everyone's into 'Staring at the Sun,' but my faves are 'Wake Up Dead Man' and 'If God will send His Angels.'

I spent the afternoon in my room, listening to my music.

And crying.

I miss my Daddy....

2:5

I'VE BEEN THINKING about something that's been bothering me a little, so I wanted to talk to you about it. You see, you might be wondering why I said those things about Lina last month; how I could claim to know that little girl's future like that. You're probably thinking it was just more of my made-up stories, like the ones I create when I'm people-watching from our window overlooking the park.

It's okay. I get it.

But here's the thing. I should tell you that every once in a while, I get this weird, random information. From the Universe. It's like something deep inside me just sits there, idle, not really making itself known most of the time. I can tell it's there, but I've learned to ignore the white noise of it humming away in the background. Then, without warning, it'll whirr to life and interrupt whatever I was doing.

It's like some hidden part of me is the same as my uncle's desktop computer that we sometimes play games on. It just sits there, quietly purring away, not knowing when it's going to get any data. Then ... *ZAP* ... a floppy disk slides into that slot and we're off and running. That computer has no idea when it's going to be fed, or what the data is going to be about. It doesn't care if it completely interferes with what you might've been right in the middle of doing. It just gobbles up that info it's mysteriously been given and spits out the results on your monitor. How you handle that, or what it all means to you, is for you to figure out.

That's how it is with me.

I've started writing down when it happens and figured out that the interruptions I get from the Universe fit into three basic types: I can feel something about my life right now, something about my future, or something about somebody else's life.

When the first kind is good, the best way I can describe it is that it feels like a warm emotional memory—even if it's something my brain doesn't consciously recall—like the day Simon Peter was born. Or it can be a mix of scents and colors that combine to make a really good feeling. But if it's something bad? I'll get this awful, scratchy sensation inside my chest like my ribs are wrapped in steel wool. Ever have the start of a panic attack? That's what it's like. Out of the blue, I'll suddenly be mega-aware of my breathing. It'll feel way too shallow. Or I can tell my heart's beating too fast and it's just the scariest feeling. I think this is what my mom calls 'women's intuition,' only mine is way stronger. It's why I have a weird way of knowing when people are lying to me, or if they really aren't my friend.

The second kind comes to me like a snapshot or really brief movie clip. The awful thing is, I never know if what I'm seeing is *definitely* gonna happen, or something that *could possibly* happen. I don't mind saying, these kind of interruptions make me feel the most nervous. I mean, how would you feel if someone was showing you your future? You'd think it'd be cool, right? But what if you didn't like what you saw? Or worse yet, what if you did? If you never knew whether that future was set in stone or whether you could change it, it'd drive you a little bonkers either way.

The third interruption I get is not about me at all, but somebody else. When I get this kind, it's something I can almost always *see*. I don't usually see enough to be able to figure it out straight away, though. At least, I haven't learned how to do that yet. Here's what I mean: imagine walking into your living room and there's a movie on cable TV. The picture will be really crisp and clear, but if the film's halfway over, it probably won't make a lot of sense to you.

Who is she? What's he doing? Why are they in that place?

There are times I can actually stay in this type of interruption for a pretty long time … if I really want to. But like I said, I haven't learned how to fine tune it yet. So, even if I keep watching, it'll be like there's a bad storm bouncing the cable up against the outside of your apartment building: you can watch all you want, but the signal goes in-and-out the whole time and you miss great big chunks of the story. So, you see, these kinds of interruptions can be super annoying because they have the potential to be the coolest.

(I told you I like people-watching!)

Now, I *was* gonna say the difference between me and that pesky computer—you know, the one I mentioned a moment ago—is that the computer doesn't know what a floppy disk is, where it comes from, or even who's feeding it all this random data. But the more I come to think about it, I guess me and that computer are pretty much the same. 'Cause I really don't know any of those things either.

My bestie, Crystal, used to tell me what I have is supernatural … like I'm a kind of psychic or something. But that girl wouldn't leave her house before reading Madam Starry's horoscope in the news-paper back in Pee Aay. We get the same column here, and my Uncle Ian (who works at the *Manhattan Bulletin*) tells me all the papers just buy that crap from some service. It comes in over the fax line and some poor sap of an intern has to sit there in an itsy little cubicle and type it all up for the week. Not very mystical.

So, listen. I don't know if what happens to me is something from the spirit world, like Crystal says, but I can tell you it definitely used to freak me out.

I'm starting to roll with it a little more though, now, and even working on how to control it a little.

Sometimes I almost can.

I'm super pumped today because I had one of my second types of interruptions this evening, one of the good ones, about something that hasn't happened to me yet. Except this time, I'm positive it's gonna happen. I was in my room reading 'The Cask of Amontillado' by Edgar Allan Poe—one of my faves; don't you just love how clever and gothic it is!?—when suddenly everything began to waver and mist over. I could smell this really nice pipe tobacco, like a mix of vanilla and warm leather.

Tobacco like my Uncle Eddie smokes.

And tomorrow is Thanksgiving. So....

I don't really care about that part of it: the holiday, I mean. Sure, I like the turkey and stuffing and all that jazz. But it's a bit of a non-event for me. I just don't see that I have a lot to be thankful for, y'know? But I'm really excited to know that my uncle Eddie must be coming. He'll probably even stay for a few days. Over the weekend, at least. My mom and Uncle Ian haven't said anything, but I know it's gonna happen.

Now, you should probably know that Eddie's not really my uncle. He's my dad's best friend. From way back. And he's been part of the family since before I was born. So, he's always just been *Uncle* Eddie. Not only to me, but to all of us. My mom even calls him that and, honestly, it doesn't sound weird. Because that's just who he is.

Anyhoo...I ask my mom about it.

"No, Deedee. I'm afraid I can't say that he is." She gets this momentary faraway look in her eyes, and I can tell that mentioning Uncle Eddie has suddenly made her think of my dad. You know how that happens, you don't think of somebody for the longest time, then suddenly you hear their name and all those memories and feelings about everyone and everything around them come all rushing back. It's like a tidal wave of emotion. Plus, I know the holidays are still hard for my mom. It's only been two years since my dad ... well ... since my dad did what he did.

It seems like forever but is probably only a second or two before my mom snaps back to the moment.

"Maybe we should call him. Whaddya say, kiddo?"

My eyes light up and I'm already plucking the cordless phone from its base that hangs on the kitchen wall. I punch in seven-oh-six as the clear, rubbery number pads light up and beep. I love that particular "do-re-mi" progression because I know it's the sound of Uncle Eddie's area code in Georgia. But I never remember the rest, so my mom recites the remainder of the number in that universal cadence people always use: Bah-bah-bah ... bah-bah ... bah-bah.

I follow along, punching the keypad. After a distant click, I hear the line connect. It rings. Then four times more. The light in my eyes dims with each one because I know by the next ring it's gonna click over to that staticky recording of my uncle's voice that sounds all stiff and monotone, like he's reading off an index card. All very adult and impersonal, and nothing at all like the Uncle Eddie I know.

I hang up, biting my lip. "No answer."

It's not just that I'm disappointed. Because I am. But now I'm wondering how I could've gotten it so wrong. I thought I was getting to the point where I could decipher my interruptions without getting them too screwed up. At least, not this bad.

Feeling like I've disappointed myself, I retreat to my bedroom and wallow in Poe's tale of wickedly delicious revenge.

III

That might not have been the best idea, me finishing 'Cask' right before bed. Because I had my bad dream again. The one that comes to me a lot. A gut-puncher nightmare, actually.

In it, I am alone in these creepy woods.

Except, I'm not. There's some*thing* else there. Silent. Motionless. Wearing a long dark robe with a cowl. I can't see this thing's face but know there is something awful—maybe even rotted—beneath that hood. It wants me to do terrible stuff. Even though I never hear it speak, I can *feel* what it wants me to do. Things like...hurting my family. It wants me to do awful things to Andrew. To my mom.

I try to get away, to make it stop, but it's like it has this connection with me that I can't break. Like it's *inside* of me. So, I do what it says. I keep hurting them in my dream. Over and over and over. Different ways each time. It's so awful, but it just won't stop.

It never ends....

2:6

AS THE GREY light of yet another New York autumn morning filters through my curtains, it takes me a few moments to recognize that I'm not in those woods. Everything about my night was so awful that I feel drained and shaky. And on the verge of crying. I remind myself that it was all just a bad dream. That the thing in the woods—the thing beneath that cowl—wasn't real. It was all in my head.

Look, I have to say to myself when this happens, internally reciting what I will see when I open my eyes. I have done this many times, to the point where it has become a kind of mantra after my nightmares.

You are not alone in some dark and venomous forest.

You are safe. At home. In bed.

You are five stories above the comforting hustle and bustle of the West Side, where a gazillion people are doing a gazillion mundane things.

Almost done with the mantra, I slowly begin to open my hesitant eyes so that I will be fully awake and aware by the time I silently mouth the last word.

You are safe, Diane. And you are soun—

My eyes open to a cowled figure looming over me and the breath escapes my chest in a way that I can't even scream.

I press back against the headboard as far as I can. The small of my back is squarely against it as I kick and claw, but I'm only entangling myself tighter in the vine-like grip of the twisted and sweat-soaked sheets. Every nerve ending is on fire, my whole body sizzling with fight or flight as the figure moves slowly closer and starts to lean in to me—

"It's Thanksgiving," the figure says flatly as it comes into focus through my blurred and overly tired eyes. "Mom says it's time for you to get up, you booger. She wants to see you in the kitchen."

Andrew—!

Trembling as the adrenaline spikes, I refill my lungs in spurts that sound like I'm about to bawl.

One more gulp, a deep breath out, and now I'm ready to let him have it. "JESUS, ANDREW! You scared the holy *crap* outta me!"

I grab the first thing my fingers latch onto and throw it as he perches nonchalantly on the edge of the bed. The plush tiger ricochets off his face. "Get outta here, you stupid little freak!"

I try to kick him off the bed, but my feet are still bound beneath the tangled sheets. The effort ends up creating a wave through the mattress that my nine-year-old brother rides like a bucking bronco, giggling as he bounces right off the bed after all. That makes me laugh, so when he gets up, I let him use the bed as a stepping stool and climb up onto my back.

We continue this impromptu game as I give him a piggy-back all the way to the kitchen. He's got my hair wrapped gingerly in both hands and is pressing the heels of his feet into my ribs, laughing as he yells, "Giddyup!"

Mom is already busy at the stove, and in his booster seat at the table, Simon Peter is joyfully muttering to himself as he plucks dry Honey Toasted Ohs from his plastic cereal bowl with great concentration, relocating them to his tray one-by-one.

"Now that looks fun," says the man's voice behind us that isn't my Uncle Ian's. Whether it's a reference to our piggy-back ride or Simon Peter's secret game, I do not know.

"Uncle Eddie!" I drop my brother unceremoniously to the floor and rush into my uncle's arms. Even though I'm almost as big as he is now, Uncle Eddie still swoops me up to swing me around in circles. Andrew smiles, pleased at the role he played in my big surprise.

"Well, hello there, Petunia!"

Uncle Eddie calls everyone Petunia. Well, all the pretty girls, anyway. But I know it means more when he calls *me* that. "I knew you were coming! I just knew it!"

"Did you?" he asks as he sets my feet back onto the cold tile floor.

"I did!" But then I remember the phone call. "I called you, but you didn't answer. It started to go to your machine."

"Because I was already on the road, silly girl. It's a bit of a drive from Georgia to the Big Apple, you know."

"You need one of those cell phones, Uncle Eddie! Then I could've talked to you on the way here. Plus, I was worried you weren't gonna come."

"Now, can you really see me with one of those things, Petunia?" He taps the end of my nose. I can tell that he's looking at my uncle Ian's cell phone on the counter behind me. "You know I like my space. Soon, there'll be no getting away from anything. Or anyone. Those things are going to take over. You watch and see."

He hesitates before saying the next thing but decides to say it anyway. "Besides, I thought you already *knew* I was coming."

It's a statement, not a question. And the tone of it feels ... off ... somehow.

"Well—" Now I feel embarrassed for a reason I don't understand and avert my eyes. I'm staring at my toes.

Realizing that he's made me feel insecure without meaning to, Uncle Eddie grabs the big brown shopping bag from the table. I'm sure he planned on revealing its contents after we ate, but now seems the right time.

"So," he begins, clearing his throat while spying my mom out of the corner of his eye. She's heard the crumpling of that bag and tosses a sly look over her shoulder before returning her attention to the stove and silently shaking her head. "I was going to wait to give this to you guys...you know I don't like to be in your mother's bad books! But is anyone in the mood for one o' these big, bad boys?"

Like a magician, he dramatically pulls away the paper bag to reveal a tray of huge, plastic-wrapped Gobs. Big, gooey, chocolate cake yummies with a good inch of icing in the middle.

Oh man! I'd forgotten about Gobs! I suddenly realize I've missed them, without even knowing that I did.

You see, you just can't get gobs in New York. Not anywhere, really, except western Pee Aay. In fact, no one here has ever even heard of a Gob. When you try to describe them to people, most will act like they know better and tell you that you mean a 'whoopie pie,' and that they're exactly the same thing. Don't let 'em fool you. They're not the same. At all. Sure, they might *look* the same—two cakey chocolate 'buns' sandwiching a layer of icing—but whoopie pie cakey bits are airy, like cupcake tops or something, and the icing between them is too sweet and sugary, not creamy and thick like gob icing. It's the Crisco that makes the difference. Yep, you heard that right. Welcome to good ol' Pennsylvania back country cooking!

Andrew and I both snatch one from the tray and I can't peel back the cellophane from mine fast enough. I force myself to slow down and close my eyes, wanting to really savor this moment as I raise it to my mouth. It doesn't disappoint.

Oh, yeah! That's no whoopie pie. That's a Gob, for sure.

I don't know how he pulled it off, but Uncle Eddie got the real deal. Somehow.

"Now, don't you kids go filling up on junk." My mom rolls her eyes at Eddie but smiles. "You can see I've got a big Thanksgiving lunch being prepared."

When she turns back to the stove, he sneaks up behind and tickles her, hitting that spot just under the ribs.

"Eddie! Stop! I have a stove going here!" She acts like she's irritated, but I can tell she secretly loves it.

It makes me a little angry.

"Why, Rebecca Cockerton," replies Uncle Eddie, chuckling that trademark Uncle Eddie laugh of his that you'd swear to God was Muttley from the *Wacky Races* Saturday morning cartoons. "I dare say the lady doth protesteth too much,"

This is exactly when Uncle Ian steps into the kitchen.

"Hey. What exactly is going on here?" He sounds concerned. More than concerned, he actually sounds angry as he lays down the sack of potatoes he was sent to fetch from whatever corner shop might still be open this morning, price no objection.

His face starts to get all scrunched.

Now he doesn't just sound angry. He looks it, too.

Is Uncle Ian jealous—like really *jealous? And while we're putting people under the interrogation lamp, am I feeling jealous too...of my own mother?*

Uncle Eddie moves away from my mom, and I can tell she feels self-conscious, glancing at her feet as Uncle Eddie takes two slow and carefully deliberated steps towards Uncle Ian, the mirth in his eyes gone. His face deadpan. "You got a problem, Cockerton?"

Now Uncle Ian takes two steps toward Uncle Eddie. They've become two gunfighters about to face off. "Yeah, I do," he says. "You're getting a little too fresh with my gal, there. Don't you think?"

Your gal? Wait. Isn't my mom my dad's *gal? I mean, I know my father's dead 'n all, but still—*

"Yeah? Well, why don't you come here and do something about it then," Uncle Eddie threatens.

So, my Uncle Ian does. With a face like thunder he leans into Eddie...and gives him a huge hug. "Holy smokes, Eddie. It's so great to see you!"

Smiling big, Uncle Eddie reciprocates, opening his arms and patting Uncle Ian on the back. "It's great to see you, too, you great big sack-o-shi—" Suddenly conscious that Andrew's, Simon Peter's, and my eyes are all on him, Uncle Eddie cuts the cheeky insult short. "Sack-o-STUFF, you."

"Good save," my mom congratulates him in dripping sarcasm without turning from the stove.

The Muttley laugh again.

II

"When did you get in, Eddie?"

(By the way, my Uncle Ian is the only one that doesn't call him *Uncle* Eddie. Funny, 'cause my dad never did, either.)

"Oh, you know. I've been around town a couple days. But I waited until you left this morning to come on in. Thought Becca might enjoy some alone time with good ol' Uncle Ed, here." He winks and gives my mom a pinch on the rump, chuckling.

My mom gives him a playful slap in return. "I would enjoy no such thing."

Ewww. Has it always been like this? Why haven't I noticed it before? Because, I answer myself, this internal dialogue as natural for me as conversing with a real person ... sometimes more so. *You're fifteen now, Diane. It just went over your head before.*

Did it? Now I'm debating myself over the suggestion of my own naivete. *The last time I saw Uncle Eddie was back in Pee Aay. When my dad was still around. Were Mom and he like this around Daddy, too? Or are they just like this in front of Uncle Ian ... ?*

I'm momentarily lost in the back-and-forth of this idea (um, yeah, it can get a little busy inside my head sometimes) when Mom makes a point of giving Uncle Ian a romantic kiss. She then gently wipes the lipstick from his lips. It's way too intimate for this situation, which I realize is on purpose. Her way of saying—to Ian and Eddie both—that all this flirtation is just innocent fun.

"But seriously," my Uncle Eddie continues. "I had some things I needed to see to and thought you wouldn't mind an old pal of your brother's coming to visit for the holiday. I hope that's cool?"

"Of course it is," Uncle Ian assures him. "And an old pal of mine, too, Eddie. After all, we go back a long ways."

"That we do, Ian. That we do." Uncle Eddie's eyes are staring at something that isn't there. I can tell it's a memory of a place and time far from this one. He snaps back to the moment when Simon Peter toddles over and begins climbing into his lap. "And of course, I needed to meet this one!"

Scooped into Uncle Eddie's arms, Simon Peter stares at this new face, literally nose-to-nose. Filled with an intense fascination, his little fingers play over the topography of the features: over Uncle Eddie's nose, beneath his eyes. I always find it incredible watching him learn. It's like witnessing a little miracle every day.

"Yes it is," Uncle Ian softly agrees with me.

But the thing is, I hadn't said that out loud.

III

Still in our pajamas and snuggled-up together on the sofa, Simon Peter, Andrew and I are glued to the TV, watching the Thanksgiving parade and devouring hot glazed cinnamon rolls fresh from the oven. After seeing it all my life back in Pee Aay, it's still weird to think that all that activity is happening just thirty blocks away. You'd swear you could see those balloons from here, being so big and flying so high and all, but all you can see is the buildings. Like always. That view never changes—just all those great big grey and brown rectangles, with these windows that shimmer like scales. Inanimate monsters neatly lined up, one after the other. I think that's one of the big reasons why I like it here; ironically, why it feels safe. There's a sense of this city never changing, and that feels secure to me. That, and you're just never, ever, alone.

Which I like.

Uncle Ian says he took me and Andrew down to the parade in

person last year, while Mom stayed home with Simon Peter, since he was only a year old at the time. Andrew remembers every detail about it and says it was really cool. But, like I've shared with you, I was still coming out of my zombie phase back then, so I don't remember it.

Like, at all.

A part of me sort of knows that I was there. I credit that to my interruptions, you know, giving me a sense of emotional memory. But I can't actually tell you a single thing about what it was like. Anyway, everyone says it's much better on TV because you can see so much more than you can in person. And those crowds?

Fuhgeddaboudit, as they say.

In the kitchen, my parents' muffled voices (well, I think you know by now that I mean my Mom's and my Uncle Ian's) mix with the velvety tone of Uncle Eddie's—along with the occasional outburst of Muttley—as they swap memories over Bloody Marys. There's something oddly comforting about hearing their glasses chime as they place them down, or when my mom absentmindedly taps her nails against the side of hers. Every once in a while, a warm peal of laughter erupts in unison over a story from their shared past: a story I know will include my dad.

For the first time in a long time, everything is right in the world. It's heaven.

IV

It doesn't last....

2:7

AFTER DINNER, UNCLE Ian went down to the Major League sports bar in midtown. A guy named Tony Lamont runs it. My uncle calls it 'Old School' New York. I've heard so many stories I feel like I actually know this Tony guy personally even though I've never been there. Being as I'm only fifteen 'n all.

Hanging out there with his best friend Felipe who he works with at the *Manhattan Bulletin* has been a Thanksgiving tradition ever since Uncle Ian moved to the city. And like I've said, that was *way back*, long before I was even born. It might seem odd to some people that he would just up and leave us like that after dinner, now that we all live together as a family. But my mom doesn't mind.

If you ask me, I think she enjoys the time to herself.

I've gotten to know Felipe pretty good this past year. He's a nice guy. Funny, too. And he always brings us something when he drops by. Last time, it was this big Toblerone for me and Andrew to share, and a little dollar toy for Simon Peter.

They invited Uncle Eddie to come along this evening. You know, make it a guys' night out. But Uncle Eddie said he was tired and might catch up with them later.

But everyone knew that was a *porky pie.*

That's what my dad always called a lie. I once asked him why, and he said it was rhyming slang from these blue-collar people in the East End of London, called Cockneys. They also say funny things like *the ol' dog and bone* when they mean the phone, and *brown bread* when someone's dead. Dad picked this up from his British grandfather who immigrated here a million years ago, in the nineteen-twenties or something. Mom thinks it's a silly way to talk, but I think it's colorful. It tickles the aspiring writer in me.

So, instead of going to the bar, Uncle Eddie napped for about an hour in my dad's leather recliner in the reading nook. Until, that is, my mom felt he'd had enough sleepy time.

"Go and wake the old snoring machine in the corner," she instructs Andrew, who does so by pinching and holding the end of his nose until Uncle Eddie coughs and splutters to consciousness.

"Come and play with us," Andrew says and is already pulling him toward the living room, Uncle Eddie half-stumbling behind and still clearing his sleepy eyes. At the coffee table my mom is setting up a fun new game with dominoes, called Mexican Train. On her lap, Simon Peter is mesmerized by the TV while she peers over his head to spread the dominoes haphazardly across the table, preparing them for player selections.

Andrew plops down on the floor near her feet. And of course, I take a seat next to Uncle Eddie on the couch.

"Do you know how to play?" I ask him, my happiness at his being here impossible to mask and I know he senses it on a deeper level.

"Do I know how to *play*?" he repeats with fake incredulity. "Petunia, my girl! At this very moment you are looking at the Mexican Train champion of Lumpkin County, Georgia, eighteen-sixty-six!"

Of course, I realize he's joking because that was, like, a hundred years before he was even born. That, and the fact that I doubt there's even a Mexican Train championship in Lumpkin County. But I play along anyway. Tilting my head and resting my cheek on my hand, I flutter my eyelashes as emphatically as I can until I've transformed into a bashful but adoring admirer.

"Why, Sir," I croon in my best Southern Belle. "I do pray you'll take mercy in our challenge upon this poor, ignorant country girl."

He Muttleys, pushing me away as my mother rolls her eyes.

"Okay, you losers," she taunts and rubs her hands together before choosing fifteen dominoes as though her life depended upon it. "Let's play."

Did I tell you my mom can be pretty competitive?

The first game is mine, though.

Mom really hunkers down after that and wins the second.

I have the third in the bag—down to only my last two dominoes—when Andrew, having at least thirty tiles left (not joking) jumps up with a huff. He gets so easily frustrated when he doesn't do something well. But to be fair, this is a pretty taxing strategy game for a nine-year-old. Plus, I tend to win a lot.

He bumps the corner of the game board as he stands, and everyone's neat line of domino 'trains' jostle into everyone else's.

Game called, due to an Andrew-quake.

I know he didn't mean to do it, but this makes him even more frustrated. He stomps away and I can feel how disheartened he is. It's like this connection we share.

"Andrew, come back . . ." I call after him, but Uncle Eddie holds up his hand to stifle my plea, winking with a soft smile. I reckon he wants me to just let Andrew cool off for a minute.

"Well, I guess it's past this little fellow's bedtime anyway," my mom declares and gingerly lifts an already sleeping Simon Peter to her chest.

"Let me," Uncle Eddie offers as he takes Simon from my mom, and I stifle a giggle as he carries my infant brother in two outstretched arms, exactly the way Uncle Ian carried that sack of potatoes into our kitchen this morning. My mom only manages to stop herself from laughing by pressing her fingers to her lips. She shushes me and we both silently crack up.

Andrew is already in his top bunk, still sulking but reading when

Uncle Eddie puts Simon Peter in the lower bed. My uncle doesn't know I've followed them. Peeking around the door, I want to see how he's gonna deal with Simon Peter's *instawake*, as we call it. (Just when you think he's sound asleep, you can bet your bottom dollar he'll snap wide awake, lurching up from his bed the moment you least expect it.)

It used to be frustrating. Now Mom and I just go with it.

"Sleep tight, my sacred little lamb," Uncle Eddie wishes as he gently lays Simon Peter's sleeping head on the pillow. He leans down to kiss him on the forehead and whispers something in his ear. It's barely audible, but I hear it. You're exposed to a lot of different languages around the city, and I actually like that. Makes it feel more worldly. But I've never heard this one before. It sounds a bit like gobbledygook to me. Also a little like the type of thing you'd hear a priest say in a scary movie. It sounds like, "*Ad tenebras lucem producat.*"

And right on cue, Simon Peter springs—I mean literally springs—up from his pillow. My uncle reels backward and clocks the back of his head against the rail of the top bunk, letting out a little yip. This draws Andrew from his self-hosted pity party, and he curls down over the top rail like a monkey, openly giggling.

"Oh, you think that's funny, huh?" Rubbing his scalp, Uncle Eddie is feigning an authoritative tone, but even he sees the humor in how he was startled. He reaches up to the top bunk for Andrew, his hand transforming into a playful monster claw that grabs and tickles.

My snicker in the hallway gives me away.

Uncle Eddie crouches down and places a finger to his lips. "Gentlemen! It appears we have a spy in our midst—"

"Yeah!" Andrew is bolt upright in his bunk, pointing towards my hidden position just beyond the door. Rigid and proud, he looks every bit the faithful hunting dog identifying a target. "I see you, Deedee!"

"Deeeeedee!" Simon Peter repeats over and over, his little chipmunk voice carrying throughout the apartment until my mom decides it's time to put an end to all these shenanigans. She appears in the doorway like the wind, hands sternly on hips.

"Uh oh," Uncle Eddie mutters, placing his hands dramatically on his hips and barking: "Shhhh, boys! C'mon now. I told you two that it's bedtime, not playtime!"

Of course, my mother sees right through this. Her face hardens. But it's a farce and everyone knows it. Most of all, my uncle.

And so, Muttley makes his final appearance of the evening, which softens my mother like butter in the sun.

Uncle Eddie just seems to have that effect on people.

"Okay now, guys." Mom fluffs Andrew's pillow and pats it, directing him to lie back down. Sliding her wedged hands between his back and the mattress, she tucks in the sheets nice and tight, just the way he likes. Squirming in the bottom bunk, Simon Peter then gets a kiss as she playfully tweaks his nose. "What does Simon say?"

Simon Peter giggles. I think he's suddenly embarrassed to perform in front of Uncle Eddie. It's actually kinda adorable.

"C'mon buddy," I encourage, knowing he won't properly go to sleep until the nightly ritual has been completed. "What does Simon say?"

My mom winks at me, a nonverbal *thank you*. It doesn't go unnoticed by my uncle. He seems genuinely touched by this bond between us.

Mom leans close enough to my baby brother that I know her gentle breath is washing soothingly over his ear. "Simon says what?" she coos so softly that the words caress even my soul. I feel all warm and tingly inside.

Then, in the smallest whisper that a whisper can be, Simon Peter shyly prompts, "Simon says...goo-nigh, Mommy."

"Goodnight, my sweet Prince," is her dutiful reply and he grins with pride as she kisses first one cheek, then the other. "That's my special son."

"Goo-nigh Andwew ..." he repeats, his voice a little bolder.

"Goodn—" Andrew starts to answer but catches himself. Eyes wide, he claps a hand over his mouth.

In the bunk beneath him, Simon Peter giggles, thrilled that he nearly tripped his brother up this time. A moment later, he gives the proper command, his stage fright all but gone as he declares with easy confidence, "Simon says goo-nigh Andwew!"

"Goodnight, Simon," Andrew replies and cozies back into the sheets.

Simon then repeats this intimate family routine with me, completing the pattern. To everyone's surprise, he won't let my mom turn off the light before he does so with Uncle Eddie, too, even though he's only met this man a few hours earlier.

And by the way, when he calls him 'Uggle Eddeee' it just might be the most adorable thing I've ever heard in my life.

The light switch flicks off and the room is instantly awash in cartoon fish and seahorses swimming in an array of blues, the scene cast by the rotating lamp on the boys' bedside table. My mom pulls the door mostly closed, leaving it ajar just enough so she can hear either of the boys should they need her. She says something about calling Uncle Ian's cell phone to see when he's coming home, then recants when she realizes he's left it on the coffee table.

"Right then." She winks at Uncle Eddie. "Guess that's his loss. 'Cause I've got a twelve-year-old Scotch just waiting to be drank." She invites him to join her in the kitchen where a crystal decanter is calling their name.

I stay back a moment. The whiskey isn't calling *my* name. Although my dad offered me a sip once, a few Thanksgivings ago. I made myself such a nuisance pestering him to try it that he figured he might as well teach me a lesson. And he did, because that tiny taste was enough to make me almost puke. I'm fifteen now, and I can still remember that horrible acid burn on my tongue. *Blecch!* Even the smell of it makes me feel sick now. I have no idea how they can just sit there and drink that stuff and act like they actually think it's good? So, no. I have no interest in joining them in the kitchen, thank you very much. Plus, I have a feeling Mom and Uncle Eddie would appreciate some adult conversation for a few.

To be honest, though, it's neither of those reasons that makes me stay here, outside the boys' room. Something else tells me to.

Not quite one of my interruptions, but it's close.

I cast no shadow in the darkened hallway, making it easy to eavesdrop unnoticed as long as I don't go any closer or try to peek in. They're whispering to one another, which makes me smile. At first, it's hard to make it out. Then I realize they're still playing 'Simon Says.'

"Simon says, coun' fish!" my babiest brother commands.

"One. Two," Andrew reports. "Eight-nine-ten-eleven ....Fifteen!"

Simon Peter applauds his older brother's counting prowess, clapping excitedly though his soft hands make little sound. "Your turn, Andwew. Your turn!"

Andrew internally debates what command he might give. After all, Simon Peter is only two years old—there's not a whole hell of a lot you can challenge him to do that he'll really understand. But, as always, Andrew manages to connect perfectly with the baby brother he so adores.

"Okay, okay! Here's a good one for ya! Ready?" He pauses to ensure Simon is on the hook. Just when the giggling from the bottom bunk has escalated to the level of potentially alerting my mom, Andrew commands: "Tell me how many people are in our bedroom?"

For a moment, I wonder if Andrew has chosen that because he's spotted me. Then I realize there's no way. Their bunk beds face away from the door, which is almost fully shut, and I'm carefully concealed behind it in the unlit hallway. He's just making this an easy one for his little brother.

"Ummm," Simon Peter deliberates briefly before starting to answer. "There's—oh! Huh-uh!" the two-year-old squeals with delight as he cuts himself short, realizing he nearly lost the game. I dare to peek through the gap in the door to see he's pinching his little duck lips together. Because, as you know, that's the only way to guarantee the words won't come out. The same way that no one can see you if you cover your own eyes.

"Haha!" Andrew chuckles. "Almost got you! Okay then. Simon says, how many people are in our bedroom?"

"One .... Two ..." Simon Peter answers as he counts on his tiny fingers, the words spoken slowly and carefully just above his breath. I'm smiling so big at his cuteness at this point I can't stand it and decide I'm just gonna go in and join their fun, my mother's wrath be damned.

What happens next stops me dead in my tracks, my hand gripping the doorknob so tight that my knuckles go white.

Because another voice finishes Simon's answer for him.

"... Three," it rasps, low and guttural.

My breath is stolen from me, my chest tight as a snare drum.

Chill out, girl. That was just Uncle Eddie in the kitchen, my mind quickly rationalizes. *Or some guy's voice on the TV. Maybe Uncle Ian is already back.*

But these are all stupid justifications. Because that voice wasn't either of my uncles'. And it not only came from the boys' room ... I can actually tell that it came from the window alcove next to their closet. The one place where the lamp light doesn't quite reach.

The one place where the shadows live.

"S-S-Simon?" I hear Andrew stutter from the top bunk.

There is no reply.

"SIMON."

Silence.

"I'm not messing around anymore!" Andrew swallows hard,

unaware he's holding his breath. His pitch rises an octave. "This isn't funny!"

Only a stilted and labored wheezing replies from the shadows. It's wet air through a pinched balloon. Quiet, but so shrill it's almost...

...*Whistling.*

In the lower bunk, Simon emits a little giggle.

"Stop it, Simon! Stop it. Stop it. STOP IT! You're scar—" Andrew runs out of breath, gulping in uncontrolled little spasms.

Run away! Get help! my head screams as every cell in my body presses me to get away from here. *Do anything but go in that room!*

But something's drawing me in like a magnet. Beckoning me to come closer, to see with my own eyes the origin of that voice lurking in my brothers' room.

It doesn't make sense why I burst through that door, or why I've regressed to the logic of a two-year-old and close my eyes as I do, as if doing so will keep me from being seen. But I'm charging in and have already lost my balance on the throw rug. My legs fly out and up, and the wind knocks out of me as the small of my back slams squarely against the floor, the base of my skull clapping polished hardwood to accentuate the sound.

My eyes jar open and I'm left sucking for air like a beached fish. I don't feel the pulsing pain in my head yet. Or the thick, warm ooze about to matt my hair. All I'm aware of is Andrew's frozen stare.

On the shadowy figure in the corner.

In my mind I scream louder than I ever have in my life—for my mom, for my uncle, for anyone to hear me—but no sound comes out. My throat is sand, my tongue cotton. I can't even swallow.

"*Dzhee*—" the figure wheezes and takes a step toward me as I lie twisted on the floor. The blue seascape of the projector lamp grows brighter to reveal a cowled robe as it moves closer, oblivious cartoon fish swimming in-and-out of focus across it. "*—Dzhheeee.*"

It's so close now I can almost touch it, and my burning panic has flooded through every part of me. I begin scrabbling backwards for the door, kicking my heels and scratching the glossy hardwood for purchase, but still I go nowhere ...

... For the manic effort is only in my mind. My arms and legs have not moved. In fact, the only physical act I muster is my left hand digging into the floor so hard that several of the nails bend backwards, one peeling a third of the way off.

I don't even feel it.

My entire world is now the decayed and blistered face beneath that cowl as the figure looms over me, exactly as it does in my dreams. A grotesque purple in the lamp's underwater glow, oozing lesions crisscross its flayed and rotted cheeks, maggots rippling from one of its dead eyes.

Eyes I recognize as my father's.

"Dzhee Dzhee!"

The sound of my name whistles through a small puncture in Daddy's cheek, a hole the size that a pencil—or a bullet—might make, but most of it wheezes through a gaping cavity at the back of his skull. Thin ribbons of scalp flap with each of his sour breaths.

My mind fizzles and pops, a million neurons that should never be connected arcing in painful, static electric shocks inside my brain. Pins and needles are multiplying down my spine, a thousand biting ants, until I can no longer feel my arms or legs.

Is this what a stroke victim feels like? is all I manage to think before my foundering rationale finally exits stage right. *Because that's not your dead father, Diane. You know it can't possibly be! The same way you know that none of this is really happening. Oh my, no! You're just dreaming. You creative, silly girl, you ....*

As if privy to this internal monologue, a satisfied snarl twists across my father's decomposing mouth. Extending a hand from the cuff of his robe, he plays a grey, pus-filled fingertip over my face. It brushes my cheek; teases across my cracked and quivering lips.

My brain doesn't care. Now entirely unfazed, it insists with cool indifference that what I'm experiencing is a harmless, if grotesque, hallucination. A distorted reflection in a funhouse mirror. *Smoke and mirrors,* it now finds comfort in repeating over and again until I begin to drift away on a tropical blue sea, the sound of the mantra fading until the words become the gentle ripples of my fingers trailing lazily across the water's glasslike surface.

… My father's rotting fingertip playing across my face…

The remotest part of my awareness that hasn't fully checked out knows my brain's peddling some dangerous bullshit. Because far from floating atop some idyllic waterscape, I'm on my back in my brothers' room. Pinned to the floor. An oozing gash on the back of my head. Staring into the milky dead eyes of my father.

His face is so close I can taste his breath—the rancid pickle of biology class dissection frogs—and my stomach heaves. He smiles at this and sniffs the air, his still-perfect teeth gleaming against the dark, rotting hole of his mouth. He licks his tongue across them, then flicks it from withered lips that once peppered my face with a dozen wet raspberry goodnight kisses. Impossibly long and thin, the end of that tongue twitches as a snake's, testing the stale and unmoving air just above my nose and mouth. Even through his cataract stare, I can tell he likes the way the stagnation tastes.

Tears well into my eyes.

What used to break my Daddy's heart now elicits just another flick of his tongue, and I realize what he savors is the fact that at some point—

—I've stopped breathing.

I don't know when. Or how long it's been.

But something in that distant part of my brain, that same tiny part stubbornly unimpressed by my delusion of the tropical waters, tells me if I don't take another breath soon, then I will have already taken my last.

Daddy…. I cry, but nothing comes out.

Desperate for oxygen, my empty lungs are on fire. They only

burn hotter with every gulp that doesn't fill them. My palms are slapping the floor, my feet jerking uncontrollably. Pinned against the hardwood, my body twists and writhes until the repeated, useless attempts to fill my lungs reduce to nothing but pathetic goldfish puckers; the violent spasms tapering to random twitches.

My father slowly tilts his head. First one way. Then the other. It's the detached curiosity of a hyena watching the life drain away from the convulsing hare beneath it.

Everything's out of focus. Spinning into dark.

Then the ribbons appear.

Far from ebbing away to nothingness, an inner spark of light wisps from my mouth. Growing into a wave, it flows and dances like colored smoke in the air. Every hue I've ever seen swirls around me, but mostly deep blues, indigo and violet. And then the white. So much bright, crystal white! A calm like none I've ever known wraps around me like a blanket, eclipsing the searing pain in my chest and the thrumming which has begun to cycle at the back of my skull. None of it seems to matter anymore. Not even the cowled, rotting shell of my father overtop me.

Until Daddy's mouth draws impossibly long, shrieking while the jawbones unhinge in a series of snaps like fresh kindling on a campfire. Uncoiling his snake-like tongue, he spools my ribbons of light from me like cotton candy round a stick. They are drawn into the black void of its mouth.

And I am falling.

Deeper.

Faster.

Into darkness.

No … not darkness. Emptiness.

Serenity strips away to expose cold, slicing fear. I am becoming nothing. All that I am, or ever could be, absorbed into the putrid thing writhing inside the body of my dead father. I thrash and struggle to hold onto the final threads of my life but feel them unravelling, just beyond my reach.

Consumed.

The last thing I hear is a yelping laugh that gurgles up into my Daddy's blistered and peeling throat....

2:8

MY GOD! DIANE!" The voice is faint to me, though I can tell it should sound loud and brusque. I think it's my mother's. I open my eyes and the light is so bright its whiteness blinds me. But I am too afraid to close my eyes again. Or maybe they're frozen open, so I can't? It feels like I'm turning my head away. But I'm not sure if I am.

"Come on, baby! Wake up! Breathe!"

A slap. A shake. A pressing sensation on my chest.

I suck in air with a sudden and violent gasp, my back arching.

Now I'm blinking; it's a spasmodic fluttering of my eyelids. I'm groggy and confused as the blaze of white light slowly softens to the warm, overhead light of my brothers' room. Shapes and colors slowly appear and a face, mere inches away, is blurred and weaving like I'm seeing it underwater through a strong current. Or the way movies always show the world through a drunk person's eyes.

A moment later, I recognize those pleading eyes.

I clasp my arms around Mommy's neck and start to bawl, rivers of tears wetting my face.

II

I'm on the couch. From the kitchen, voices ebb and flow. I can make out the odd word here or there. *But truthfully?* I'm afraid to know how they fit into the rest of the murmured conversation. Because the ones I pick up on are lots of 'un' words: like 'unsettling' and 'unstable.' Most of these are in my mother's voice, which sounds panicked and fearful. Some are in the vaguely familiar voice of our occasionally seen neighbor from the eighth floor, Dr. Patterson, reiterating that he's found nothing of concern about my *physical* health, then adds something about a 'voluntary admission' just before lowering his voice to a near-whisper. But the one 'un' word I hear that scares me the most is spoken by Uncle Eddie:

"Unsafe."

I think there's a question mark at the end of it, but I'm starting to cry so can't be sure. Even through my hiccupping tears I can still hear his flat and authoritative tone repeating my brothers' names. That, and the awful sound of my mom quietly sobbing in reply.

III

Leading me slowly into my brothers' bedroom, my hand feels small and clammy in Uncle Eddie's big, warm grip. Sensing me bristle as we cross the threshold, he pauses to caress my back before we take another step forward. The curtains opposite us ripple and waft from the window left half-open, the cold November air billowing them toward the center of the room. And despite Uncle Eddie's overt care, I still expect him to say something condescending. Or dismissive. Something along the lines of, 'There's your boogeyman.'

But he says nothing at all.

On the throw rug is a small blotch of my blood, drying to a near-brown, and I'm again conscious of the rubber-tipped mallet tapping the base of my skull with every heartbeat. I reach for the bandage at the back of my head. The cut and pulsing lump aren't unbearable, but they don't exactly tickle either. It's the scraping nausea which accompanies this thick, sadistic beat that makes it feel worse than it really is.

We stand still for a moment to watch the curtains lift and fall.

"But—" I blurt out as they momentarily hold a shape like a person. *A man in a cowled robe.* Smiling cartoon fish swim out of focus across them before the drapes fall back to rest against the wall in their dark little alcove. "The window wasn't open. It wasn't!"

Uncle Eddie unknowingly purses his lips. It's the worst look he could ever give me, reeking of disappointment and disapproval. "Petunia—"

"NO!" I yank my hand out of his so hard that I nearly lose my balance again, sliding on the rug. "It was here! *HE* was here!"

"Diane . . . sweetheart. Your mother's told me about the window lock being broken. This isn't the first time she's come in here to find the bottom pane shimmied up a few inches from the warm updraft off the street."

He doesn't believe me.

The one person left in my world who makes me feel closest to my dad—closer than Uncle Ian, in some ways even closer than my mom—and he thinks I'm making this up.

Or that maybe I'm losing my mind.

. . . Unstable . . . Unsafe . . .

I feel the void closing in on me again, the terror as that putrid thing extracted my ribbons of life: the very essence of who I am. The hopelessness as it seemed to absorb them, empowering the sick thing inside it pretending to be—

"My Daddy!"

Running from the room, filled with fresh tears, my uncle calls after me. Mom's face is haggard as she rocks Simon Peter in her arms, Andrew falling asleep on the sofa next to her. I tear past them and out the front door before she understands what's happening.

I can't wait for the elevators. My uncle will be right behind me any second. So, I slam open the internal fire exit and take the stairs, bounding down them two and three at a time. I'm panting by the time I rush past the evening doorman and out the main entrance.

I'm still wearing only my PJs, never changing after watching the parade on TV this morning, and the night air hits me like I've opened a freezer door after a long, steaming bath. Shocking and exhilarating at the same time, I dodge in and out of unconcerned passersby as the wind sweeps the tears from my face. Only after I've made it all the way across Central Park West do I dare glance behind me. Uncle Eddie is just now darting from our apartment building. He slides to a stop at the bottom of the steps, eyes searching up and down the busy street. But I'm already lost in a group of pedestrians.

I hop the low stone wall into the park.

And disappear into the dark safety of the trees.

IV

The limbs are mostly bare, the pretty autumn colors all but gone as we march toward winter. Normally I wouldn't take much notice, but I do tonight. Sitting on my special boulder at the edge of this wooded tract of the park, I can easily see our apartment building between the trees.

That doesn't mean my uncle can see *me*.

At first, I'm self-conscious about being spotted, so I press low against the rock as I spy Uncle Eddie pacing frantically up and down the busy main thoroughfare. It isn't long before I appreciate just how camouflaged I am in here: a grey and black pajama-clad shape behind a line of trees, amidst a tangle of brush and undergrowth, crouching atop a huge, craggy boulder. Emboldened, I sit fully upright and follow his progress as he ducks in and out of side streets, shielding his eyes from streetlight glare and raising himself on his toes (as if those few extra inches will enable him to see that much farther). Coming up empty, Uncle Eddie finally makes his way back to our apartment building. Just when I think he's giving up, he pivots and stares motionless across the street south of the playground. His eyes search the darkness at the park's wooded edge, in the exact spot where I'm hiding in my special place. I'm certain that he sees me. But just when I think he does, he slowly turns and retreats quietly back into our building.

I don't know if I feel relieved or rejected.

The cold night air I found so life-affirming only minutes ago now creeps into my bones, and I start to shiver. It makes me grateful I chose my flannel PJs today instead of my light cotton set. Mom always keeps the house way too warm in the winter months—the heat blasting to nearly eighty on days like today—so the cooler cotton PJs would have been more comfortable. But I wanted to get into the holiday mood as my brothers and I watched the parade, so the cozy flannels were perfect as we all snuggled up together in front of the TV.

I pull my legs up to my chin, taking the shape of a tight little ball, and blow on my fingers. Rub my arms. It helps, just not a whole lot.

At least the wind has died down.

Catty-corner across the street, I spy the rectangle of light that is the boys' bedroom window, glowing like a warm golden beacon on the fifth floor. Others in the building are illuminated, but I can spot this particular window in a heartbeat because of the way it sits at the corner, just above the decorative stone ledge that wraps around the building. It's a narrow sill, maybe a foot deep at best, but really adds a touch of class to the face of the old building. And I like that. I think it's cool that developers spent the extra time and money to add things like that back in the old days. My dad used to point out those kinds of details to me anytime we visited a town where there were older buildings. He'd absently caress his chin while staring in admiration, then shake his head and tell me how they just don't make an effort like that anymore. I wasn't really sure what he was saying at the time, but now that I live in New York, I get it. Because we have a lot of super cool old buildings here, buildings that made an effort. I really like the gargoyles on ours: gothic little monsters crouching at each corner of the ledge, with grimacing faces and long snouts to help drain the rainwater away. When it's really storming out, they spit the water in an arc that lands a good four or five feet from the building by the time it splashes down to the sidewalk. Mom and I once saw a man lose his umbrella to it. He wasn't watching where he was going (or maybe he just couldn't see through the rain, being as he had his head down 'n all) and when he walked beneath that heavy stream, his umbrella just folded in on itself. It was kinda funny at the time ... but now that I'm out here shivering, I'm thinking maybe it wasn't so much fun for him.

Perched atop my rock, I'm still seeing that scene in my mind when suddenly a twig snaps somewhere in the dark and wrenches me back to the moment. I swing my head around and search the darkness. As still and silent as one of those gargoyles, I hold my breath and listen. For a moment, there's nothing but the muted sound of the city.

But then ... crunching leaves. I think I spy movement in the dark. Now I hear the unmistakable sound of footsteps—coming straight towards me—and my gut tightens.

Has Uncle Eddie come back for me, after all?

But I know he hasn't. Because impossibly, there's hardly a soul on the street. Like, no one for a few blocks. So, if my uncle had come back out, I would've noticed him crossing Central Park West; a lone, heroic figure in the darkness. Since that isn't what's happening, this is the moment I realize that when Uncle Eddie turned back into our building it was complete, numbing rejection I felt after all.

Because, let's face it, you and I both know that all I really wanted was to be found ....

The thing is, none of that matters now. Because whatever's heading toward me hasn't come from the street. It's coming from inside the park behind me, the deepest, darkest part where the trees grow close and girthy trunks strangle out the last of the city's determined glow.

The sound of another heavy step.

I'm sure I hear a wheezing breath, and fresh panic skewers through me, my clenched fingers digging into my palms.

Do I run? Hide?

But I know it's too late for either of those options as nearby branches press aside, the ground snapping beneath sizable feet. Biting shivers freeze my spine, the dank night feeling more and more like a paralyzing ice bath.

"—Diane?"

My Uncle Ian's voice. Instant relief spikes my adrenaline, blurring my vision and trembling my hands as I cover my face.

I begin to laugh hysterically.

A moment later, I'm almost crying.

Uncle Ian climbs up onto my rock. He's a little unsteady on his feet, a thick smell of alcohol reaching me before he does. He slides next to me and nestles in close, opening his coat and wrapping me up into him. It's warm. And makes me feel safe.

"I'm sorry babygirl. I didn't mean to scare you." He pauses, carefully considering what he's about to say next. Then he adds, as easily as if apologizing for drinking the last of the milk or something, "And sorry about what happened tonight. I know that had to be terrifying. And frustrating, for no one to believe you."

Wait—what?

He hasn't even been home yet. And didn't he leave his cell phone behind? But maybe Mom called Felipe's? I've never seen him with one, though, so how could Uncle Ian possibly know what happened? Inundating myself with these questions, and more, faster than I can answer them, I take a stuttering breath to calm my nerves.

"Diane! That's enough." The intensity in Uncle Ian's voice is startling, but at least it's curtailed my own mental interrogation.

I swipe away a thin line of tears with the heel of my shaking hand, slowly lifting my eyes to meet his stern gaze.

"You already know how I know," he insists. Except his mouth isn't

moving. The words are somehow coming from inside my own head like I'm hearing them through a pair of headphones I don't have on. *"We've both known, Diane. For a while now. Haven't we...?"*

Fresh anxiety tightens my chest.

"Haven't we?"

Saturating my thoughts.

"Haven't we."

And my rational mind clicks another notch further from my grasp. Because this can't be real. Sure, I've told you that sometimes I get my 'interruptions,' but those come to me as feelings; emotional sensations; puzzles I need to decipher. Not as full-blown conversations I can actually hear inside my own head.

That's just straight-up impossible.

"Impossible?" Uncle Ian immediately counters, not a breath of air escaping his motionless lips. His eyes lock onto mine, but I see no love or safety in them. Only a faraway emptiness. *"Impossible, like the reanimated corpse of your father, Diane? Coming back for you... to consume you?"*

I don't know how he's managing this sadistic mind trick, but it's twisted and wrong and makes me feel dirty from the inside out. Without thinking, I slam both of my hands into his chest—hard— and push myself away. But I'm more exhausted than I realize and all I manage to achieve is Uncle Ian strengthening his grip around me. Pulling me closer, even tighter to him. A predator holding its prey captive before devouring it.

"Oh, my dear Diane! I'm not the predator. This is all about you. Don't you understand that yet?"

His eyes widen but reveal no whites; his smile stretches in each direction until his face is a perverse, inhuman mask.

"Don't you see that? It's always been about y—"

"STOP IT!" I shout as loud as I can and claw his face, one of my nails stripping a layer of skin from his cheek. It's not deep, but it's enough of a shock for him to loosen his grip, and I slide from his stifling embrace. He reaches for the inch-long scratch which begins to seep red as I shuffle across the top of the rock, beyond his reach.

Not that he tries to stop me.

We've both been to my special place in the park many times before, and he knows the boulder drops away to a small ravine at this end. It may be just twelve or so feet down, but it's a big enough fall to snap an ankle. Or worse. Concealed by the dark of night, the ground beneath the overhang is littered with thorn-ladled briers strangling a menacing array of snapped and fallen tree branches. Look closely and you'll see how the thorns gleam like shark's teeth; the broken sapling tips reflecting the shifting moonlight. It's almost beautiful in its chaos. But make no mistake, it's a beauty of impaling, skin-piercing spikes.

I don't care.

Swinging my leg over the edge, I back hastily over the precipice. My shoeless foot seeks whatever purchase it can get on the cold rock, and I find that my toes grip the craggy vertical face better than expected. Now I swing my other leg over, aware that a single mistake could end with my arms and legs shredded to pieces.

"Wait!" Palm out, Uncle Ian raises the hand which was examining the scrape on his face. He holds up his other. With both empty in front of him, he's illustrating that he's not a threat.

Then why does my gut feel like a washing machine churning a bowling ball round and round?

I've experienced this before and it catches my attention exactly as it's meant to, the intensity of it forcing me to take notice of my breathing which is way too shallow; my chest which is starting to burn like it's being stuffed with steel wool. I'm having one of my interruptions. It's the bad first kind, designed to warn me that the person I'm with is no longer my friend.

Both legs over the ledge, I descend a few inches to the next tiny outcropping. Despite the jagged stakes and briers that hungrily await my fall, I never once take my eyes off my uncle. My left foot plays blindly across the stone, my toes finding a narrow shelf so I can release my right.

It gives way the moment I place my weight on it.

The jolt of downward momentum jerks my left hand from the rock ledge above me, the grip of my right all that's keeping me from plunging.

Uncle Ian does not flinch as I hang here, gasping.

Staring with dark intensity, his focus is on my hand as less and less of my white-knuckled fingers remain visible atop the boulder, fatigue relentlessly sliding each tip closer to the edge.

The first to release is my thumb.

Then my pinkie.

My eyes clenched tight, just three fingers hold the weight of my entire body as my bare feet kick and scrape, seeking a way to latch onto the unseen rockface.

Pebbles and shingle fall away.

I'm picturing myself plummeting and how I should stick the landing for least injury, when my uncle's rough hand wraps around my forearm.

With a single, effortless tug he hefts me to safety.

As I lay on my back, wild eyed and panting, he wets his cracked lips and releases a sharp breath of his own. Again I'm hit with the stench of stale beer and liquor as he opens his mouth, hesitates, then considers how to force from his throat the words which refuse to come. But the vibrations he's broadcasting can't be stifled.

They bombard me in low, bass waves.

I know he's unaware he's projecting them, because they're exposing some kind of truth he's struggling with, an unthinkable revelation wrapped inside a cyst of deceit. I can't feel exactly what that truth is, but those sickening waves are drowning me from the inside out. Something about them makes me feel like everything I am is a lie. And just like that, what little foothold I'd regained in my life over this past year starts to crumble away again, as easily as that rockface just did.

Except this time, I might actually plunge right over the edge.

My entire body tenses, a fierce energy shuddering through me. It's telling me that if I want to keep from sinking back into that mental abyss, I have to get away.

From here. From him. Right now.

But there's nowhere to go.

He's still blocking the only way off the rock.

Watching me squirm, Uncle Ian clears his throat. I can't tell if his eyes are moist with sympathy, or if that's only wishful thinking on my part. Either way, they're wide and unblinking when he tilts his head to a curious angle, first one way and then the other. He sidles over to me, his lips in a thin smile as he leans in and so quietly whispers in my ear: "I'm going to tell you what really happened to your father...."

2:9

THINGS AREN'T ALWAYS what they seem, Diane." In my moment of confusion and emotional shock, he's seized the opportunity to wrap his arm around me again. To anyone else it would look like affection. To me it feels like captivity. But too stunned and disoriented to resist, I do nothing to stop it.

"W-What do you mean, 'what *really* happened'?" Not only is my stomach doing somersaults, but now my heart's pounding. I know he has to sense it. And that makes me feel even more vulnerable. But my fingers are turning blue, my toes numb, and I realize as I sit here shivering, so intensely my teeth are actually chattering, that I'm more grateful for the warmth than I am afraid of what he might say next. So, I lean into him as he opens his coat and wraps half of it around me.

"I had a puppy once," he says after gently lifting my chin so I'm forced to look at him. "Which of course means your dad did, too. I was, oh I dunno, maybe eight years old or something. Which would've made your dad around eleven, I guess."

He releases my chin but surprisingly, I don't look away.

"Man, we sure loved that little dog. Our dad, your Grampa Hare, brought him home one day after work. Just out of the blue. He told us his name was Duncan. And being a stupid eight-year-old kid, I thought he was saying 'Dunkin.' You know, like the donut shop? So, every time someone called out for Duncan, I'd shout out, 'Donuts!'

right after. And I guess it stuck, because before too long, that's what everyone called him: Donuts."

I see it all as clearly as if I'm there, actually watching Uncle Ian's memory play out as if it were my own. There's Donut's brown and cream patchwork fur. The lolling tongue. And the game of keep-away my dad and uncle are playing, innocently teasing him with a rawhide bone in the house where they grew up back in Pee Aay ... the same house my grandparents sold to my Dad, and where Andrew and I grew up too.

That little puppy is still frolicking in my mind when Uncle Ian's words trail away and I'm returned to my surreal reality: barefoot and wearing only my PJs at the onset of winter, perched on a boulder in Central Park.

Everything has become ... quiet. The usual stream of traffic noise has faded into the background and all I hear is the sound of the breeze wafting leaves over the ground; the odd watery ripple against the shore of the reservoir. It's nature's soothing musical score and in it, I begin to feel at peace. To the point that I'm starting to forget the awful thing that's happened.

Or maybe I'm just becoming numb again.

"Anyway," Uncle Ian carries on, a relaxed smile lifting his eyes. "We sure did love that silly puppy. Did your dad ever tell you and Andrew about Donuts?"

I find myself unwittingly shaking my head in response, giving myself over to the moment and not even questioning how I've gotten here or why I'm so content to ignore the unmistakable warnings of one of my more frightening interruptions. Because right now, that bowling ball feeling in my gut seems like it was a lifetime ago. Not mere moments.

"Hmmm." Uncle Ian has a faraway look on his face. At first, I think he's deep in the memory again. But if he is, I can't see it or feel it this time, even though such an expectation would make absolutely no sense to a normal, sane person. He's actually staring blankly through the trees at the hulking shape that is our apartment building, catty-corner across the street. It's taken on a menacing air as, one-by-one, most of the lights in the street-facing windows have switched off, leaving the façade cold and lifeless. On the fifth floor, Andrew and Simon's bedroom light is among these. Previously a warm, glowing beacon, now the sash windows are two dark squares reflecting the moon's cold, blue-white light. It glimmers like a weak flashlight in both upper and lower panes, providing just enough light to reveal that the bottom window has again lifted up an inch or so. Behind it, the boys' bedroom curtain ripples in and out as the warmer air from the street rises to find its way through the small gap.

Not a demon in the undead corpse of my father, after all. Just a breeze. Billowing some long fabric. And an overactive imagination. All of which seems a lot more plausible.

Exactly as Uncle Eddie had suggested to me.

Which must make me some kind of crazy, delusional person.

Exactly as Uncle Eddie had suggested to my mom.

Which I suspect she may be actually starting to believe. And who would blame her?

I would! I proclaim to myself as I shove this creeping doubt aside. I know what I saw. What I *felt*. And it wasn't wind-blown drapes.

"I don't know what's going on!" I cry out without expecting to, my voice loud and harsh in the stillness of the night. Uncle Ian looks surprised, and I grimace a little. A moment later, I find myself tucking in closer to him as I fight off the cold ... and the idea that I'm crazy. Because maybe, *just maybe*, that thing in the boys' bedroom *was* as real as it felt. I mean, haven't I just been talking with my Uncle Ian without actually speaking?

(Or, at least, he's been talking to me that way. But I've heard it. And understood it.)

So, maybe there's more going on in my world than I understand.

"What does a dog have to do with my father? And what do you

mean, you'll tell me what *really* happened?"

When this question comes out of my mouth a second time, the air on which it travels tastes sour, like breath that's been trapped inside you for too long. Ever wake up after a really hard sleep and your mouth tastes awful and you just *know* you've got morning breath that could wake the dead? Like that.

Uncle Ian doesn't flinch, over the question or the metaphorical sourness. He just sorta burrows back into his story without skipping a beat, as if he hadn't heard me at all.

Maybe he just didn't care.

"One day, we came home from school and Donuts didn't want to play like usual." He tries to smile but now it feels forced. "He was always so excited when we got home, y'know? Couldn't wait for us to get off that school bus. We'd hear that dog barking up a frenzy before we even got to the end of the driveway. Used to make your Gramma Veronica nuts."

He nudges me with his elbow and winks with a grin. This time it's authentic. But I still feel no joy in it. If anything, I'm starting to get that bowling ball tummy again.

"You know how your Gramma liked everything to be, well, let's just say she liked everything *just so*. Anyways, on this day, Donuts isn't barking. He isn't waiting for us at the door to the garage, his tail going a million miles an hour. He isn't doing anything at all except lying in his bed behind the sofa. Bry—I mean, your dad— and me both tried to get him to play. To come say hi. To lick our faces until we'd scream for him to stop. To do anything Donuts would usually do. But he wouldn't. He just lay there, his eyes all hollow. And a little bit confused."

When he pauses, I can tell by Uncle Ian's expression that my own eyes probably look pretty much the same as Donuts' eyes that day.

"So, the next morning, Dad—I mean, your Grampa Hare—took Donuts into his arms and just drove off in that big ol' Ford LTD."

As my uncle takes a breath to finish his story, I already know what he's about to say. It doesn't stop me from having to pucker my lips over my teeth and clamp down a little so my eyes don't well up.

"Your Grampa Hare never said a word to us. Not even when he came back without Donuts an hour-and-a-half later. He just stood there. At his work bench in the garage. Cleaning his revolver."

Despite my lip-puckering, tears have already started to come. "But w-why?" I stutter. "Why would Grampa Hare do such an awful thing?"

Another long, silent pause. In it, I hear the rising wind as it blows through the trees. It's becoming intense.

Almost whistling.

"Oh, babygirl. Something wasn't right with Donuts. Your Grampa did what he had to do—"

"But how did he *know* that? He didn't give him a chance. He never even took Donuts to the vet, or anything!"

"Well ... what I guess you need to understand is that sometimes a thing can seem really bad, even if it's the right thing, and done for the right reasons. Your Grampa Hare didn't have a choice that day. He did what he had to. To protect his family ... and Donuts."

I hear it, but I don't care. I'm angry as hell at Grampa Hare now, even though I've missed him and Gramma Veronica every day since they died in their car crash two years ago. At the time, Mom and Dad kept the awful details from me and Andrew. But I had to know what happened, so I looked it up on the school library's computer last year. You know—once I sorta got back to being me again. The articles I found said the truck driver was barreling down Hamburger Hill and distracted by something (he never admitted what) when he slammed into their car head-on. Gramma was thrown through the windshield, at least twenty feet. Grampa was impaled on the steering column. One gruesome quote from an eyewitness basically said that Grampa Hare was still alive and trying to pull himself free when the paramedics arrived ten minutes later. The newspaper didn't print it that way—I can't exactly remember how they put it—but that's what stuck in my mind after I read it. Another lady told the paper she'd seen a boy standing in the road, right in the middle of the crash site. But when she ran to him, there was no one there. The police thought maybe that was the reason the truck driver jumped lanes like he did—to avoid hitting that kid—and they called for anyone to come forward if they knew who that little boy was, or if they saw what happened. But I guess they never did find out anything else, so we'll never know. Anyway, it was the next day that Uncle Ian came back home to Pee Aay for the first time in years. I mean, I hardly even knew him before that. Then all of a sudden, he's right there, in the middle of our lives. Which is a pretty strange coincidence since it was only about a week or so later that he and my dad went into the Little Woods and Daddy shot hims—

The realization hits me.

As hard as that truck.

"No. No! No-no-no-nonono NOOOOO—" I thrash and throw wild punches at my uncle as the spark of comprehension billows into a raging fire. I can't breathe. My head fills with helium. The world's spinning like a carousel out of control, a whirling blur of colors whipping around me faster and faster. They blend to become a single dirty grey light. "DHO! Dho-dho-dho-dho-dhooooo—"

My bawling denial is so muffled by his hand clamped over my mouth that it's all but an indecipherable mumble. Someone a few feet away would barely hear it, let alone a preoccupied pedestrian half-a-football-field away. The nearest are an agile couple with coats pulled over their heads, sprinting down the building side of Central Park West as they dodge the fresh November rain that's begun to slice the cold night air. Pelting my eyes wide with horror, it stings almost as much as my tears.

"Yes," Uncle Ian counters my denial, his vibrations screwing into my soul like cancerous tentacles. My mind hears his voice not as his own, but as gnarled and pitchy layers. A deep, bestial growl beneath a hyena's cry. "Yes-yes-yes-yes-YES! There was no grand gesture, no majestic act of light and love. No father laying down his life for a daughter, as we've always told you."

His hand presses even harder over my mouth and my right incisor digs into my bottom lip which is pulled so tight I can feel it cracking. A moment later the tooth punctures the surface with an audible popping sound and white-hot flash of pain.

A trickle of blood flows hot down my chin and seeps through my uncle's fingers.

"Just a stupid, sacrificial lamb. Led so easily to its own slaughter. The seventh. Fulfilling the prophecies of Enoch and the Apostle John, for their sight is now truth! And now ... and now—"

He releases his hand from my face and pushes me away with a single shove that catapults me backward. I roll end-over-end down the boulder slippery with rain, and slide to an awkward, painful stop. Two more nails have bent and sprung back as I grappled to slow my tumble; one splitting down its length.

"—The glorious reign of Darkness led by the one true Prophet!"

"You killed my father!"

"He *was* killed, yes! But are you so sure it was *my* finger that pulled that trigger?"

I feel like the wind's been knocked out of me. Not just from the fall, but from what he's saying ... or rather, what he's not saying. "You're lying! You're a disgusting piece of shit. And a goddamn liar!" I pick myself up from the soaking wet ground, trembling so hard it's visible. I try to get it under control, but I can't.

He sees this and smirks. "Can you be so sure ... *babygirl?*"

I used to like that pet name. It made me feel so loved. And not so alone after my daddy died. But hearing it now coming from his mouth makes me want to puke.

I spit at him instead.

It drops barely halfway between us, sticking to the rock for a moment then is washed away in the downpour.

Still, it gets my feelings across.

"You know, Deedee, there was someone else I once knew with that level of spunk," he says and swipes the raindrops off his trousers as he stands. "You knew her too, in fact. And she had the fight in her, just the same as you."

He begins ambling down the glossy rock face, his eyes locked only on mine as I take a step backward for every one of his steps forward. "It didn't end too well for her. Or maybe I should say, it didn't end well for her, either."

Either?

Now I *know* my interruption is right—he wants to get rid of me. Just like he got rid of her: the lady called Della, who I told you I met the day my daddy died.

I know it's her because I can see his memory again. This time, I wish I couldn't. On the floor, paralyzed in fear as he looms over her, Della's eyes are wider than I've ever thought a person's could be. She can't breathe. I can *feel* her suffocation and panic. And those tendrils. My skin crawls as that dark, ancient energy coils into her, wrapping around her lifeforce.

Just like the vibrations I feel coming off Uncle Ian right now.

"You killed her! Just like you killed my dad!" I take another quick step back and nearly fall but catch my balance just in time.

He shakes his head, running his fingers through his damp hair as he reaches the lowest shelf of my special boulder. "I've already told you. You may want to reexamine which one of us you see actually pulling that trigger. One day you'll realize the truth. But yes, I did kill Della. Well, sort of. You see—"

He hops to the ground, taking a deep breath and stretching as if he's just stepped outside on a crisp autumn morning and is ready to face the day. I, on the other hand, look like a drowned rat, am bleeding from the mouth, have a drenched and saturated bandage on the back of my head, am covered with dirt and green moss stains, and my torn fingernail is screaming. I'm also much colder than I realize. Little do I know as my intense shivering begins to stop that I'm sliding into second phase hypothermia.

"—There's even a loophole there, Deedee. Because the whole Della thing wasn't my doing, either. I mean, not really. That was actually the work of the Shadows. I was just there to clean it up."

"The way you're going to…going to…*clear* me up?" I don't know why I had to think about that word so hard, but it just wouldn't come. And when it does, I still said 'clear' instead of 'clean.' My head's getting fuzzy and I can't seem to focus my thoughts. I also can't imagine that I was able to spit so easily just a minute ago, because my mouth is a desert; my throat closing in on itself.

Uncle Ian sees this, but not with his eyes. I can feel his mind probing mine, extracting the images of those physical sensations.

"No, Diane. I'm not going to 'clean' you up. Not in that way, at least. You might come in handy one day." He thumbs the air behind him, casually gesturing over his shoulder in the direction of our building but never breaking eye contact. "Do you hear that?"

I hear only the fierce wind which drives the rain against me like an endless barrage of staples.

"Try harder!" Any feigned humor has left his face. Plastered across his brow, his hair hangs wet over his eyes in a way that looks like an animal's mane. His scrunched nose pulling his mouth into a beast-like scowl. "Listen not for the sounds, but the vibrations. Find them, Diane! I know you have it inside you. HEAR THEM!"

Wait—does he know about my special interruptions?

Without wanting to, I find myself pleading with him, telling him I can't hear what he does. That I've never been able to do what he's saying I can do. That I can't understand the sensations I sometimes get, let alone control them. That I've tried, but I can't!

Except…I've said nothing at all, the words resounding in my mind but refusing to come out. I take a grating breath. My chest hurts now, my heart feeling like it's no longer keeping a proper beat.

"Oh, but you can," he replies, his words echoing in my mind.

"You've been doing it this whole time. You're doing it in this very moment. And by the way, that sensation you're feeling in your chest? That's because your heartbeat is irregular, babygirl. It's the hypothermia doing its thing. Next comes unconsciousness. And then you'll die out here, Diane. Slowly. And alone. While I play the distraught uncle who finds you, frozen on the ground in a gut-wrenching fetal position. It'll bring tears to the eyes of all I tell."

He makes a dramatic *tsk tsk* sound with his tongue.

"But no, no. As enticing as that sounds, we can't have that, can we? I have plans for you, Deedee. And a safe place to hide you away until that time. So, listen now! Listen to what's inside you. Hear what the universe is sending you from that building across the street!"

I lurch forward to run—from here, from him.

But something stops me like I've been ensnared by a web of barbed wire. It's not a physical issue. My legs feel rubbery and weak, yeah, but they're able to move.

No, this is something else—something within me—that stops me from going so fast and so far from here.

Something like a voice breaking through the static of my mind.

A child's voice.

"Simon says... open the winnnnnndow, Andwewww," Simon Peter commands his older brother, the sing-song melody of his words rising into my mind as clearly as if I'm in the room with them.

Every cell of my body explodes in instant, white-hot panic and it's all I can do to keep from dropping to my knees. Because I can feel what's going to happen.

"Ahhhh," Uncle Ian says with an expression of recognition. "There it is." He nods satisfactorily.

"W-What is this? What are you d-doing to me?"

"I'm doing nothing to you, Di, it's all inside you. Like I've said, it's always been inside you."

"DON'T CALL ME THAT! MY DAD CALLED ME DI!"

"I know he did, *Deedee*. But if I were you, I wouldn't waste time arguing semantics right now." Unfazed and focused only on me, he is simultaneously aware of what's happening over his shoulder. For a silhouette has appeared at my brothers' fifth floor window...the dark figure materializing from the folds of the flowing curtains.

Before my mind can muster another thought I've already taken off, bolting as fast as I can towards our building.

"Your father will go down in history as the catalyst of the New Apocrypha!" Uncle Ian shouts after me as I disappear through the trees and over the stone wall to the street. "Your daddy is a hero!"

I dodge barefoot across the slick thoroughfare gleaming with rain-mirrored headlights as his decree merges into a terse score of honking cars and screeching brakes.

My ears are deaf to it all.

The only sound I hear is the bottom sash of my brothers' fifth story window creaking upward in fits and starts.

And the gentle scuffing of cloth on wood as Andrew slides one leg carefully out....

2:10

I BUST THROUGH the door to our apartment so abruptly that Mom and Uncle Eddie have no time to stop me. Pacing in the kitchen, cordless phone in hand, my mom is slack jawed as I fly by in a blur. Her words trail away to a moment of dazed silence before saying something to the person on the other end about being sorry if she's caused them any upset. Then sheepishly adding, "But she's home now."

Uncle Eddie hasn't even stood from the kitchen table before I'm already down the hallway towards the bedrooms. From the corner of my eye I see him holding my mom's wrist, mouthing something about giving me a minute.

It's cold and dark when I throw open the boys' bedroom door.

Every inch of the room awash with smiling, absurd sea creatures, the deep blue projector lamp only heightens my anxiety as a wall of coarse, baritone vibrations crashes down on me the moment I cross the threshold. The psychic sensation is so intense it drops me to my knees, making the bowling ball I had in my stomach with Uncle Ian a mild tingle by comparison.

And that smell. Rotten eggs and wet iron.

I'm heaving as I begin crawling on my hands and knees. Head down and holding my breath between violent, retching spasms, I do everything to keep this dark energy from overpowering me.

Far from sharing my agitation, Simon Peter's eyes are alight as he bounces up and down in the bottom bunk, oblivious—or impervious—to what I'm feeling. He's giggling with undiluted glee as he watches his brother compliantly duck out the window.

I want to scream for Andrew to stop, to let him know I'm here, but fear it will startle him and he'll lose his balance. I force myself back onto my feet and am nearly able to touch him.

When time slows to a third its natural measure.

I struggle to make the last few feet, trudging through a swamp of invisible glue, as Andrew slides his legs further out the window with each of my impossibly labored steps.

"   S i m o n
s   a   y   s
f   l   w   y
A   n   d   w   e   w   ,
f   l   w   y   !   "

Simon Peter's voice is like an album on a record player that's been unplugged: a deep grumble that gets slower and lower with every word. By the last one it stretches so long that it becomes a single, reverberating bass that I can feel in my stomach.

As Andrew dutifully steps out onto the slick and narrow ledge.

"NOOOO!" I scream, the frozen moment releasing, and I'm at the open window in a blink. "WAKE UP, ANDREW! WAKE UP—"

But he's unresponsive and becomes stiff as a board the instant he stands fully upright on the building's foot-deep exterior outcropping. He noticeably wavers as a blast of frigid air swirls up from the street to buffer us both.

I grab the back of his pajama shirt and it bunches into my fist.

"I've got you, Andrew! I got you!" I don't know if he hears me in this zombie-like state he's in, but I'm clenching my fingers tight around the fabric, my arm tensing to become as rigid as a steel bar.

When I feel his weight lean into my grip and I'm able to steady him by pulling him towards the window frame, a tidal wave of relief prickles my entire body, starting at my shoulder blades and flowing all the way to my toes.

Goosebumps have never felt so good! I say to myself, filled with this incredible sensation. Some might call it the presence of my guardian angel; others, a simple flood of adrenaline. Whatever it is, I embrace it as I reach through the open sash to grab his pajama top with my other hand as well.

As I do, a nervous laughter of relief bubbles up from a place deep inside me and I can't stop it, even if I wanted to. "I got you, budd—"

The blow to the small of my back knocks the wind from me.

I buckle forward, the momentum driving my fist into Andrew's spine. My fingers open. And his pajama top unravels from my grip.

"Flwy Andwew, flwy." Simon Peter flatly commands under his breath as he wraps himself around my waist, craning to witness his brother's obedience.

Arms frozen to his sides, Andrew teeters forward, and my heart squeezes so hard I feel the pain like a vice closing on my chest. But then his stiffened body angles back on its heels and slowly stabilizes, a wobbly plank finding its natural center.

Until another blast of icy air pries him from his zombie state.

Instantly aware of the nightmare he's woken to, Andrew's mouth stretches into a scream that won't come as his arms pinwheel for balance in stupefied panic. He twists toward the window, reaching for my hand.

Our fingers almost touch…

… But his feet skid out from under him.

He slips. Cracking against the stone overhang his forearm snaps, bending unnaturally. His fingers still manage to grab the sculpted edge of the narrow ledge, and for a split second he's able to hold himself there, legs dangling.

But a snaggy tip of a bone is piercing his wrist.

Before I can latch onto his arm, my brother's fingers loosen from the blood-speckled ledge. Unbelieving, his eyes lock onto mine just as the last finger releases.

He falls, the breath sucked from his chest while swimming the backstroke through the cold night air. His eyes are bulging with terror just before his body twists. Now he's facing the rain-soaked street he's hurtling toward.

The sound as he strikes it is unlike anything I've heard.

Andrew's skull fractures like ceramic. A thick, grey mass squeezes through the cracks and holes and I'm reminded of that can of white children's plasticene that's been handled by too many grubby hands and is now being pressed through a colander. The red starburst that blows from his body becomes a 3-D dome, the airborne particles seeming to defy gravity. Momentarily hanging in the air, a million red prisms twinkle in the unnatural light of the streetlamps like a swarm of overfilled mosquitos. As they settle to the ground, I see that the spine has exploded from Andrew's back.

Mouthing a soundless scream, my mother collapses in the center of the room. Smiling fish swim across her body as she quivers in terror-stricken silence.

She appeared in the doorway just as my fist slamming into Andrew's back, but too late to do anything other than witness her son falling to his death.

Arms stretched and reaching, she writhes on the carpet, emitting a reverse, sucking yowl. Her eyes are rooted in horror, a blank thousand-yard stare as she whispers three words. A mantra she chants over and over.

The last words she ever speaks to me ....

2:11

YOU KILLED HIM ...... You killed him .... You killed him ....
you killed him you killed him you killed himyoukilled
himyoukilledhimyoukilledhi—" My mother's charge
builds to a raging, hysterical wail until the words blur
into a single, awful indictment.

Even when Uncle Eddie lifts her off the floor and carries her into
the living room, it is this shrieking decree I hear. It drowns out the
screams and shouts from the city street below as I throw up
between the shaking fingers I've clasped to my face. I begin crying
so hard I choke on my own vomit.

Simon Peter is oblivious.

He's leaning out the open window, standing on his tippy-toes to
scrutinize the unfolding scene on the street below. The rain has
stopped now, and the misty air is pulsing red and blue as, one-by-
one, every fashion of emergency vehicle announces its arrival with
blaring sirens. Soon they surround our building, and the strobing
lights blend together into a purple wash. They illuminate Simon
Peter's profile, making it appear as if his puffy little infant face is
covered in bruises.

*No, not bruises, it looks like his skin is in the process of actively
decaying. And I'd swear it's ... writhing ... something beneath it
desperate to be free.*

"Andwew flwy," he informs me, turning to get my attention. The
awful words, coupled with the illusion of the face from which they

are being spoken, are even more disturbing in their contrast to Simon Peter's tiny, sweet voice. He leans out the window again. "Andwew flwy, Deedee."

I throw up a second time, yellow bile spraying through my fingers as I run from the room. In the hallway I crash headlong into my Uncle Eddie who is making his way back from the living room. Unfazed at our collision, he simply opens his arms wide and folds me into his protective embrace.

"It's going to be okay, Petunia. It's going to be okay," he repeats again and again in soft, leathery tones, squeezing me tight to his bosom as I allow the promise to wash over me. I sob for an amount of time I'll never be able to recall, knowing that bundled in his arms is the final place on earth where I still know I am safe.

It is this assurance which is rebounding through my mind when the two officers pry me from his grip.

One clamped to each of my arms, they show no emotion as they haul me from our apartment. Half-dragging, half-swinging me, I'm shrieking and thrashing and begging Uncle Eddie to help me, to save me—*please save me!*—as a swell of tears floods my cheeks, the salt stinging my lacerated bottom lip.

My world becomes a slow-motion blur as the warm light of safety grows dimmer in my soul, the sanctuary of home and family sliding further from my grasp until its flame fizzles and then snuffs out completely. Even the memories sour instantly in my mind, everything feeling like a lie and shriveling, turning to decay.

Everything except for my memories of Daddy.

Now I'm bare and shivering in the cold November night. Again. Except this time, I'm drowning in a sea of flashing light and harried, barking voices all around me as they force me on a gurney and strap me down. I don't know why, because I'm no longer fighting them. I'm just too numb now. So I do not resist as they strap my wrists and ankles to the metal rails before lifting the stretcher up to the height of the ambulance doors.

Momentarily raised above the throng of people who have come for the free show, I spy the crumpled figure of my brother about twenty feet from the corner, all alone save a couple cops who are making sure no one comes too near. The shroud they've put over him is saturated dark with Andrew's blood, but only around its border, the edges of the material lapping up the thick liquid from the blacktop like some kind of fabric vampire. The rest of the sheet is still clean and white where it clings to his body, faithfully following the contours of his face, twisted torso, broken legs and arms. The effect is a grotesque, inverted silhouette.

In my mind it's a hideous, life-size version of one of those old cameo broaches you'll see in antique stores—or when watching period dramas on PBS—where a person's profile is carved in ivory against a stark black background.

The image bumps and jars from sight as two paramedics and one policewoman slide me into the boxy ambulance and I have to shut my eyes to its sterile, artificial brilliance. But behind my eyelids I still see the image of Andrew lying under that sheet. Except now it is a film negative. The sickening, dark border of blood has inverted to brilliant white all around his body: an outline like a warm, glowing halo.

Saint Andrew, I think to myself.

First-Called Apostle. Brother of Simon Peter.

A fisher of men.

More tears run in lines down the dirt on my face, and I hold this image of Saint Andrew for as long as I can before it dissolves away to inky blackness. The sound as they begin to close the ambulance doors makes me open my eyes. I want to take what I believe might be the last look at my home.

What I see I don't expect.

It is one of our building's waterspout gargoyles, perched high up on the corner of the fifth floor. I don't know if it's the sudden and harsh change of light on my eyes, or if it's my mind finally breaking down, just like they think it is. But crouching on that ledge, less than a handful of feet from where Andrew fell, that stone gargoyle looks bigger and much more lifelike than before.

And I'd swear it's actually stooping down so it can see me....

2:12

T HE ONLY ONE to come visit me today is Uncle Eddie. He made the trip all the way from Georgia again, which makes me love him even more. Ian did try to come, a couple times, but I told the nurses I wouldn't feel safe around him, so Security finally took his name off the list of officially approved visitors. I can change it later if I want to, but why would I? Just thinking about him, or saying his stupid name, brings that bowling ball feeling back to my stomach.

(By the way, in case you've just noticed, I no longer call him 'uncle' because I don't consider him to be my family.)

I don't consider him to be anything at all, frankly. Not anymore, now that I know what he did. To my dad, to Andrew.

To me.

Uncle Eddie brought me gobs again. Security is making sure there's no contraband mixed in there with them, or anything I can hurt myself, or someone else, with. But as soon as they mark them as 'Permissible' I'll be able to have one.

"Rebecca—er, your mom—misses you." Uncle Eddie's voice is soft and gentle. "She wanted to come, Petunia. Truly she did. But with Simon Peter, well, you can imagine it's a bit much. Especially since you won't allow your uncle, Ian, to come."

"She could come on her own. Leave Simon Peter with Unc—I mean, with Ian."

"Well I guess she could, yes. In a pinch. But Uncle Ian has been pretty busy these days. There was a lot of missed work after Andrew, um...."

His voice trails away. He's clearly as uncomfortable as he is unsure of how to finish that sentence.

So, I finish it for him.

"... After Andrew, my sweet, baby nine-year-old brother was pushed brutally and cold-heartedly to his death. By yours truly, a violent, sociopathic menace to society."

"No. I didn't say that."

Crossing my arms and leaning back in my teal plastic chair, my reply is nonverbal, a perfect expression of 'You didn't have to.' But I decide I want to add something after all. "It's what my mom says."

"No, she doesn't. Listen—"

"Yes! She does! It's why I'm here!" I gesture dramatically all around me, my best real estate agent portrayal as I draw Uncle Eddie's attention to my lovely new home's institutional design elements, which include its behavior-calming sea foam green palette on concrete block walls.

My uncle breathes out, a sigh of genuine dismay. Otherwise, he remains silent, chewing on his lip without realizing he is.

"She came to the doorway, heard me laughing, then saw me push Andrew off the ledge ... was running across the room to stop me but was a split-second too late." I'm staring him down, my eyebrows low. "That was her statement on the TempOrInComMin. Forgive me if I'm paraphrasing at all."

"Temper in common, Petunia?"

"Temp. Or. In. Com. Min," I repeat slowly, emphasizing each syllable in a short, staccato burst as if I'm teaching him another language but frustrated because we've already gone over this damn lesson a dozen times before. It's condescending. And I know it. "Temporary Order for Involuntary Commitment of a Minor."

There's a whole slew of abbreviations they use in here, like they have somewhere to go and just don't have time for the longhand versions. Lord knows why. Time is all anybody in here's got.

Uncle Eddie nods and is about to say something, but I cut him off before he can even open his mouth: "And let's not forget her screaming 'YOU KILLED HIM' at me, over and over and over, at the top of her lungs. Wasn't exactly holding her cards close to her chest there, was she."

"She just watched her son plummet to his death."

"SO DID I."

There's an awkward silence during which the guards glance in our direction. This kind of conversation is nothing new to them, but they're always gonna keep an eye out in a place like Barrow Moor. You know, just to be sure.

Uncle Eddie breaks the deadlock by clearing his throat, which allows him to slide back into the conversation more comfortably.

"I know you did, babygirl. But can you blame your mother for what she said, after what she'd just seen? Anyone would make that mistake. She's human." He leans in and touches my clasped hands. I bristle at first, but then relax into it. "And. She. Does. Miss. You."

His big, warm mitt of a hand covers both of mine. It feels nice. I wiggle my cold, dry fingers into his and it feels safe. Even though I know he's telling me porky pies.

Uncle Eddie never was much of a liar.

And now I'm suddenly reminded of my father again, and how he used to use that phrase because he liked how colorful it was. And how much less judgmental it felt. "Because," Daddy would say to me, "everyone tells a little white lie. Every now and then." Exhibit Number One: Uncle Eddie's whole 'Mexican Train Champion of Lumpkin County' tall-tale.

This brings a smile to my face, the first real smile I've had in a long time, and Uncle Eddie thinks it's because I believe my mom misses me.

I decide to just let him think that. "I love you, Uncle Ed."

"I love you too, Petunia. Oh, and I almost forgot . . . ." He reaches beneath the corduroy sports coat he has draped over his lap. "Close your eyes!"

I do as I'm told and extend my arms toward him, both palms up. Now I'm really smiling. Something smooth and soft is laid into my hands. But it's also sturdy and rigid at the same time and has some real heft to it.

A leather-bound hardcover book.

I open my eyes to find I'm holding the complete and unabridged works of Edgar Allan Poe. It's black with this awesome red debossing all over it that looks like vines. (I learned that term last year in my advanced Literature in History class. Printers call it debossing when a hardback book has sunken-in parts stamped into its cover.) I'm sure the red vines must be Palomino grapevines, because that's what Amontillado is made from. I looked that one up myself. The edges of all the pages are silver. And it has one of those awesome fabric bookmarks already attached to the spline.

"I love it! Oh my God, Uncle Eddie!" I thumb through its pages and the scent of fresh paper and ink wafts up on a current that feels like adventures yet to be taken. It's freedom. And the best gift anyone in the world could give me right now.

Barring my actual freedom from this place.

"It's over a thousand pages," he says and turns the book over, flipping up its back cover. "See? So, enough stories there to keep you occupied for quite some time."

His lips are smiling, but there's sorrow in his eyes.

"Let's just hope, Deedee, that you're not in here long enough to finish it."

I give him a closed-lip smile of my own. "Let's hope."

"How's it going with your weekly sessions? Any word about when that date might be?"

By 'weekly sessions' he means my one-on-ones I have with the Psychiatric Doctors here. Usually, Dr. Maddox. But Uncle Eddie doesn't like to use that word ... *psychiatric*. So he'll dance around it.

I guess it makes him feel the way I think most of us do when we hear it: a little bit icky. Because anything that follows must surely be referring to the realm of crazy people.

After all, normal, healthy people don't have psychiatrists, right?

I know that's not true. But it's what people think. And in this case, they would be right, because Barrow Moor is a Forensic Psychiatric Hospital.

Which basically means an insane asylum.

Built for criminals.

"They're going ok." I answer his question but am instantly deflated. You see, during my initial psych hold last month I told them everything that happened. I mean, why wouldn't I? They were there to help, and I finally had the ears of a group of adults wearing all kinds of serious uniforms. Adults who could actually help me.

So, of course I told them.

I told them that my uncle (I still called him *Uncle Ian* when I first got here) confessed that he killed my father two years ago. That he'd done it after something like a monster took me into the woods. And how everyone kept saying that Daddy had killed himself there to protect me, but now that was all bullshit.

I said my mom got pregnant even though she couldn't have a baby anymore, and then gave birth to Simon Peter in only a few months.

I cried when I shared that my dead father came back to me and tried to eat my energy. Except it wasn't really him: I knew it was some kind of demon inside his animated body.

I exposed Ian for admitting to 'cleaning up' the murder of that pretty lady with the southern accent, and that something he called the 'Shadows' were the ones he said actually did it.

I told them how he talked to me telepathically and had plans for me but wanted to hide me away somewhere until he needed me. That he then projected into my mind the boys' game of 'Simon Says' from all the way across the road, and that it had to do with this

'Dragon-Something-or-Other' he started rambling about like a crazy person.

Most of all, I recounted moment-by-moment how Simon Peter was able to use that game to control Andrew's mind, making my nine-year-old brother climb out the fifth-floor window and onto that narrow little decorative ledge. How Simon then pushed or head-butted me from behind when I grabbed hold of Andrew's pajama top and was keeping him from falling. I said that one of the rainspout gargoyles on the side of our building came to life and was leering at me as I was being taken away in the ambulance.

I told them all of these things, filled with a sense of relief that someone was finally going to help me.

Instead, they 2PC'd me.

Two Physician Certified.

That's what they call an involuntary admission after two Psychs (psychiatric doctors) sign off that you're in such bad mental shape you need involuntary medical treatment.

Basically, that you're a legit nut case.

And since I'm the one who killed Andrew, that meant not putting me in just any old hospital, but a facility where the inmates—I mean patients—can't just up-and-go as they please. A place where they have guards. And barbed wire. And screams.

Lots and lots of screams. All the time. And I don't mean the good kind, like you hear at an amusement park.

A place where you don't get out. Ever. Unless they say so.

Even prisons have a maximum sentence. But not here. At Barrow Moor, you're at their mercy.

In Limbo, as the Catholics say.

"Any mention of when you might be coming home?" Uncle Eddie asks, a look of creeping hope lighting across his face as my fingers unconsciously trace the cover of my new Poe book.

Under the table my legs swing back and forth. My Bob Barkers (the rubbery, standard-issue slippers we all get) squeak as they scuff the dirty grey-and-white checkerboard floor. The sound echoes off the cinder block walls.

It reminds me that I'm not going anywhere. Anytime soon....

2:13

THERE ISN'T GOING to be a trial. They've dropped the charges against me since there was no actual proof I pushed Andrew off his bedroom ledge, let alone that I did such an awful thing with intent. They tried to get me to plea for involuntary manslaughter, making all sorts of claims that they'd go light on me, but I told them to go to hell.

And by the way, if it sounds like I'm full of legalese all of a sudden, I guess you'd be right. When someone's trying to pin your brother's murder on you, you learn those kinds of terms real fast.

I didn't hear much for a while after that. Then the word 'suicide' started bounding about, and that made me feel sick. Because Andrew would *never* do that. Geez, he was only nine. And he was happy. To even suggest he could do such a thing was terrible and I wouldn't stand for it. I told them that, too, even though they hadn't yet completely cleared me. If I'd corroborated that terrible theory of theirs, it would have exonerated me immediately rather than leaving me to stress all these months about what they might still try and do to pin his death on me.

But I just couldn't disrespect Andrew's memory like that.

I'm glad I took the high road, 'cause they've pretty much gone away now, anyway. Thing is, I'm still in here. And I'm going to be, for I don't know how long. Just because they're not charging me with his death doesn't mean I can just up and walk away from Barrow Moor. If I'd been sent to jail, then yes, that would be true.

But I'm in this place instead, and I've been diagnosed with Paranoid Delusional Schizophrenia.

And no, that doesn't mean I'm a bunch of different people inside. I don't know about you, but I always used to think that's what schizophrenia meant. But that's actually this other thing called Multiple Personality Disorder, which is a whole other kettle of fish. The weirdo in *Psycho*, that Norman Bates fellow? I think he's what they mean by MPD.

That's not what's happening to me.

What they say I have is a mental condition where I suffer from Persecutory Delusions, the kind where you believe you're being watched, or harassed or maybe even chased by someone.

Or some*thing*.

They also say I have delusions of Control, Reference and Grandeur. In other words, I have these fantasies that the thoughts in my head aren't always just my own but can sometimes be controlled by someone else; that I believe I get messages from the world meant just for me; and, deep down, I believe maybe this is all happening to me because I've been purposefully chosen.

I dunno, maybe they're right.

I've had a lot of time to think about it. And yeah. I mean, all those things sound like a lot, but at least they're something with a label. And if you ask me, once something's been labeled, it usually means there's some kind of way to handle it.

Right?

So maybe it wouldn't be too bad if I am what they actually say I am. Because I sure don't know how to grasp what's happening if I'm not the whack job they claim me to be.

And all of this turns out to be real, after all ....

2:14

Friday October 13, 2000

T HESE EVALUATIONS ALWAYS take place on a Friday. I think their mindset is that if they can get rid of one (or more) of us before the weekend, then Facilities—just a fancy word they use around here for 'janitors'—can have a couple days to clean up our personal space to make room for the next wackos in line.

My birthday is the end of next week and I'm going to be eighteen, so I'm thinking they might finally let me go.

But then again, that also sorta freaks me out.

I've kinda gotten used to it here . . . .

"So, Miss Cockerton," Doctor Maddox starts off, spying me over the top of her glasses while her fingers flip with an admirable adeptness through a folder with my name on it. They come to a particular grouping of paperclipped pages, and she pulls them from the binder without looking. "Let's see now."

I always expect to see her behind her desk during an Eval. You know, looking all authoritative. But she's on one of these stupid plastic chairs just like I am, and we're facing each other. Not having a barrier between us is supposed to be less threatening and more conducive to me sharing my feelings, or something.

She pushes her glasses up the bridge of her nose and reads the file swiftly, her rusty red lipsticked lips moving just perceptibly as she scans the various notations. Her legs are crossed, a black skirt coming just above the knees of her tanned and toned legs.

Gosh, I wish my legs were like that. Maybe I should get on it, you know, spend some more time in the aerobics room?

In more than a couple ways, Dr. Maddox reminds me a lot of my mom, Rebecca. 'Cause my mom was smart, too, and also used to work out a lot. And like Dr. Maddox, she always had great legs. Before Simon Peter, anyway. After that, everything changed. In all sorts of ways. For all of us.

Dr. M's waggling her left foot up and down as she reads, and I'm drawn to the wedges she's wearing—pretty, but sensibly low. Even these manage to look sexy on her. It's no wonder every pimple-popping turd of a boy in this place jerks off to her in their gross, pubescent little fantasies.

Oh. Yeah. I don't think I mentioned it before, but Barrow Moor is a co-ed psych facility. We don't sleep in the same units or anything—the boys have one wing, and we have another—but we're all on the same Juvie floor.

"So, how are things, Diane?"

I grin shyly, squirming inside a little at what I was just thinking. If she only knew what I know about all those disgusting little animals masquerading as boys around here and what they do, I wonder what she would think. Would she be grossed-out about it, the way I am, knowing she's spank-bank material? Or instead, would her analytical mind find it all a perfectly normal, healthy component to a boy's mental and physical development? Maybe, just maybe, I wonder if she might actually be a little bit flattered to learn the effect she has on them all?

I wonder....

She beams back at me. Confidently.

Maybe she does know. And maybe feels a little bit of all three of those things ....

Dr. M scribbles something and I suddenly feel exposed, like she's able to see what I'm thinking. I clear my throat and smooth the crease in my skirt which, by the way, is much longer than hers.

"I'm … fine. Good. I'm good."

Dr. Maddox says nothing in reply, tilting her head to a gentle angle and waiting for me to go on.

"Sorry. Yes," I add, pushing the small of my back into the chair and becoming aware of my slouching shoulders. I raise them and lift my chin and chest simultaneously. "I've felt really clear and level these past few months. No concerns, really. And I'm excited about my birthday next week."

"Your eighteenth, I see. Congratulations, Diane. That's a very special time for a young lady."

I'm sure it is. If you're not institutionalized in a criminal psych ward. "Yes. I suppose I really am looking forward to it."

"And does that bring up any thoughts or feelings about your future?"

I wait for some kind of prompt, some indicator of what she's looking for here. None comes. "I suppose I'm starting to think about what I might like to do when I get out, sure."

"And what does that look like to you, Diane? What do you see, *who* do you see, when you glimpse that future?"

"Hmm. I think I see someone happy. Someone who's got their shit—er, I mean, *stuff*—together." Dr. M smiles at this. She never does mind that I have a propensity to swear. Every now and then. "Someone who's not still stuck in this place."

The pause that follows kills me.

She presses her lips together as she scribbles a few more brief notes … then puts her pen down. In fact, she takes the whole binder, squares the papers all together, and sets it neatly on the floor beside her. "I want to talk to you about that part."

II

"How many times have you seen your uncle—and I mean Ian, not Eddie—since you've been staying here with us," Dr. M asks.

Staying with us.

I can't believe the words she's chosen. As if she's merely a congenial host of some quaint little upstate bed and breakfast inquiring how many Dark-eyed Juncos her bird-spotting guest from the city has seen.

She's also fully aware of the answer.

I find myself sloughing back down in my chair, the little shoulder-perching figment of my longtime bestie, Crystal Riley, suddenly appearing to whisper in my ear. *"See! Classic passive-aggressive adult bullcrap, right there. I swear, it's some kind of law that they all take lessons in it."* In my mind's eye Crystal is not the young lady she must surely be today, but perpetually the twelve-year-old girl she was the last time I ever saw her.

Dr. M pulls her chair closer, relaxing into it as she claps her hands to her knees, giving them a little rub. "I'm going to be frank with you, alright?"

I nod. It's the tiniest physical motion that a nod can be and still be considered a nod. Dejection is written all over my face.

"A big part of your healing, Diane, is accepting your past, the good and the bad alike. That's not only to—quote unquote—get outta here," she explains, making air quotes with her fingers. "It's also incredibly important to your overall sense of wellbeing. Do you understand?"

I say nothing, staring at the floor. Tears threatening.

"And coming to terms with what you claim your Uncle Ian did is probably the biggest component of that healing." Dr. Maddox allows that to resonate. Even though I don't like what she's saying, I do actually trust her and think she genuinely has my back. "You do still believe that your uncle killed your father, and had something to do with your brother's accident...?"

Now she not only reminds me of my mom in the way she looks but in the way she sounds, too, asking questions when, really, there's only one right answer.

So instead of replying, I say nothing.

Eventually we hash this out, but the bottom line is that she wants to see me make a real effort with Unc—with *Ian*—before she'll recommend to the other Psychs that I'm in a healthy enough place to be safely released back into the wild.

She also wants to know where I would call home, with whom I'd be associating, what I'd be doing to support myself, etcetera. Integral to this she makes it clear that in her professional opinion a halfway house would not be a good fit for me.

"So, the best option by far, at least for the short-term," she declares while simultaneously noting in my file the condition she's about to stipulate, "would be for you to go back and stay with Mom and Uncle Ian. And to do that, you need to confront your ghosts."

Dr. M stands, indicating that the eval is over. As is any chance of me getting out of here by my eighteenth birthday next week.

"Make peace with your uncle, Diane."

III

I'd rather die in here first ....

2:15

June 27, 2005

SIMON PETER PERFORMED his first miracle today. At least that's what every media outlet in America is saying. But I know this isn't his first time. Remember, years ago I was witness to the two-year-old birthday boy using some kind of innate mix of precognition and telepathy to stop little Lina Sonoro from decorating the grille of an MTA bus with her guts. When he did that, Simon Peter not only saved that little girl's life, but also altered one small current in the vast tide of history. Tiny though that ebb may be, its rippling repercussions—both good and bad—will go on and on throughout time.

Until now, only three people in the entire world knew how that really went down: Simon Peter, me ... and yes, Ian.

Well, I guess that's not *strictly* true.

Dr. Maddox knows. As I said earlier, I've been sharing everything with her since my TempOrInComMin back in ninety-seven. It's been in my file all these years, and they discuss everyone's case at every quarterly assessment. Which means the eight other Psychs here at Barrow Moor know about it as well.

So, I guess that really makes twelve of us in total.

Funny how numbers and spirituality so often go hand-in-hand, for I find myself suddenly thinking of the twelve apostles. The big difference here is that only three of us are believers.

At least, that used to be the case. I'm pretty certain the others are believers now, too. Because today, the whole world knows what

Simon Peter's capable of. Just like I've been telling them all along.

And the more I think of it, isn't that exactly how Jesus converted a bunch of fishermen, tax collectors, partiers and thieves who were also nonbelievers?

Dr. Maddox has already sent a message via one of the nurses, requesting we have an unscheduled eval tomorrow, and I know this is going to be the topic. Just like I know we'll also be discussing an actual release date. At last. Because the seeds of truth I've been planting all these years have finally begun to sprout, the seedlings visibly rising up from the soil for all to see.

Before, only I knew where they laid beneath the dirt.

Now everyone does.

Which means that I'm *not* a paranoid schizophrenic. Because if I am, then the rest of the world must be, too.

Either way, I'm no longer some freakish subvariant of society.

So, yeah. I know that I'm finally getting out of here. Probably in the next few days, if I want to. But to be honest, that scares the shit outta me almost as much as it did when I was first locked in here. Because, and let's be straight about this, what exactly does a twenty-two-year-old girl with a documented history of psychoses, an education that barely exceeds your basic G.E.D., and no allies left in the world ... actually *do* out there?

She does anything she damn well pleases, I chastise my waning confidence, reminding myself that I used to be fearless. Smart. Full of curiosity. Creative. *So, yeah, she does anything.*

As long as whatever it is, is as far away as possible from the reach of her fucked-up family ....

THIRD
DISCIPLE

And now was acknowledged the Presence
of the Red Death. He had come like a thief in
the night and one-by-one dropped the revelers...
... And the flames of the tripods expired.

—Edgar Allan Poe, *The Masque of the Red Death*

The Devil can cite Scripture for his purpose.

—William Shakespeare, *The Merchant of Venice*

The Red Shadow

3:16

08:57

I
T HAPPENED BEFORE a national television audience, in the third hour of the network morning show, *New Day, USA!* Broadcasting live from New York, the program was about to cut to its last commercial break when a rapid series of pops came so loud that their snare drum sound breached even the heavily insulated wall of studio glass looking onto Times Square. On the other side of this enormous street-level window, a throng of bystanders jostled and waved in the hopes of being one of the blurry shapes spotted on camera over the shoulders of the polished and charismatic morning show hosts. In an instant, all but one of these sign-sporting fame seekers dropped to the sidewalk, hands instinctively clasped over their heads in self-defense.

The startling blasts caught both presenters off guard, and they simultaneously jumped in their seats. Analise Gonzalez, America's morning show sweetheart and *ND-USA!'s* undisputed celebrity heavyweight, flinched—a short but sharp paroxysm—and the 'coffee' in her show's branded mug sloshed over the brim. Clear liquid splashed across her silk blouse, and could the viewers at home have smelled it, they would have been greeted with the tangy, sweet aroma of white rum wafting into the air. Analise stuttered, tripping over her lines, then lost her train of speech altogether as the teleprompter segued to the next commercial break without her.

However, in a bold and unprecedented move, Rachel Stoltz, the Studio Floor Manager, did not go to break. With Monday's show effectively over and the Director stepping away for his weekly budget meeting, Rachel was in charge.

And she kept the live feed running.

"Let's get a shot out the window," she directed Camera #2 which panned over the shoulders of the three flummoxed presenters, zooming in on the blurry crowd just beyond the wall of thick glass. Most of the bystanders were cowering or scurrying from view.

But one curious individual remained standing.

The cameraman drew this nine-year-old boy into focus at the precise moment that another man, not part of the group, stumbled into shot. This man reeled to one side, spun a seemingly perfect pirouette, then slumped to the ground on his side, his arms and legs twisted and contorted beneath his body. His head cracked the curb of the sullied sidewalk just inches from the boy's feet, and a spray of blood plumed from the man's temple in a fine red mist. It turned into a thick, pulsing stream which coursed down his face, over his mouth; pooling upon the greasy concrete.

Prone for but a moment, the man's body slowly untwisted—a spring reverting to its natural, resting state—starting with his feet. This release of tension traveled up his legs, then his waist. His torso. As he rolled from his side onto his back, his right arm dislodged from beneath him and flopped lifeless to his side.

The man's neck was the last part of the spring to uncoil, and his head slowly turned to face the sky. When it did, his breath hissed from his lips in a single, long sigh.

08:59

In the process of rolling onto his back, two more patches of red rotated perfectly into focus of Camera #2. Each was between the man's shoulder blades, and burgeoning like crimson rose petals from two small holes in his crisp, white T-shirt.

This was also the precise point in the reel where nearly every broadcast network in the country would later edit the replay to overlay two oval blurs ... while also slowing down the footage for dramatic effect. The cable networks did the very same, minus the blurred overlays. They defended their choice of doing so by claiming the American viewer had the right to an objective, unbiased perspective of the holes made in the man's back. Holes made by rounds from the NYPD's standard issue Glock-19.

Holes clearly made as he was running away.

Staring into the heavens, the man's eyes glazed over. Despite glinting in the dazzling glare of morning sun, his pupils dilated until all but the thinnest stroke of colored iris remained. His mouth fell open. Tiny red bubbles foamed from his lips. And then stopped. His rich chocolate complexion grew sallow grey as pint after pint poured from beneath his torso to bathe the plaza in deep red pools.

The man, a British expatriate later identified as Antoine J. Washington, lay dead at nine-year-old Simon Cockerton's feet.

09:00

"Don't you *dare* go off air!" Rachel announced to the control room and entire Studio Floor. "And you two," she added, speaking directly to the show's presenters who were watching in slack jawed astonishment along with so many others. "Keep yourselves exactly where you are! We're staying live with this!"

ND-USA!'s Camera #2 kept rolling as screaming bystanders scattered, their cries muffled behind the thick studio glass. They dispersed to leave Simon Peter alone and perfectly centered in the frame of the shot, gazing down at the corpse's empty eyes which stared vacuously back up at him. Here Rachel cutaway the live shot to Camera #1, which was also now trained upon the unfolding scene, as two police officers skated into frame. Guns still drawn, they trained their Glocks on Washington's dead body, shouting commands which the studio mics received through the wall of glass as little more than muted, indiscernible bellows.

One officer nudged Washington's torso with his heavy black boot and the empty shell of a body gave no resistance. The second officer crept closer and cautiously did the same but chose Washington's head as the target of his boot's square, reinforced toe.

Antoine's face rocked to the side, his other temple clapping against the concrete. His tongue lolled from his gaping mouth. And his dead, unfocused eyes stared directly through the window into Camera #3. (The Corpse Cam, as it would quickly become known across the trending threads on Myspace).

Camera #1 (the Cop Cam) followed every move of the two officers as they absentmindedly pressed away young Simon Cockerton from the immediate vicinity then proceeded to search the dead man's body for any weapons, drugs, or other contraband. They pulled a tattered wallet from his front left jeans pocket, a set of keys from his right, and a snub nosed .38 from his back pocket where its shape had worn the jeans material into a light outline from repeated insertion into the same pocket, same position.

The officers removed it with care, spinning its cylinder and tapping out each of the six rounds. Three were still live. Three were only brass casings from which the distinct odor of freshly fired gunpowder was apparent. After securing the weapon, they proceeded to check Antoine for a pulse but found none in his neck or his wrist. They checked for a heartbeat, one officer placing his ear close to Washington's chest while the other officer held the man down, just to be safe.

There was none.

The officer repeated this procedure at Washington's lips, but no breath emitted from them.

09:05

Following the direction of the Studio Floor Manager, Camera #2 (the Kid Cam) kept Simon Peter as its sole focus. While everyone else had moved far away, pointing and gasping and creating a shifting, bustling and growing perimeter around the scene, Simon Peter remained alone near its epicenter. Standing resolute. Calm. Steadfast.

It was when the officers stepped away from the body for mere seconds—waving off the paramedics and shouting for the Medical Examiner—that Simon Peter stepped up to it. He gently lowered himself to the ground and knelt before the dead man, facing the great wall of glass where all three of *ND-USA!'s* cameras now focused upon the boy and what happened next...

09:06

Kneeling, Simon Peter settled comfortably back onto his heels and held his hands out before him, his downcast palms hovering just inches above the man's chest while never actually touching it. He slowly closed his eyes, speaking softly over the corpse. Zooming tight on Simon's face, one of the cameras caught what appeared to be a pattern to his speech, the boy's lips moving in a cycle of about six or seven seconds before repeating the words once again.

Damn, I wish we had a lip reader on set! Stoltz thought to herself then immediately began to run through her mental list of production contacts for anyone who might have a reason for one to be in the building. She drew a blank, tossing the idea on the backburner to focus her attention on matters at hand. *Maybe Burke* (the Director) *can get someone in post-production...?*

As Simon Peter chanted, his hands started to tremble. It wasn't seen by anyone else—and could have been forgiven as nerves if it had been—but Rachel Stoltz noticed. And she *knew* it wasn't anxiety she was witnessing. What she found curious was the way the trembling intensified the longer Simon Peter held his hands over the corpse. For a brief moment she thought perhaps she'd even begun to feel a kind of tingling within herself. That, of course, was absurd, and she dismissed the sensation outright while directing another of the cameras to focus only on the boy's hands.

Doing so left one final angle to set, and Rachel ensured this one would cover both Simon Peter and the dead man in a single, continuously filming frame.

Let's just see what this odd little dude's up to....

09:08

It didn't take long to find out.

Simon Peter's lips moved furiously, his entire body beginning to twitch with the intensity of the chant he repeated over and over. His trembling grew to such a ferocious shudder that it became obvious now even to the crowd which had amassed on the plaza. The gawking perimeter fell to a curious hush as they intently watched the young boy on the verge of convulsing as he performed some kind of bizarre ritual over the dead body.

It was this unnatural silence, almost a sound in itself, which alerted the two officers. Now girdled by a half dozen or more others, they pushed back the perimeter to find the nine-year-old on his knees and quaking. *This time,* thought the cop who had booted the side of Antoine's head, *I'll happily justify having to forcibly remove this weird fucking kid from our crime scene.* He was already in the process of unleashing a pair of handcuffs from his belt, midstride.

He never had a chance to use them. For Antoine J. Washington's corpse sat bolt upright with a sucking, horrifying yowl....

09.10

Like a dozen toy flutes being blown off-key, the dead man's shriek penetrated even the hefty studio glass ... and the ceramic mug of show host Analise Gonzalez dropped from her hands. It exploded into a thousand rum-drenched shards.

As the inside of the studio had fallen to eerie silence during these past eleven minutes, the sound engineer ramped up every available microphone to maximum input, desperate to capture at least a small portion of the audio taking place just beyond the heavily insulated windows. So, when Analise's mug crashed to the floor, its sound red-pegged the digital meters on every one of the mixing board's channels.

Floor Manager Rachel winced in pain, snatching the thundering headphones from her ears with a curt, reflexive wail of her own. Camera Operator #1 did the same, and the camera angle dropped, the shot of the live feed becoming the dirty studio floor instead of Simon Peter and the squealing, thrashing corpse he'd resurrected.

"Jesus H. Christ!" Rachel Stoltz shouted, barely believing what she was watching as Antoine's body shrieked and writhed on its back in a pool of thick, oily blood. "Get on that shot, goddammit! GET BACK ON THAT FUCKING SHOT!"

09:11

The paramedics pushed through the ring of police and pedestrians who stood frozen in disbelief. They now attended to Antoine as they should have at the outset, rather than obeying the officers who shooed them away. In reality, their inaction had made no difference, for Washington was dead by the time they arrived. However, an immediate trauma analysis would have eliminated the one variable upon which disbelievers would later hang their hat, claiming that Antoine had never died at all but had merely been unconscious.

The younger of the two EMTs slipped as he strode into the slick red puddle. He corrected his balance at the last moment, narrowly avoiding plowing into both the man and boy as the other medic took Simon by the shoulders and began lifting him to his feet.

Simon Peter did not resist. As he rose, he leaned forward and whispered into Antoine's agitated ear. His words were not audible to anyone but the man he'd resurrected. However, his moving lips were clearly visible to one of the three cameras which had zoomed tight on the shot.

Immediately Washington ceased jerking and wailing. While still quaking from head to toe, he leaned back onto his elbows and settled into a confused, yet almost stoic, aspect.

The first paramedic donned nitrile gloves and began running through standard trauma protocol. The first thing he did was ask Antoine his name. It was an oddly calm interaction, and from afar one might be forgiven for thinking that Antoine had merely taken a small tumble and was having a twisted ankle examined.

09:13

Camera #1 swung back to the three presenters inside the studio as Rachel Stoltz worked her earphones and microphone back onto her head. She pointed at the hosts, an assertive and full-armed gesture, as the small light atop the camera's body turned white to indicate they were live.

A deer in the headlights, Analise Gonzalez appeared stupefied. She stuttered once or twice, struggling for the words that wouldn't come, then shot a terrified look at her two co-hosts.

Beau Wilson chortled awkwardly. Straightened his tie. Cleared his throat. Did his best to compose himself.

"Well," he forced from lips which quivered noticeably. "That was a wild fifteen-minutes to start your morning. Heh, gang?"

If he had stopped there, perhaps the public would have forgiven such a minimizing response and allowed it to drop by the wayside sooner than later.

But Wilson did not stop there.

Perhaps it was the barely masked racism which had become more and more prevalent since experiencing a negative situation on the street a few years ago. A skepticism aimed not at an individual, but at an entire group, and which had begun to govern more and more of Wilson's daily interactions these days than he would ever openly admit. Add to this his natural disposition to use (what Wilson considered to be) humor to deflect his anxiety in times of crises, and the presenter chose to add: "At least your day is going better than this piece of crap's right here! Haha!"

Aghast, the entire studio was silent in disbelief as Beau Wilson thumbed over his shoulder to Antoine J. Washington who was being lifted onto a stretcher and rolled onto his side so he wouldn't choke on his own blood. The back of the man's entire body—from his hair matted thick with congealing clots, down to his stained basketball shoes—appeared as if he'd just been removed from a vat of melted crimson wax.

In the background, the perimeter of bystanders cast their eyes to the ground, their mouths wide with horror. Some turned away altogether, unable to bear the sight. Others had their attention diverted as uniformed police pressed them back, methodically dispersing everyone from the plaza.

Everyone, that is, except Simon Cockerton.

Unyielding, the nine-year-old stood alone before them all. He stared past Antoine and the paramedics, and straight into the lens of the TV camera as if he knew which of the three was broadcasting live, as well as its precise location deep inside the *ND-USA!* studios.

Rachel Stoltz instructed its operator to zoom in, cutting to a tight shot of this young hero.

Wondering if she were the only one to notice the dark, recalcitrant affect growing in his eyes ....

The next morning the head of thoracic surgery at Saint Michael's University Hospital announced to a room full of reporters and TV cameras that Antoine J. Washington had lost more than seven of his approximately ten-and-a-half pints of blood. Various tests had established that he may have received no oxygen to his brain for more than five minutes. And a pair of nine-millimeter rounds had been successfully removed from Antoine's chest cavity. One had struck his heart. The other, a lung. But each had subsequently backed out of the respective organs ...as if drawn away by a magnet. The trauma to both remained evident, as well as the bullets' pathways through his chest. However, their points of penetration into heart and lung had begun some kind of catalyzed self-repair, the initial damage to the tissue appearing as if it had been carefully and expertly reconstructed.

The surgeon admitted it was like nothing he'd seen before.

He then ignored every hand which shot up, every incredulous voice which shouted out a question, as he pressed his glasses up the bridge of his nose and continued with his report.

"The patient has been in the capable hands of our ICU since nine p.m. last night," the surgeon calmly relayed. "His condition this morning is stable, and he is in remarkably good spirits, given what he's been through."

He shuffled through his notes.

"Mr. Washington has also requested—stipulated, in fact—that I share the above information with you, as well as the specific details of our care. Numerous though may they be, the procedures we have undertaken have been relatively routine and have included ..."

After reeling off a litany of proceedings, the surgeon relaxed and leaned into the podium, placing his notes to one side and adjusting his microphone.

"Look. Just like you, I've seen the footage. And I know what you want me to confirm."

The cameras snapped and flashed as thirty photographers reeled off dozens of shots each, the bright white lights a swarm of blinding fireflies. The surgeon blinked, his eyes watering.

"Given what we've all seen," he began again, raising his voice to be heard above the growing clamor. "Given what we've witnessed, combined with the critical volume of blood lost; the two rounds we recovered from Mr. Washington's chest. And the fact that those objects had entered his heart and lung, I am willing to say …."

He hesitated, the weight of his words already upon him as every camera in the room flashed, the frenetic energy building to a mad crescendo.

"…Willing to say that, yes, Mr. Washington had to have been biologically dead, at least for an uncertain length of time, prior to being brought to us here for treatment."

The room exploded into a turmoil of shouts, reporters holding mini digital voice recorders high and screaming out an array of impossibly overlapped and indiscernible questions. The surgeon closed his eyes until the flashes and voices subsided.

"However, ladies and gentlemen. *However.* What I am *not* willing to do is enter into conjecture about how Mr. Washington's vital organ operation resumed, given all that I've just shared. His blood loss, above all. It's unprecedented. That being said, there are a few potential phenomena that might provide an explana—"

The sentence was never completed. The roar of the reporters had risen to a cacophony, flashes lighting the small room as brightly as the summer sun ….

3:17

WHILE EVERY MEDIA outlet across the country had clambered to secure an interview with Simon Cockerton and Antoine J. Washington, the first to succeed, not surprisingly, was *New Day, USA!* Exactly one week after the incredible events had unfolded on live TV, the morning show had secured both individuals for an exclusive interview which would air in prime time later that night. To promote this highly anticipated hour-long segment, the two were in the studio this morning with *ND-USA!* dedicating thirty full minutes as a live teaser of the nine-p.m. taped show. So, as the nation awoke, one out of every four households began their Independence Day celebrations by turning on their TV sets to see the young boy people were already hailing as a new prophet, and the modern-day Lazarus he'd brought back from the dead. As a result, the *ND-USA!* team was celebrating a number one ranking, exponentially exceeding its nearest competitor by over twenty-three million viewers. Landslide ratings unparalleled by any other show bar the biggest game in football itself.

For the first time in her professional career, Rachel Stoltz was actually nervous. The morning show's British director, Burke Cummings, was an equitable man if nothing else, and he'd given Rachel the reins.

"And jolly well deserved too, my love. Well-deserved indeed," he'd commended her at the prime-time special's planning meeting just days after the incident. "Just don't get *too* comfortable on that bloody high horse of yours. I still need a cracking good floor manager when this whole hullabaloo is over."

But for now, Rachel was in the driving seat as she readied herself for the most pivotal show of her career.

"Oh, hey. You must be Mrs. Cockerton." She extended her hand as she greeted the woman who accompanied Simon as they were led through the labyrinth that was the backstage.

Rebecca released her son's hand and shook Rachel's.

"Yes, Rebecca. Please, just call me Rebecca." She glanced around her, seeking her husband through the dark jungle of wire vines and lighting rig trees. "And, uh, Mr. Cockerton, of course," she stated nervously, "is Ian. He'll be here in a moment. And I know he'll feel a lot less intimidated if you greet him by his first name as well."

"Then first names it is. In which case, I'm Rachel." She released her hand from Rebecca's and offered it to Simon. "And you! You must be our very special man of the hour!"

Simon beamed and shook her hand with a plucky vigor that was difficult not to find charming. His easy manner only further accentuated his disarming, inherent charisma. "Yes, Ma'am. Good morning! You can call me Simon Peter."

Rebecca Cockerton chuckled inwardly, the resultant smile lighting her face despite the creeping anxiety gnawing at her gut. "I'm much more nervous than Simon, I'm afraid you'll find, Rachel," she confessed to the floor manager.

Stoltz responded with a wave of the hand and a shrug.

"This?" She swept her hand casually before her to indicate the expansive, soberly illuminated backstage. Bustling bodies dodged tangles of long black cables which snaked between intimidating, high tech electrical equipment most people only ever saw in movies. "You have nothing to be nervous about, Mrs. Cocker—uh— Rebecca. Just think of all this as an adult version of show-and-tell."

"Ah! I used to love that day in school!" The unfamiliar voice had come from behind, and Rachel noticeably flinched before spinning to see a man in his late thirties in tidy blue jeans, white button-down shirt and tweed jacket replete with suede patches on the elbows. "I'm—"

"—Ian," Rachel finished for him, her hand already outstretched.

Instead of shaking it, Ian Cockerton lifted the woman's hand to his lips and gently kissed the back of it. Rachel blushed, pulling it away immediately and looking to see if Rebecca had witnessed the interaction. Fussing over Simon Peter's outfit and hair, she hadn't.

Somehow, Rachel imagined Ian wouldn't have cared if she had.

II

The family sat in the green room and watched the first ninety minutes of the show from a surprisingly small television with the volume permanently set just low enough to be a frustration. Their half-hour slot was at the top of the eight o'clock hour, when they would be joined by Antoine J. Washington. As the show airing later tonight had been filmed in two separate interviews, this morning would be the first time Simon Peter and Antoine would see each other in person since the miraculous resurrection. It would also be the first meeting between Antoine and Simon Peter's parents, and Rebecca Cockerton looked forward to an introduction in the green room prior to going live on the air.

Rachel Stoltz had other plans.

"I want the world to feel the emotion when Simon Peter and Antoine meet again," she explained. "That's really important. So that moment has to be real. It'll be okay, though. I promise. You're going to like what Antoine has to share with you."

Rebecca wasn't so easily convinced. With competing media quick to dig up dirt on the man who had been given a second chance at life, a lot had come out about the British expatriate in the past week. It was revealed almost immediately that Antoine had a list of convictions to his name. Mostly misdemeanors. But one felony for which he had served seven years by pleading guilty to a class D charge. Avoiding a costly and time-consuming trial, the State of New York, in return, downgraded Washington's sentence from armed robbery in the first degree for intimidating the victim with a deadly weapon (in this particular case, a folding knife) to felony robbery in the third.

The thought of a man she did not know, and who was capable of such a crime, being part of Simon's life made Rebecca more than a little nervous. At the same time, she also found herself wondering if she would feel the same innate defensiveness had the man been Caucasian with the same murky history.

She immediately rebuked the thought, convincing herself that she would be in Mama Bear Mode regardless of the color of the man's skin. *Red, purple, blue, black, brown or white doesn't matter,* she defended, perhaps too vehemently, in a mind that raced with conflict and uncertainty. Her fingernail absentmindedly scratched the grey, commercial grade fabric of the armchair in which she sat. *If you have a history of doing bad things to good people, and then become close to my son, I'm going to sit up and take notice.*

"I understand how you're feeling," Rachel reassured, bending down and speaking softly to the mother while Ian and Simon Peter giggled at something they were watching on the show. "I would feel the same way if my child were involved, in any way, with a convicted felon. Any mother would be crazy not to. All I ask is that you trust me. Please?"

After a moment's consideration Rebecca reluctantly nodded, her countenance slowly relaxing into mild acceptance.

The floor manager mouthed a silent but appreciative *thank you*, then announced to the others: "Five minutes guys. Everyone ready?"

Ian winked and gave two thumbs up. Simon Peter nodded with enthusiasm, never taking his eyes off the TV.

III

"Alright, we're back!" Analise Gonzalez announced to the cameras with genuine excitement as she set her mug upon the side table, once again surprised by—and equally proud of—the warm, creamy taste of arabica coffee on her palate. "I know you've all been waiting for this, and so have I! So please now let me introduce to you..."

The live camera panned to the settee to Analise's right and in the sound booth the engineer played a realistic digital effect of an audience full of people clapping.

"...Dad, Ian. Mom, Rebecca. And their miracle-maker nine-year-old son, Simon Cockerton!"

On the studio floor, dozens of members of the production team had amassed from the shadows and roared into genuine applause.

Simon Peter chirruped something, his words muted by the hearty welcome. As the clapping and exuberant hoots slowly died away, Analise leaned toward him and, winking, asked him to repeat himself.

"Simon *Peter*," he said again, louder but smiling. "I'm named after the apostle, Simon Peter. The fisherman who was the brother of Andrew. The one that Jesus called a Fisher of Men and promised him a special position in the Church."

"Oh my," Analise Gonzalez exclaimed as she glanced at her teleprompter, her left hand reflexively fingering the dainty gold crucifix which hung from her neck. Already off-script and having to think on her feet, the host was never more grateful than she was in this moment that she'd chosen to fill her mug with a stimulating dark roast as opposed to thought-stifling rum. "You know, that connection never even crossed my mind. You're certainly aware of your Christian history, Simon. What a wonderful story!"

"Simon *Peter*," he corrected her again.

"Yes, of course." Analise chuckled. "Simon Peter! So tell me, Mom.

Has Simon...*Peter*...always had an interest in his faith? Would you consider yourselves a fairly religious family?"

Rebecca Cockerton stumbled over her words as she began to answer, appearing as surprised as the presenter over her son's revelation. She looked to her husband.

Ian took her hand in his.

"We're very *spiritual*, Analise. I find the word 'religious' very constraining, don't you? I prefer to view our spirituality in terms of a universal balance. Light and dark, good and bad. Both, together. For one surely needs the other ....And the world needs them both."

It wasn't in the slightest the answer Analise Gonzalez expected to hear. Especially in response to what would normally be a quick throwaway, almost rhetorical, question. "Hmm, uh-huh. I see." She was nodding, allowing a moment for the statement to process.

Only three minutes into the interview and it's already going off the rails, Analise thought and reached for her mug. It got barely halfway to her mouth before she put it back down, having seen its warm brown liquid instead of the crisp, cool clarity it normally contained. *C'mon, Analise. Think. Think! You've got this. Just take a beat and think about how his answer makes you feel. The words will come. They always do.*

"Well, I certainly agree that world needs more good in it: more hope. Hope like your amazing son has brought us all. But are you saying the world actually needs the bad, too? Do you mean that, Mr. Cockerton, or am I misunderstanding you?"

Thattagirl, Lisi, the presenter praised herself. *Back on track!*

"Maybe I should clarify." Ian's eyes were drawn to the crucifix around Analise's neck. It glimmered under the bright studio lights. And for a moment, his confidence wavered. "Um, I. Okay ... here's what I'm trying to express. Your cross there, that you're wearing around your neck. What does that mean to you?"

The presenter didn't hesitate. "It means   hope. It means forgiveness. It means sacrifice, and the highest love." She looked deeply into Ian's eyes, engaging him at a depth she'd never achieved in an interview before. "It means ... *everything*."

"Yes, it does," was his response. "And it should. But have you ever stopped to consider? That symbol would not be around your neck; it would not have the meaning that's been ascribed to it; indeed, the memory of Christ himself would likely have disappeared into the dark abyss of obscurity, the creed of Christianity dead before it ever took hold, had your savior simply chosen to ... *live*."

Gonzalez had stiffened, her posture defensive. "That's correct! It was the greatest love, manifest in the greatest sacrifice. The living Son of God the Father and the Holy Ghost giving his own life that we may live!"

Behind the dark shadows of hulking cameras, Rachel Stoltz nearly passed out. Her presenting host was not only espousing religion but was using the broadcast to promote one very specific doctrine in particular.

So much for my one big shot, Rachel decried, and if she hadn't known better, might've even suspected Burke Cummings himself for putting Analise up to it. Of course she knew better. For Analise's ratings were Rachel's ratings were Burke's ratings. Sink or swim, they were all paddling this rowboat together. Unfortunately, it had just sprung a leak—a really big one—just as the waters had become a whole lot choppier. Rachel thought she might even see the silhouette of a circling shark or two.

She pleaded over her comms channel, praying that the booth had the commercial tracks ready.

"You better believe we do," was their unquestioning response.

So, it was her call whether she cut Analise off or allowed the show to devolve into an unscheduled catechism class. While it would appear achingly unprofessional to simply cut to commercial, perhaps the two-minute break would allow her to get the show back on track. And get Analise back to the concise, expertly crafted questions waiting on her teleprompter.

"Listen," Ian Cockerton's voice broke through her thoughts, essentially making the decision for her. Almost as if he could read her mind. "I don't want this to devolve into a religious class. We agree that Christ needed to die on that cross you're wearing, and suffer horribly in the process, for the power of his enduring love to be understood and recognized. But here's my point: that wouldn't have happened without a sadistic, bloodthirsty group of Roman soldiers willing to beat, torture and humiliate him. What Christ went through came from the depths of Hell itself, of that I can assure you. And those soldiers wouldn't have had the opportunity to take out their frustrations on Christ if Judas hadn't given him up to them . . . for a paltry thirty silver coins. So you see, the rise of Christ and the Christian faith was as dependent upon the evil of man as it was the good of the Savior."

Analise Gonzalez, as well as Rachel Stoltz and every member of the *ND-USA!* team, could only respond with numb silence.

"But hey!" Ian Cockerton proclaimed with a bright smile as he turned to face the live camera. "Why don't we get Antoine out here and get this party started." He winked at millions of stupefied Americans at home, still in their robes and pouring coffees. Then winked again. Beyond the cameras.

At Rachel Stoltz.

She sent the broadcast to break and allowed a safe margin of a second or two before screaming with all her might into her hands.

IV

During the break, one point three million more viewers tuned in to the show, word on the grapevine traveling fast. Seems everyone wanted to tune in to see the train wreck firsthand, whether they believed in the modern-day resurrection or not. Regardless of their motivation, Rachel Stoltz was now directing the most watched morning show in television history. Anywhere in the world. She breathed a sigh of relief and gratitude, sending a quiet and cursory prayer of thanks to the heavens.

Just before Analise Gonzalez walked off set.

This was too much. *Way too much*, Gonzalez had proclaimed as she marched to her dressing room without stopping, forcing Rachel to stride briskly alongside her. Something felt very, very wrong, Analise added. Just being near the Cockertons was flooding her with an intense, overwhelming anxiety. And while she couldn't quite put her finger on it, she could *feel* it, the way some people say you feel when something terrible happens to your significant other.

Or to a twin.

You just know.

Analise's male co-host, Beau Wilson, had barely escaped the hot seat after the base, and likely racist, comment he'd made about Antoine J. Washington the previous week. But there was no choice: he'd have to take over the remainder of the interview. Which also meant he'd be the one presenting the segment in which *ND-USA!* would introduce Antoine (a.k.a., Wilson's 'piece of crap') to both the Cockertons and the world.

"God *damn* it!" Wilson proclaimed as an intern affixed a lavalier mic to his lapel. "I mean, really. What in holy goddamn? Now *I* need to play nice to that piece of garbage Washington and eat his shit pie…all because the Puerto Rican Princess decides now's the time she wants to thump on her bible?"

"Well, they say karma's a crafty bitch," answered Rachel, finding more than a little joy in this rare opportunity to rub Wilson's nose in his failed marriage to co-host, Analise. Accusations of his serial infidelity, almost from the start, made Analise Gonzalez's success in the year since their divorce all the more poignant, her career outshining Wilson's these days by leaps and bounds.

"Yeah? Well, fuck that bitch," Wilson said in reply, and whether he was referring to karma or Analise, Rachel wasn't sure.

"No, Beau. That's what got you into trouble in the first place."

She patted him on the shoulder, secretly reveling in his angst. It was barely a moment before she despised the feeling, wanting no joy from his distress—from anyone's, for that matter—regardless of who they were. "But hey. Maybe this was supposed to happen, y'know? Think about it. You pull this off and every person in America will not only forget your *faux pas*, they'll actually admire you for the way you've recovered from it. Takes a real man to stand up to his mistakes."

Wilson knew the floor manager always admired him, so was definitely referring to his comment of the previous week. Still, he couldn't help but equate it to the recent dark years of his marriage.

V

Ignoring his jangling nerves, attention focused solely on the teleprompter, Beau Wilson settled into his patter. The fact that he was once again top dog—while his ex-wife watched from the wings—did more than a little to bolster his confidence.

"And now I have the honor to introduce a man to whom I owe an apology, the size of which I could never fulfill. But I hope he will accept the depth of its sincerity, as it comes from my heart. Ladies and gentlemen, meet our modern-day Lazarus, Antoine . . . J . . . Washington!"

More than paying his dues, it was evident Beau Wilson had realized the powerful impact it could have upon his career if he were to successfully pull off this interview. Transformed into a gushing sycophant right before America's eyes, the presenter grinned like the Cheshire Cat as he stood to lead the applause for Washington who bounded across the studio and up onto the stage.

Nothing like a forty-three-year-old who had been shot in the back—twice, just a week prior—Antoine was as sprite and agile as a teenager. In fact, if you'd tuned in to the morning show at this point without already knowing the program's subject, you'd be forgiven for thinking he might be an up-and-coming comedian, or perhaps a trending new hip hop artist.

At least, you might have thought that until he stopped in front of Simon Cockerton, dropped to his knees in supplication.

And burst into a flood of tears.

Rising from the sofa, Simon Peter hugged the man kneeling before him, a deep embrace without reservation.

Partially muffled by the boy's shirt, Washington gushed his humble adulation. His native East London accent was thick and clipped with THs at the beginning of words articulated more like Fs; the Ts in the middle of most barely spoken at all. "Thank you, thank you, thank you little man. You brought me back, bruv. My wife thanks you. My baby daughter thanks you! I don't deserve it, mate, but *I* thank you."

On the sofa next to her son, tears formed in Rebecca Cockerton's eyes. Rachel Stoltz had Camera #1 cut in tight as the woman wiped them away with the tip of her finger, conscious not to smudge her makeup. She accepted a tender embrace from Antoine as well, the stranger whispering something in her ear before taking his place next to her husband.

As he sat, Antoine pumped Ian's hand up and down so many times the floor manager lost count. The whole exchange was everything Rachel had hoped it would be.

"Antoine," Beau Wilson started the conversation once the emotive introductions had settled. "There's been a lot of talk centered around your past this week. I'd like to start our chat by addressing that before we move on. Is that okay with you?"

Blinking away the moisture from his eyes Washington shuffled in his seat, his apprehension as sudden as it was apparent. "Well— uh—yeah. Mr. Wilson, yeah, it is," he answered, his Cockney accent disarming. "And you know, I seen all that and heard it myself, so I appreciate you givin' me the chance to say my piece. But before I do, I got something to say to *you*, a'ight?"

The breath caught in the co-host's throat. He steadied himself. And while he appeared graciously attentive and receptive on the outside, on the inside Beau Wilson's chest had tightened like a snare drum skin across his ribs.

Experiencing a similar, if significantly milder, sensation Rachel Stoltz quickly addressed the booth through her comms to make sure the sound engineer had his bleep censor ready.

That intuition was about to pay off in spades.

"You see, I know what you said about me, guv," Antoine revealed to the simpering presenter. "After them cops shot me dead, right. I know you made light o' the whole situation like it was nothin'. Like me being shot and left for dead on the bloody street was entertainment for all the goddamn latte-sippin', cereal crunchin' motherfuckers out there in TV land." He gestured wildly at the tens of millions watching in the unseen audience at home, while making aggressive eye contact with the camera.

Of course the viewers didn't hear it that way. After the infamous 'Wardrobe Malfunction' of the Super Bowl halftime show the year before, the network had introduced a new seven second 'Decency Delay' for all of its live broadcasts.

Rachel found it an indictment of the country's mores that there was no actual mandate in place for her to censor the pool of blood last week as Antoine lay dying on the sidewalk. 'Use your best judgment,' Corporate had explained regarding the airing of matters of violence. But God help you if you showed a bare female nipple or let a sexual swear word slip through the net.

So, Antoine Washington's tirade was actually broadcast as:

"…Like me being shot and left for dead on the bloody street was entertainment for all the *[bleeep]* latte-sippin', cereal crunchin' *[bleeeeeeeeep]* out there in TV land."

Beau Wilson bristled but did not interrupt him.

"And what I want to say to you, Mr. Wilson, is—"

Here Antoine rose from the sofa and crossed to the presenter, his hands clenched in sizeable fists that flexed with every step.

Beau Wilson bolted to his feet, eyes darting, as he considered an escape route from the stage ....

VI

Secretly, Rachel Stoltz hoped Antoine would clout Beau right there in front of the world, smacking the disagreeable presenter straight out of his Italian leather monk strap loafers. She hadn't cared for the co-host's self-serving, egocentric behavior at the best of times. Even less after the whole marriage-to-Analise-fiasco. And she was far from alone in that sentiment. So, watching Antoine knock some sense into Beau would've definitely made for great television.

Wishing violence upon anyone, however, was not in Rachel's nature and disappointment in herself roiled sour in her stomach for even allowing such a thought to surface. More so when she caught the fear and panic in the presenter's eyes.

Security had already rushed to the stage, keeping just out of the camera's frame but ready to spring into action. One of them later admitted to Rachel that rather than prevent it, they were going to let the tussle go down first. 'You know,' the guard admitted with a wink. 'Give Antoine a chance to at least throw a punch. Maybe two.'

It never came to that.

Instead, Washington threw his arms around the presenter. Pulled him close. And looked Beau straight in the eyes, his gaze unwavering and sincere. "What I want to say to you, Mr. Wilson, is ... *I forgive you*. You are my brother. And I forgive you ... for *all* of your sins. I love you. And I want you to know that it's all gonna be okay."

VII

Beau Wilson was a different person from that moment, his transformation immediate and evident. Almost physically tangible.

He not only managed to carry the segment, but far outperformed anything that Analise Gonzalez had ever done. It was astonishing not only to Rachel, but to Director Burke Cummings as well.

"I was going to ask you about your past run-ins with the police, Antoine. The producers have a whole slew of questions queued up," the presenter conceded as he pointed toward the teleprompter. "Particularly centered around your past felony conviction for which you served some pretty serious time. But, whaddya say we just focus on what happened last week, how's that sound?"

Bringing his hands together as if about to pray, Antoine leaned forward. "Yes, Mr. Wilson. That sounds good, mate. That sounds like the reason I'm here." Craning past Ian and Rebecca to catch Simon Peter's eye, he patted his chest and laid one hand over the other, miming an embrace.

Simon Peter mirrored the gesture back.

"Wonderful," Beau acknowledged, and Antoine settled back into his spot on the sofa, centering his attention on the presenter. "Rather than play the ratings game and drag this out just to keep people watching, let's go straight to the question everyone in America—no, scratch that; the question every human on the planet—wants me to ask. Because you, Mr. Washington, are the one person in the world who may actually have the answer that all of mankind has been seeking. Since the start of time itself...."

Washington was unconsciously nodding as Wilson spoke, eyes cast down as he squeezed his hands between his knees. He jostled on the sofa next to Ian as if he couldn't quite get comfortable, then took a deep breath. He did not look up.

"What the world wants to know is ...." Beau leaned forward, elbows on his knees, his focus on Antoine intense. The whole world did the same, leaning closer to their TV sets with bated breath.

Wilson paused until the silence drew Antoine's eyes to his own. His voice softened. Almost to a whisper.

"What did you experience, Antoine...*after* you died...?"

3:18

INTENSELY FOCUSED ON the grainy picture of one of the old Zenith TVs mounted over the counter, Diane washed down her breakfast burrito with another sip of coffee. She shook her head without speaking when the waitress asked if she would like anything else before they closed up shop. Normally open from early morning 'til late, today the diner would be closing by lunchtime so they too could participate in the Fourth of July fun.

"Oh, wait," Diane interjected as the waitress began to turn away. "I'll take another Bloody Mary . . . . Oh! And some Pie! I'd like your lemon meringue pie. Please."

"Whole? Or just a slice, cariño?"

Diane smiled, the girl's natural charm endearing. While she'd never met Felipe's daughter before, Diane had heard about her more than once. In hindsight, she realized, it had been a lost opportunity as she had a feeling they could have been great friends.

It was too late for all of that now.

"As much as I'd love to take a whole one, I hafta hit the road after this and I'd have no way of taking it with me. So, just a slice please—" she leaned forward, acting as if she were squinting to see the girl's name tag, already fully aware that her name was "—*Lucia.* Oh, and would you mind turning that up for me? Please?"

Lucia Menendez snagged the brick of a remote from under the bar and clicked it at the TV. Nothing happened. It took a brisk tap against the Formica countertop for the volume level to appear on the screen, just in time for *New Day, USA!* to go to commercial break.

"You know, my family knows these people," revealed Lucia, still gazing at the screen. "Well, sort of. I mean, *I* don't actually know them. But that guy they just showed ... the father? His name is Ian and he used to work with my dad. In fact, they were really good friends at one point. Can you believe that?"

"Oh? Wow!" Diane feigned surprised, her voice louder and rather more dramatic than she wanted. "Yeah. No, that's crazy."

"Right? They used to hang out here. This place was their local."

"Local, as in, bar? You mean that kind of local?" Of course, Diane knew full well that she was having the first breakfast of her newfound freedom in the place where everything had started, so long ago, in the days before innocence had died.

Back then the worst thing that could happen in your life was your adopted brother ripping up your gaudy, oversized Valentine from Handsome Robbie Hanson.

Not your uncle blowing your father's brains out in the woods.

Lucia nodded as she grabbed a pie from the chill case. "Yeah. Used to be called The Major League. Another friend of theirs, a guy called Tony Lamont, owned it. Like, forever. One of those old school bars that aren't really around much anymore. But I bet you can probably tell—my dad hasn't done a whole lot to modernize it. I mean, just look. Even these nasty old TVs are still the same. Zeniths. Have you ever even heard of that brand? Like we're stuck in a nineteen-fifties time warp. And that one over there?" She pointed to the other end of the long expanse of counter. "That one's never worked. Not since he bought the place."

Diane chuckled. "So how did all that come about?"

"What, you mean how'd he get this place?" She slid a massive triangle of lemon meringue in front of her guest. "Well, he used to work for the *Manhattan Bulletin*, before they started laying people off. Not a lot of folks get their news from reading a piece of paper anymore. And I don't know about you, but I've always hated the feeling of that cheap ink on my fingers. Anyway, I guess it was sometime in early oh-one when he bought the place. Their friend, Tony, died around Thanksgiving a few years before that. I guess it sat empty and boarded up until—"

"—Until your father couldn't bear to see it gathering any more cobwebs and decided to turn it into a diner."

Lucia winked, tapping the side of her nose. "You got it! And besides adding a kitchen, he hasn't done a thing to the décor. You see that?" She waved the pie cutter at a small hole in the wall to Diane's left, about the size of a quarter. "You know what that is?"

Diane shook her head, shrugging.

"That's a damn bullet hole, girl."

This time Diane didn't have to fake her surprise. "No *shit*—"

"—Yeah." Lucia confirmed. "That Ian guy I just told you about? He and my dad were blowing off work one morning. This was like, oh, probably two or three years before Dad took the place over. And some crazy guy comes in and just starts shooting. Because of a baseball game. I mean, I love my Yankees. But what the hell."

Diane leaned across the red vinyl stool to her left, braced it from spinning, and examined the hole in the flaking plaster wall. She ran her fingertip around the edge polished smooth by countless other curious fingers that had poked and prodded it for a decade.

"Yeah, everybody does that," Lucia informed her as, suddenly self-conscious, Diane withdrew her digit. "People are fascinated. We get true crime nerds here a lot. Oh, and even a couple requests from ghost hunters. Guess we're on some kind of online list. Anyway, the hole's a lot bigger now than it used to be. And that stool you're propped up on? This poor old guy—the one the psycho shot—died right there. Blew out the old man's chest then half his face as he slumped right there against the wall."

A jagged vibration spiked through Diane's gut and she recoiled as if she'd received an electric shock. Behind it came an oppressive feeling: a weight like impenetrable loneliness. The image of a weary, grey-stubbled face she didn't know. And a sickening, inexplicable odor that overcame her as quickly as it was gone.

The stool nearest the wall spun as she reflexively but too quickly withdrew her weight. It threw off her balance and she nearly face planted right there on the black-and-white checkered floor before she managed to shift fully back atop her own stool.

She gasped, her face blanched.

"You okay, cariño?"

Diane knew some of what had happened, but not that level of detail. She'd pieced together portions of it back in Pennsylvania when she was only twelve and Andrew had just turned seven. Back then, there wasn't even a Simon Peter yet. Her uncle Ian had called out of the blue, and the jarring sound of the phone at night had awakened her. She'd snuck down the hallway and listened to her father talking to him on the cordless handset at the bottom of the stairs. She continued to listen as he then relayed the conversation to her mother. Some of it she couldn't hear. Other parts she did, but not everything made sense at the time.

That same fateful night her grandparents were killed in their car wreck. And the next day Uncle Ian had shown up at their doorstep, back at the childhood home to which he swore he'd never return.

One summer evening a couple years later, as she and her uncle strolled through Central Park eating ice creams, Diane asked if he'd be honest with her about what really happened that day. He didn't reveal much. But he did say this guy they simply called Anonymous (because the authorities never did figure out who he was) just came into The Major League that lunchtime and started shooting. Ian admitted that he, himself, had been very close to being killed. His good friend, Felipe, too. Another man, a homeless man, actually was. And then Tony, the bar owner, shot Anonymous dead.

Ian claimed that all he could recall were these blinding white flashes . . . accompanied by a series of booming echoes. Then an awful smell of hot iron and sulfur. That evening he had a terrible dream about Diane's Gram and Pap and learned in his late night phone call to her father that it had come true. He didn't wait. He caught a bus back to Pee Aay that very night. 'So, that whole awful incident is the reason I came back,' he told her. 'Thank God, too. I can't imagine how things would be today, for all of us, if I hadn't been there when your father, well, when he did what he did. The rest of the story you know. And now here we are.'

Of course, she'd believed him at the time, and was as grateful as he that he'd been there when her father died. If she'd only known then that it was he who had pulled the trigger. He who had taken her father; her brother—even her mother—away.

He who had brought the darkness into their lives....

Which is why, out of a whole world of places to set the tone for her first full week of her freedom, Diane had chosen to be here, at the old bar. Because if anywhere was a good place to draw a close to her old life—and finally start her new one—this place had to be top of the list. The other obvious choice was the old family home on Central Park West. But there was no way she could go back there. She had briefly considered scouting around the outside, maybe even sit on her special boulder, only to see if she might catch a glimpse of them going in or coming out. But the thought of seeing that fifth floor window again, and that spot on the pavement beneath it, was too much for her conceive. Plus, if her uncle Ian knew she was being released—and she was certain that he did— going to her special place was far too risky. He would surely be checking to see if she'd show up there. Just like he had that Thanksgiving night. And besides, even if she felt the risk were worth it, Lord knows if her family even lived there anymore. It had been more than seven years, after all.

Nope. The Major League—or should she say, the new Home Plate Diner—was the place to finish. And the place to start. It was at this very counter where the course of her future had been predetermined. Even if she hadn't known it at the time. So here she would allow it to lead the way today.

She shook off the introspection and attempted a smile. "Gosh. Yes ... I'm fine."

"Sorry," Lucia apologized. "Maybe you're squeamish about these things. Anyway, me and Mama" (she pronounced it 'ma-MA,' and spoke it so sweetly that the uncomfortable feeling in Diane's tummy was eradicated by the warm goosebumps rising between her shoulder blades) "are constantly saying Papi's got to spruce the place up if he wants to attract a better clientele." She cringed as she remembered that she was, in fact, telling this to a customer. "Present company excluded of course, mi cariño."

Cariño, Diane considered. That's the third time she's called me that. *'Sweetheart?' Maybe 'honey,' if Señora Grazer's middle school Spanish serves me correctly?*

"Of course," Diane commiserated, her eyes smiling. And in that moment, she realized that the feeling she was experiencing was genuine, unfettered affection—as casual and inconsequential as it may be to anyone else—for possibly the first time in more years than she wished to count. "So, Lucia. You say you don't personally know the family that well?"

"No, not really," she answered while refreshing Diane's Bloody Mary. "It's all very sad, though. And weird. They had—or have—a daughter who's close to my age. Papi was always saying he wanted to get us together on a play date, being that she was the niece of his best friend and new to the city. I'm glad it never happened."

"No?" Diane's disappointment was almost palpable. "Why?"

"Because the girl was nuts, cariño. She pushed her five-year-old little brother out a nine-story window. Or so they say."

Well, Diane corrected her mentally. *Got that wrong. He was nine and the floor was the fifth. Not the other way around.*

And I would never hurt my brother!

Pangs of sorrow began to weigh heavy in her gut, and she forced the feeling aside. There had been too much mourning already. And anger. And remorse.

Years of it.

"But she was never charged," she reminded Lucia. "At least that's what the papers are saying...?"

"As far as I know. She was committed to Barrow Moor, though. So I guess that tells you everything you probably need to know about the girl, y'know?"

Oh, my dear, sweet, naive Lucia. If only that were true,

Diane pushed the pie to one side, her appetite gone. She downed half the Bloody Mary instead.

"Did you ever meet this Simon kid?"

Lucia shook her head, holding up her index finger to indicate that she'd be just a moment as she greeted two customers. While she took the couple's order, Diane scribbled in her notebook. She didn't notice Lucia's return, the waitress hovering over her while scanning the notations Diane was making on the page.

"Doin' some kinda research about this?"

Diane flinched, quickly closing the journal's cover and sliding it into an inexpensive bag dangling from a hook beneath the counter.

"No, I-uh-I'm—"

"Hey, it's okay," Lucia assured her and propped herself on the counter by her elbows, her chin in her hands. "Nunya. Right?"

"Nunya?"

"Yeah, cariño. Just say, it's nunya. As in, nunya business!'" She giggled and helped herself to Diane's pie, swiping a huge fork-full of stiff, peaky meringue off the top. "Best bit, the meringue. Don'tcha think?"

Diane did think. And instantly forgave her: both for stealing her meringue *and* for making a snap judgment about her being a psychotic murderer. After all, who could blame her? To Lucia, the girl known as Diane Cockerton was just some stranger who got committed for killing her baby brother. With all the news about it and, of course, hearing it from her father, Felipe ... who heard it directly from Ian ... why would she believe any differently?

Christ, even her own family—her own mother—believed it.

"It *is* the best bit. You were saying ... about that boy, Simon ...?"

Lucia used the fork to nip off the tip of the pie's deep yellow triangle and lifting it to her lips as she closed her eyes.

"Mmmm. The lemon pie part is pretty damn good too, though. You really need to try this. Here—"

She heaped a decent amount of both pie and meringue onto the fork. For a moment, she considered actually feeding it to Diane, an oddly agreeable sensation flooding over her as though she not only knew this girl, but that they had been lifelong besties. The idea was as confusing as it was pleasant, and she shook her head to quash it. She spun the fork's handle toward Diane instead.

Diane felt the connection too. She said nothing as she took the fork. "Yes. Mmm, so good! Maybe I will have some, after all."

"Have the rest, cariño. On me. After all, I've already demolished half of it." She pulled an order pad from her pocket and scribbled out the line item as Diane polished off the rest of the slice. "And to answer your question—the one you asked before we dove into that little slice of lemon meringue heaven there—no, I've never met that Simon kid. But I gotta say, something doesn't feel right to me about him, y'know? People are calling this kid everything from a miracle worker to a modern-day prophet of God. But me? I think there's something ... *off* ... about the whole thing."

At that moment the picture on the old Zenith wavered in and out. It flashed brilliant white then became a bristling display of static, the sound of the white noise exploding from its tinny little speaker. When the image finally materialized, it was Simon Peter's face that appeared, except it was grossly disfigured. The same electrical interference had distorted Beau Wilson's voice to something eerie and inhuman as he welcomed back his viewing audience at home.

Lucia shuddered as if warding off a sudden, intense chill. "Well, well. Look at that, cariño. Speak of the devil ...."

3:19

T HE CONDITION OF the boxy old television in the Home Plate diner had nothing to do with it acting up. Across the country, millions of people watching *New Day, USA!* covered their ears as an intense burst of static crackled through TV and surround sound speakers which had been turned up in anticipation of Antoine J. Washington's response to the Beau Wilson question. Many turned away, the accompanying flash of light temporarily blinding. Others remained transfixed as Simon Peter's face undulated beneath the wavering lines and disassociated pixels, the interference seeming to modulate the hero's appearance into something dark and disturbingly sinister and entirely at odds with the smiling visage of a sweet young boy.

Some claim they saw a bestial face obtruding from his features. Others, the countenance of a magnificent angel. A few would later swear they witnessed a skull-like image with a number of small bumps projecting from its head like the nibs of antlers. In support of this view, one now infamous picture—a fuzzy still shot isolated from the footage of Simon Peter reviving Washington—was plastered across the front page of the *National Inquisitor* along with the headline: BUTTON BUCK BOY BRINGS BACK BRIT BADDIE. The tabloid claimed that the image captured an inhuman skull beneath the boy's flesh, with a very pronounced formation of horns. As clear as an X-ray, the picture was embraced by a handful of extremists as indisputable proof that, far from being a prophet of

God, nine-year-old Simon Cockerton was, without question, a boy possessed by a demonic entity. The fact that an almost identical digital image of a satanic skull could be found on an online stock photo website did little to dissuade this particularly extreme faction. Nor did the confession of the image's creator, a graphic design student at UCLA, admitting that he had Photoshopped the demonical skull, superimposed Simon's face over it, and submitted it to the *Inquisitor* as a joke.

What the greatest majority of people saw, however, was ...

... *Nothing.*

Static interference. A broadcast glitch. Bad weather interrupting the TV signal. Therefore, what was never openly acknowledged (as no single incident could be directly connected to any other) was the fact that every metro region across the country had received a tremendous influx of 9-1-1 calls in that moment. Desperate, screaming pleas for help as women were dragged from their phones under a hail of their husbands' punches. Panicked cries for ambulances from helpless parents watching as their children writhed on the floor in inexplicable pain. Thousands with no prior history of it suffering a panic attack so intense it was both mentally and physically incapacitating, dropping grown men to their knees.

Most commonly experienced and universally ignored, however, was the sweeping unease which overcame millions of individuals at once—a dark, disturbing sensation akin to déjà vu—only for the malaise to be dismissed once it receded as swiftly as it had come.

II

Diane Cockerton clutched the edge of the counter, her knuckles whitening as the disturbance tore through her core like a spear. She grimaced as the pain came hot from a place deep inside, fighting to keep control of her faculties. This time the interruption was more than she could bear—too sudden to prepare for; too intense to govern—and she doubled over, the seat of the red vinyl barstool rotating beneath her.

Losing her balance, she spun to the side and dropped to the dingy black-and-white floor with a hollow *thud.* This was followed by the collective gasp of a small handful of remaining diners who had yet to finish their breakfasts.

"Jesus, cariño!" Lucia cried out as her new friend slid from view. "Papi! Papi! I need you!"

She darted around the counter as Felipe Menendez, perplexed, appeared at the double swing door to the small kitchen.

"Dios mío, Lucia! What *happened*?" He rushed to his daughter's side as his customer convulsed on the floor, her eyes rolling back into her head. "We gotta turn her on her side! Here! Lucia. Help me roll her over...!"

Like his daughter, Felipe Menendez had no idea who this young woman was. The last time he had seen Ian's niece, Diane Cockerton had been every bit the pimply fourteen-year-old teenage girl. Not an attractive, if rather pragmatically dressed, twenty-two-year-old woman. Still, as he and Lucia gently rotated her onto her left side, he couldn't help but feel as though he knew this woman from ... *somewhere.*

"Stay with her. Make sure she doesn't choke," he instructed Lucia. "I'll call for help ...."

His fingers shaking, Felipe punched three numbers into the wall phone and awaited the concise but reassuring greeting from the operator asking him what his emergency was. Instead, he was met with the distorted, cyclic beeping of a busy signal.

But that wasn't possible.

He pulled the handset from his ear and stared at it with confusion while processing the fact. Emergency services call centers are always available. They have dozens of dedicated lines, and every call is routed from one to the other until picked up. The number just doesn't register as ... *busy.*

The only other time in his life Felipe had experienced anything like it was when he called 9-1-1 on that fateful day in September, 2001. The day which so poignantly will forever be known by the same three numerals.

He slammed the receiver in its wall cradle and immediately plucked it back off to listen for a dial tone. An F-major chord trilled in his ear before he punched the numbers again, more carefully this time. The droning tone gave way to silence, and Felipe released a sigh of relief in anticipation of the detached, dispassionate voice of the dispatcher which would come next.

Except it didn't.

This time the line went dead. No sound at all. Not even the busy signal. Not even a click.

"Papi! Please. She needs an ambulance!"

III

Deep in a place where only she existed, Diane Cockerton was falling through the void. She did not understand how she knew that she was falling, for engulfed by only emptiness, there was nothing against which she could gauge such motion. Yet that terrifying sensation of plummeting rolled her stomach like a tumbler as she fell through the darkness.

She heard a voice as she plunged faster and faster through this abyss: a faraway sound which also came from within her.

Faint.

Slow and garbled.

Like the time she'd played one of her mom's scratchy old 45 records on 33 speed and thought it was funny at first. But then it began to sound eerie and creepy, the low, gravelly voice making her skin crawl. She'd covered the record player's small mesh speaker with one shaking hand while attempting to raise the needle with her other. The player's arm bounced across the black vinyl with a series of explosive pops until it skidded against the paper label at the record's center. There it lifted and fell, over and over, like an electric heartbeat.

Now that sound was the rhythm of her own heart as, no longer plunging through the darkness, Diane floated stationary, suspended in an infinite sea of emptiness.

"Deedee..."

The tone of the voice had become clear. Childlike. Pleading.

Was it Simon Peter's? Andrew's?

Confused, Diane opened her eyes. First hazy, then wavering as if she were underwater, the perpendicular horizon of the diner's black and white floor swam into focus as she lay curled on her side in a tight fetal position.

"H-Hello?" The question was strained, her voice shaky and thin with her cheek pressed firmly to the cold, dingy floor. She attempted to lift her head but found the task impossible as though it had been braced by an invisible spine board, the type she'd seen on TV when footballers were carted off the field. She tried rising to her elbows, but her body had become as heavy as lead, rooted to the floor and unable to move.

Searing panic rose in her chest, pushing the plea more forcibly from her throat.

"Hello...! Lucia? *Anybody*. Please! HELLO."

The stark and empty diner offered only the weak echo of her own voice by way of response.

Within their restricted framework, Diane's eyes darted with frantic appeal from booth to booth; stool to stool.

But she was alone.

No hungry patrons scraped forks against sturdy ceramic plates while sharing eager plans for this Independence Day. No smiling Lucia chatted them up while topping off mugs of lukewarm coffee and wiping the counter in anticipation of the early closing.

All was still and silent, save the sound of Diane's own labored breathing. That, and the morning show host's droning voice which crackled incoherent from the old TV she could no longer see from where she lay rigid upon the grimy floor.

C'mon, Diane. Get up! she commanded herself. But frozen in place, her muscles would not move. *No, not frozen. Paralyzed. God help me, what's happening?!*

Hammering in her neck, Diane was aware of every agonizing thrum of her pulse as it pounded faster and harder with each passing second. Yet her breath had reduced to a thin and ragged wisp. What little there was now caught in her throat—

—As the foot appeared before her.

Grubby, bare and smaller than an adult's, its color was a bloodless, lifeless grey. Torn, desiccated flaps of skin lifted from raw lesions seeping thick yellow pus, the discharge moistening the dirt smeared into them.

Now a second foot appeared, adorned by a dress shoe. Tattered and ragged, clods of mud sloughed from its sole as it slid across the floor at a grotesque angle, the bone above it splintered and snapped. The foot now serving little purpose, the fibula of the boy's lower leg stumped against the floor as he shuffled slowly closer, bone scraping against tile like that old record player's needle stuck in a scratched loop.

"I see you, Deeedeeeeee ..."

Now the boy's scorched dress pants entered her frame of vision. Patches of dark blue polyester had melted into his skin, making leg and fabric indiscernible for much of its length.

In her mind Diane scrabbled wildly to get away, frantic arms and legs pressing her from the thing which stood before her. But reality proved that she had not moved at all. Instead, eyes transfixed and wild, a violent, tensing wave swept through her body, constricting every muscle. In an instant her knees had snapped up to her chest, both shoulders drawing violently in toward her neck like bat wings. Her hands were rigid claws, nails at the tip of each bent finger gouging the grimy checkerboard floor.

Her breath released in a choking, shuddering blast, dozens of small, opaque bubbles frothing upon her lips.

"Oh, my. What's the matter, Deedee—cat got your tongue?" The corpse of the boy leaned down to peer with one lidless eye, one empty and rotted socket, into hers. "It's been so long. *So very long*. But it's finally time for you to come out and play. Just like I played with your slut mother."

He tilted his head slowly to one side.

"Oh, you didn't know that Rebecca and I played? Yes, oh yes!" While the timbre of his voice remained that of a child's, the creature's speech had taken on the phrasing and cadence of an adult. "In the shower! It was I who beheld your mother's ungodly thoughts. I who guided her hand as we inserted the impure seed. 'And, lo, the angel appeared. For she had found favor to give birth to a son,' isn't that how it goes? 'He who would succeed the throne of David, commanding the house of Jacob forever. He whose kingdom will have no end!'"

The thing that had been Matt Chauncey threw back his head in laughter. It lolled unnaturally to one side atop its elongated neck so that a shrill sound—*a whistling sound*—trilled from its throat where the noose had long ago torn away the larynx.

"Oh, wait. No...that's *your* destiny, Deedee. *You*, to be the womb of the Dragon Lamb. The chosen vessel!"

Reaching for the woman with a wizened hand, charred fingers extended from the muddy cuff of the suit which had dressed the boy's body in the casket. Their cold, bony tips played over Diane's abdomen as she lay powerless; ragged nails snagging her crisp white cotton shirt as they slid between the buttons.

Continuing to seize, Diane's eyes rolled back into her head. A silent cry caught in her constricted throat as its fingers forced their way beneath her jeans, strips of dead skin flaying from bone to cling to her snug waistband. A moment later they found the soft flesh the creature was seeking, and it plunged them deep inside.

"Ah yes. Yes, that's it! Fort Pitt. Tag, you're it!" the thing inside the corpse of Matt Chauncey howled with a buoyant excitement unparalleled anywhere outside the exuberance of youth.

And the scream finally released from Diane Cockerton's lungs.

A long and harrowing wail ....

3:20

BEAU WILSON

Okay, we're back! As I'm sure you know, I'm here with the incredible young man many are calling heaven-sent. Some, a prophet for our modern times. A few have been so bold as to call him a Messiah for our age. Well, I don't know if any of that is true, but I do know this: he's a pretty special individual. And I'm certainly proud to have him here with us on *New Day, USA!* along with his family and the very man he was able to bring back from the brink of death. Ladies and Gents . . . Simon Cockerton!

SIMON PETER COCKERTON

Hi!

BEAU

(chuckling)
Well, hello!
(leaning in, relaxed but somber)
Now, Simon. We all saw what happened just outside our window here last week. But here's my question to you, and I want you to be honest with me in your answer, okay? Do you think you can you do that for me?

SIMON PETER

Okay. And my name's Simon *Peter*.

BEAU

My apologies. Simon *Peter*. Isn't it the truth that you didn't really bring Mr. Washington back to life? That you were just administering some kind of CPR...some kind of medical technique we may not be familiar with? And, gosh-darn it, because we're all just so eager for that elusive thing called 'hope,' we misinterpreted what we saw? Isn't that the truth of the matter here, Simon...*Peter*?

SIMON PETER
No.

BEAU
(contemplative)
Then surely, the truth must be that Antoine—er, Mr. Washington—wasn't really dead. And when he came to the way he did and found you waving your hands over his chest, that was just a fluke. A matter of you being in the right place at the right time to make it look like a resurrection.

SIMON PETER
(silent)

BEAU
So you're affirming that what we saw was real: you brought Antoine J. Washington...back . . . from the brink of death.

SIMON PETER
No.

BEAU
No?

SIMON PETER

Not the brink, no. Antoine's soul had left the body which could no longer host it in this realm. I reunited them.

BEAU

Them?

SIMON PETER

Them, yes. Body and soul. I brought them back together. As one.

BEAU

That's quite a sophisticated concept, Simon. Are you sure you're only nine years old?

SIMON PETER

I've already told you, I'm Simon *Peter*. And I'm almost ten. Will be, in October. So I'm nine and three-quarters.

BEAU

(laughs)

Well, I guess that three-quarters makes quite the difference!

(to Antoine J. Washington)

Antoine. We can all sit in the comfort of our personal space and say whatever it is we think, but there's only one person in the world today with the real answer ... and that's you. So, tell me. Do *you* believe you were dead, Antoine? Or do you think you , perhaps, had just passed out. In shock. After all, you had just been shot in the back. Twice.

ANTOINE J. WASHINGTON

(nodding, snickers uncomfortably)

Right? Well. I'm gonna make this clear. A'ight? I hear all that talk from folk who weren't even there, know what I'm saying? They're

ANTOINE (cont)

talking all kinds of smack like—like—I wasn't really in that bad o' shape. Or, just like you say, I was in shock. Just happened to come outta it in front of the cameras. Bruv...I even heard this one dude shooting off his mouth 'bout how we set the whole thing up. Like me and this rich-ass kid here had the whole bloody thing planned. You believe that? Like some kinda con. Bruv, can you even *imagine* me having anything to do with these people if [CENSORED] didn't go down the way it did?

(to the Cockertons)
No offence, Cockertons, a'ight?

BEAU

So, that kind of talk. That's all false? What you're confirming to America—to the world—right now is that you were shot to death. Just outside those windows. On that plaza ....

ANTOINE

(nodding, eyes downcast)
Yeah, guv. I left this world. Right there.
(pointing)
Like, gone. And this angel
(embraces Simon, tears welling)
right here says, 'No! Not today, man. Not on my watch!' I mean, God knows I don't deserve it. 'Cause I done some bad stuff in my time, y'know? I got a record. But I saw that you know that. I hurt some folk, back in the day. But I've done my time for the terrible things I did. And now that's all behind me, y'know? I'm done with all that! This right here? This. This is my future. Right. Damn. Here. I owe this lil' dude my life, like literally. And I'm gonna follow where he leads. 'Cause this one? He's special, y'know? So yeah, I'll say it, guv. He's a Savior.

BEAU

Savior...?

ANTOINE

What else you gonna call someone who can bring y'all back from
the dead, bruv? I was a goner. Lights out. Said hasta la vista to this
world. God help me. And I gotta say, I don't ever....
(pauses, face morose, shaking his head)
I. Do. Not. *Ever.* Wanna see...what I saw when the lights
went out. Not ever again.

BEAU

(almost a whisper, leaning towards him)
Let's talk about that. Can we talk about that, Antoine? Because
what the world really wants to know is...what did you
experience, Antoine...*after* you died...?

ANTOINE

(clears throat, hesitates)
Wow. Mate. You know, I sure didn't see the good place.
(points skyward, studio chuckles)
But for reals. Everything just went...dark. And it's true what they
say. I seen this light. Then my lady was there. And my little boy. I
seen all the [CENSORED] I done in my life and the more I see, the
farther they get from me. It was bad! Mate, it was so bloody bad.
There was this valley...of writhing things. I can't even call them
people, y'know? They were just in misery. No, they weren't *in*
misery. They *were* misery. You get me? And screaming. God help
me, I can still hear it
(mimes covering his ears)
and in the sky is this battle going on. I wish I could describe it,
right. It was so messed up. But I'ma try. So...there were these

angels. At war. And they were flying all around above me. Above this sewer of misery I's walking into, even though I didn't want to. But I can't stop myself. Thing is, Mr. Wilson, the good guys weren't winning that war. They weren't winning. And those angels, they just kept falling outta the sky. Dropping. Like flies. Everywhere I look, another'un's falling and I hear their screams as those beautiful wings go up in flames when they hit that squirming mass of [CENSORED] I'm slowly becoming part of. And them people—that sea of screaming *things*—just jump on 'em and tear 'em to pieces and those angels are crying and screaming and ...

(pauses)

And then I feel myself being pulled back. Like I's being sucked from that [CENSORED] by a vacuum. I can't explain what it was like, bruv. All I know is a moment later, I was back. Laying full o' holes and bleeding out on the street with this ... *Messiah* ... kneeling by my side. And he's talking to me even though his lips ain't moving and he's telling me it's gonna be a'ight and not to be afraid, 'cause my life's got a purpose, guv.

(gets to his knee and kisses Simon's hand)

And now I'm on my knees by *his* side. 'Cause I know that purpose I'll find is only gonna come by following him.

BEAU

(after a judicious pause, to Simon)

Well, I'd say you got yourself a fan there, Simon ... *Simon Peter.*

IAN COCKERTON

(interjecting)

I'd think he's got himself a *believer.* That's what I'd say, Beau.

BEAU

A believer? So, then you agree. I mean, you feel there's something,

BEAU (cont)

let's say...spiritual...about Simon Peter then? Of course, you're his father and we all know that comes with a certain element of—

SIMON PETER

—He's not my father.

BEAU
(taken aback)

Oh, I'm sorry. Uh, I...I misunderstood then. I was told that Ian and Rebecca were both your parents.

SIMON PETER

My Father is not of this world. I am in my Father, and you in me, and I in you. We are one.

BEAU
(speaking as if to an adult, seeing beyond the boy)

We are one. Is that why you...I'm sorry, I'm still having a hard time saying it out loud. But I'll—I'll—get used to it....Is that why you *resurrected* him? Of all the people in the world. It's been a hot topic. Why give a monumental second chance to an individual with such a, let's just say, *checkered* past?

SIMON PETER

To judge any amongst our number is to judge all, just as we ourselves are judged. Surely you know the disciples of Jesus were thieves; murderers. Corrupt officials. Drunks, carousers and pleasure-seekers. It was not the pious in whom he was interested, but those believed unable to be saved. My Father has chosen Antoine, and like the willow, I bend to his will. Now Antoine shall bend to mine. He has been restored...for his surrender.

SIMON PETER (cont.)
(looks directly at the camera)
Antoine is the first. I assure you, he will not be the last.

BEAU
Is that what you're looking for? Followers?

SIMON PETER
Our time has been millennia in the coming, Mr. Wilson. But now the world is finally ready. To see the truth. To look upon God and life as no others but the angels have before you. So it is that those who are willing to open their eyes shall be rewarded. They shall inherit the earth.

BEAU
Interesting choice of word: *rewarded*. So, we can expect even more from you like the Antoine resurrection? Is that even possible, Simon Peter? Is it an ability you can *choose* to use?

SIMON PETER
Do you believe that I am able to do this?

BEAU
(transfixed, held in Simon Peter's gaze)
You know what? Um, I—*yes*—I believe I actually do.

SIMON PETER
(rising, cups the crown of Beau Wilson's head)
Then according to your faith let it be done to you. All that you have lacked you shall now have in abundance. All that was dirty is now clean. See that all with ears shall hear this.

~ END OF TRANSCRIPT ~

3:21

SWINGING AND CLAWING and kicking in wild arcs, Diane emerged from the seizure a cornered animal fighting for its life. Her scream shattered the silent tension amongst the remaining patrons as her eyes opened to a nightmare unfathomably worse than the creature she had encountered in her interruption. For it was her uncle, Eddie, who knelt before her in the diner. Her uncle's hand exploring where it never should.

Her scream muted as concisely as if the lungs themselves had been torn from her chest, abject terror frozen upon her face.

"*Nooooooo—*" The sickened denial hissed from inside a sucking wheeze, the sharp intake of breath fighting her hysterical refusal to accept it. She swung at her uncle's hand; raked her nails across his face. But it was Lucia's cheek that opened in three thin lines; Lucia's hand which was nowhere near her except to stroke Diane's back in gentle circles while propping her new friend on her side to prevent her tongue from filling her throat.

Lucia winced as Diane's nails swiped at her a second time, ducking to the side before they could make contact again. Felipe and one of the other patrons restrained Diane's flailing arms until, moment by moment, the young woman's consciousness steadily returned. As it did, a unified exclamation of relief rose from a half-dozen remaining diners. This sound comingled with the *New Day, USA!* interview running in the background, and both were received by Diane as high-frequency trills riding atop muffled waves. Slowly the ringing diminished and the muted speech became clear but overlapping fragments that blended and competed for her awareness to become a surreal, audible kaleidoscope.

Diner 1: "... thank God. Do you think she'll be alright...?"

Beau Wilson: "...so the gun was yours, Antoine?"

Diner 4: "... poor girl. Never seen anything like that, up close ..."

Antoine J. Washington: "Yeah. It was mine, a'ight. I was emptying that raghead's register when—"

Lucia: "Cariño, can you hear me?"

Antoine: "... turns out the cops was just 'round the corner the whole time 'n I didn't know it. Never saw 'em. So, they come in, guns drawn, and I leg it. The rest y'all saw firsthand. Two to the back. Live and unfilter—"

Lucia: "It's gonna be OK, cariño, I got you. Can you—"

Beau: "... then, Ian, there's the story of what happened with your own daughter, Diane. She was—"

Ian Cockerton: "—My niece. Not daughter."

Diner 3: "... betcha any money she's got a pocketful of drugs ..."

Beau: "... had some trouble of her own. Accused of killing her brother and committed to Barrow Moor high security insane asyl—"

Felipe Menendez: "... I still think she should be seen by someone, don't you, Lucia? I'm trying 9-1-1 again ..."

Ian: "... several years, yes. She absconded last week and we really just want her home. I fear she's still suffering from delusions, so she's safest with us. Where she's loved and—"

Lucia: "We're going to get you to a hospital, OK cariño?"

Diane squeezed her eyes tight, concentrating hard to press away the tumult of sound. "No ... hospital." In her mind the declaration was bold and clear. Not the four mumbled syllables which actually passed across her parched lips.

Lucia gently swept the hair from Diane's eyes and forehead. "What's that, sweetie?"

"No .... No hospital." Diane forced the air from her burning lungs, raw throat, as the diner momentarily spun. "Please, Lucia."

Beau: "...a request you'd like to share, Mr. Cockerton? Millions are watching as we speak. I'm sure our caring viewers can help bring her back home."

"Papi? I don't think she wants an ambulance ...."

Ian: "... if you're watching, Deedee, your mother and I just want you home. Your brother, too. I'm sure you must feel lost right now. But you don't have to. You're never lost to us, Diane. Never. So hang tight, babygirl. We will find you."

While received as benevolent, even loving, by the ears of the millions watching, to Diane it was a thinly veiled warning.

We.

Will.

Find.

You.

Toxic barbs to her soul, Ian's words spurred her to clarity. Taking Lucia's hand, Diane rose from the floor upon legs loose and rubbery, concentrating harder than she had in her life to shake off the neural static which sizzled inside a thick mental fog.

"R-Really, Lucia. I'm okay," she assured her after a strenuous moment of concentration. The lie tasted acidic and foreign upon her lips. "I promise, I am."

Diane focused on her breathing, stood tall, shoulders back, and showed Lucia her hands to prove they no longer shook.

"See?" She illustrated, holding them out before her. "Steady and solid. It was just an episode. I'm so sorry." She could feel her fingers threatening to tremble, so she dropped her hands to her sides and feigned brushing grit from her jeans. "I didn't mean to frighten you. But please, *please*, ask your father not to call an ambulance. I can't go to a hospital. I can't ...."

Reluctant to leave her side, Lucia responded with a modest nod but spoke no words at all, studying. Watching Diane's hands. Evaluating. Listening to the way she breathed.

Her eyes met Diane's as Diane perched on the edge of the stool from which she'd tumbled, picking up her handbag. She smiled, ensuring the fake emotion travelled to her eyes.

"Really, Lucia. I'm fine. *Please*. No ambulance." She was shaking her head slightly from side to side. A subliminal tactic to encourage Lucia to mirror her body language. Once she did, her compliance would naturally follow. It was one of the few things for which she actually appreciated her Uncle Ian. In charge of sales at the Bulletin for so many years, he'd learned a thing or two about persuasion.

But Lucia did not nod in return.

Still, after a considered hesitation, she approached her father at the other end of the counter who continued to struggle to secure a line to 9-1-1. Gently sliding the phone's receiver from his hands, she hooked it back in its wall cradle. Rising to her toes, she whispered in Felipe's ear, relaying something quietly in Spanish.

Diane studied the interaction closely but was unable to read Lucia's lips. *That's what you get for not opting into Barrow Moor's evening Spanish class,* she admonished herself and, again smiling, pretended to casually search through her handbag. Only when Lucia's eyes were averted did she allow herself to turn to the old Zenith and the closing dialog of the *New Day, USA!* presenter to which her attention had been increasingly, anxiously drawn:

"*—about to show you a recent picture of Diane Cockerton, courtesy of Barrow Moor Hospital,*" Beau Wilson announced as he looked directly at the camera, appealing to the millions at home. "*This photo was taken just hours before her daylight escape from the institution last week. If you've seen this young lady, she may be confused and frightened. Please don't approach her. Instead, you can help her worried family by calling one-eight-hundred—*"

Swinging wide, the front door opened to bright summer sun which promptly flooded the diner. Whorls of gently floating dust sparkled like fireflies in the stale air as the perpetual sound of the street wafted in atop a blistering wave of July heat. A silhouette appeared briefly in this blinding rectangle of light then blended swiftly into the throng of people on the busy sidewalk beyond. In a moment it became just one more faceless form occupied with the important task of hurrying from one part of the city to another.

Slowly, the door shut of its own accord. Juddering and creaking on its hydraulic hinge, it reclaimed the glaring sun in a diminishing triangular wedge until the restaurant's dim incandescent bulbs were again all that illuminated the space.

And, just like that, Diane Cockerton was gone.

II

She did not know if Lucia or her father had seen the cold, artless hospital I.D. which had been plastered across the screen of that old Zenith as she slid out the door. If they had, Diane reassured herself that the haggard, grey-skinned patient it portrayed would have borne little resemblance to the vibrant young customer who'd just enjoyed Lucia's company over a shared slice of lemon meringue pie. Because that woman boasted bright and hopeful eyes beneath the bangs of her shiny, raven-black hair. Not the dull, murky gaze of the girl in that photo who peered out at a world she no longer trusted from the unkempt tangles of a clipped, dishwater-blonde nest.

Or at least, that lack of similarity had been the case before Diane had succumbed to her interruption. She required no mirror now to appreciate that seizing and writhing upon the Home Plate's greasy floor had stripped away the depth of her disguise until her appearance had rolled back to within a degree of that tragic girl's.

Not that it made much difference. Not in the grand scheme of things. In of a city of ten million people it was incomparably long odds for anyone to think that Diane and the wretch on the TV would, in fact, turn out to be one and the same person.

Add to this the fact that very few people possess confidence enough in their observational skills to draw such a conclusion, and there you have it: instant anonymity.

Even when a resemblance is clear and obvious. Most people will shrug off the similarity as an uncanny coincidence before trusting their own observations as proof of such a slim probability. Now throw in a simple change of attire and you'll shrink down the number of people willing to go out on a limb until it's next to nil.

Still, Diane accepted that she had spent a fair bit of time chatting with Felipe's daughter, and who was to know if Lucia was part of that very small minority? What if she were to recognize more subtle detail in Diane's facial features than the average person might? It could be the color of her eyes; the line of her jaw; the way her smile curled at one side when it was unguarded and real.

There was no doubt Lucia was a smart cookie. It was one of the reasons Diane had been instantly drawn to her, and why she'd felt such a pang of remorse for the long-lost opportunity to develop what surely would have been an effortless friendship.

It was also why Diane knew she'd have to expedite her timeline now. Surprisingly, the one thing she hadn't anticipated was her photo being plastered on almost every TV in the country. Looking back on it, it was an obvious chess move she should have expected her uncle would make. And long odds of being recognized or not, it was a bold stroke for which she should have prepared.

I guess that's why they say hindsight is 20/20. She shook her head and nearly chuckled at the cliché for its core truth. *Damnit. Why hadn't I thought of that?*

She'd have to get as far away from the city as possible. As quickly as possible. Just in case.

Not that she believed Lucia was the type who would rat her out to the authorities, even if she did make the connection. But she did have to accept that she didn't know the girl. Not really. And she couldn't afford to be so naïve as to think that a half-hour's small talk, as pleasant as it may have been, equated to actually *knowing* someone. Even though their time together hadn't set off any intuitive alarm bells; no interruption of the first kind warning her to get away.

In fact, it had been quite the opposite.

Diane could feel in her gut that Lucia just might turn out to be a good ally to have in her corner one day. And that was just about the best indicator of trust she could fathom.

But still … you never did know.

Of that, her uncle Ian was living proof.

She swept a hand over her wig, smoothing and adjusting it in just the right places as she quickened her pace up 6th Avenue. With the other she rummaged blindly through the mélange of items bulging her handbag as she dodged artfully in and out of tourists as adeptly as any native New Yorker.

There was just one thing left to be done before she could fully implement her plan. A promise she'd made to Andrew, a long, long time ago. Then, New York City, and this life, would be gone forever.

No different from everything and everyone I've ever loved.

The cold realization surfaced in a rush of stomach-tightening emotion as Diane became wedged in a bottleneck of visitors alongside Radio City Music Hall, the crowd 'oohing' and 'aaahing' at the iconic landmark.

She took the opportunity to pore more efficiently through the contents of her bag, pulling its mouth wide and fumbling deep inside, concerned only that she find one item in particular.

God, where IS it? You'd swear there's a damn black hole in there.

'The dreaded purse of infinityyyyyyy!' her father used to joke about her mother's oversized handbag on those occasions when he'd catch Rebecca doing exactly as her daughter now was.

Funny how the most trivial moments in life so often pack the most powerful punch, she considered. And this one, about as innocuous as it gets, warmed Diane's soul like a blazing sun.

She beamed with unexpected delight as she returned to foraging through the handbag, identifying the jumble of objects half by sight, half by feel. A fresh pack of light menthol cigarettes; the obligatory foil of breath-freshening gum. Her journal; a pen. Another wig (this one a convincing ginger). Another pen. A crumpled one-way bus ticket to Helen, Georgia (open-ended and unused).

Then, buried beneath a jangling plastic bottle of pills caught in the tangles of a clean but rumpled change of shirt, her fingers brushed against something cool. Something smooth.

Something metal.

With a sigh of relief she closed her eyes while forcing her thoughts to picture something other than what she knew it to be. She did this as a defense against inadvertent telepathy that could reveal her intentions to precisely the wrong person.

Into focus sprung a field of bright red poppies, a thousand flowers swaying in unison upon a warm, springtime breeze. A segment from a program she'd watched at Barrow Moor about the farms of Lincolnshire, England, she'd found the documentary incomparably soothing despite the frustrated outcries of all around her to change it to anything else at all.

Soon the poppies faded, to be replaced by the warm sepia memory of a puppet show, a sweet moment from her childhood.

Now this brief image morphed—with no little irony—into the saucy banter of a comedian she'd stumbled upon one night at their Pee Aay home while everyone else was fast asleep and she was discovering the forbidden fruit that was cable TV. She had been far too young for most of the subject matter, making the taboo experience all the more delicious, even though she did not understand all the jokes. Still she laughed when the others in the recorded audience did, and that made her feel the way she imagined adults feel all the time. That was back in the days of innocence. Back when everything was still ... *right* ... in the world.

So it was that one after the other, image upon disparate image, Diane forced distraction and nostalgia to the surface of her consciousness: a collage of camouflage projected where the foreign vibration she now felt prying inside her mind would readily find it.

She thought of everything.

She thought of nothing.

She thought of absolutely anything at all.

Anything, that is, but the handgun nestled at the bottom of her bag, her fingertips running reassuringly over its long, cold barrel ....

3:22

AS THE SKY filled with clouds and the streets were made clean by a new downpour of cooling summer rain, New York City was transformed into a shimmering tableau of itself. And with every raindrop that fell, seemingly another check arrived at the post office box of the newly established Church of the New Apocrypha.

Far from waning, interest in the boy prophet had only grown in the weeks since the *New Day, USA!* broadcast. Proof that a forlorn public yearned for Simon Peter's unique message almost as much as it thirsted to be at the receiving end of his miraculous ability.

The day after the world watched him offer a dead man another chance at life—live before their very eyes—letters for the 'Modern Jesus' or the 'Miracle Maker' flooded the *ND-USA!* studio. Even more arrived following the exclusive interview. And every day thereafter until the morning show, having received more bags of mail than they had manpower to process, was relieved to announce the address of the Cockertons' new P.O. box.

Party to this outpouring of affection, the Cockertons' new family attorney swiftly filed for 501(c)(3) status on their behalf.

And so, the new church was born.

The volume of letters received continued to parallel the public's feverishly waxing interest. In them were revealed line after line of personal detail and intimate struggle, most invariably concluding with a desperate plea for Simon Peter's healing hands. Some of the letters' more industrious authors, having anticipated the sheer volume of mail and their ever-diminishing odds, chose to accompany their requests with a handwritten check.

The percentage of these, as well as the average number of figures which were scribbled before the decimal point, grew with each passing week.

As did the multitude of devotees and diseased who crowded the steps of the Cockertons' apartment building at West 93rd and Central Park, despite every effort by the family to conceal their personal address. Men, women and children of every age, race, nationality and physical or mental affliction poured down the stone stairs and onto the sidewalk like a disfigured, melting mass of humanity. It was little stretch to imagine it a Dalí painting: equally enthralling as it was disturbing.

Among these acolytes there had been two natural deaths (if one were to classify tormenting, debilitating illness as 'natural') in as many weeks. Both of the bodies had been discovered of a morning as the throng had begun to rise from its sleeping bag, layered blanket, cardboard shelter slumber.

Additionally, there occurred untold numbers of fights. One mugging... and a non-fatal stabbing.

It wasn't until the latter that the city agreed there was a need for a visible police presence outside the building. This was now a continuous affair, with the regular rotation of officers becoming familiar faces to Ian and Rebecca. Even Simon Peter knew many by name, though the boy was no longer allowed to go outside except in the strictest, most guarded circumstances.

"Look at them all." Ian spoke rhetorically as he and Simon Peter stared from the fifth floor living room window at the sea of desperate faces milling about the wet, steaming sidewalk.

"Yes. Isn't it wonderful?" the nine-year-old replied. A Cheshire cat grin which he had no compunction to hide brightened his face. "I'm deciding who I favor next." He scratched the side of his head, biting his lip. "Who do *you* think, Ian?"

From the first words he'd spoken, Simon Peter addressed Ian Cockerton as neither father nor uncle. But simply, Ian. Rebecca, however, was always Mom in one form or another.

Mother, now.

But Mommy for the first five years.

"Gee, I really don't know, pal. Are you thinking about doing this *today*?"

Simon Peter nodded with enthusiasm.

"You sure you're up to it? That teenage girl took everything you had in you. Last thing we want is for you to overextend yourself. You were sick for days afterw—."

"Last thing we want is to leave these people suffering," Simon cut him short. "I want you to decide. Who do *you* feel I should favor?"

"I could go down there first. Speak to Roberts." Roberts was the Officer in Charge today. "See if anyone has a donation?"

Simon Peter shook his head. "Huh-uh, no donation. Not today. Pick somebody," he patted his chest over his heart. "Pick from here."

Ian silently nodded. He peered at the crowd more closely, examining so many bent and broken humans. Each with a mother, a father, a sister or brother, a cat or dog that loved them. Each with a story. A terrible story. Unfair, grueling, and soaked in pain.

Among these, one in particular stood out. A man in his twenties. Well-built, if not athletic. He suffered no apparent issue with mobility, Ian witnessing him rise effortlessly from his knees while gesturing the sign of the cross over his chest.

He had been here for days. Perhaps even weeks.

"Ah, yes. I see him as well," Simon confirmed, though Ian had said nothing to identify at whom he was looking. From this considerable height, any effort to read his gaze would have been equally futile, for his eyes drank in a dense grouping of more than three hundred individuals. Knowing which precise person he was focused upon would be beyond the realm of possibility.

Yet Simon knew.

Just like his unnatural, archaic precocity of language which exceeded the vocabulary of most adults, Simon Peter's ability to step inside your mind—at will, and seemingly uncontested—was just another uncanny aspect of the boy which Ian had gotten *mostly* used to over the years.

"And yet you are still surprised when I do it," Simon mocked while gazing up at him, his eyes filled with an impossible depth of wisdom. "Did your brother and you not share this ability? Then why do you question my own?"

"You mean your father and me."

Simon bristled, his cheeks instantly flushing. He made a *'grrrrr'* sound like a small animal and stomped his left foot, his hands on his hips. In this respect, he was every bit the typical child.

"He's ....Not ....My ....FATHER."

"Well, *I'm* sure as hell not. So let's just go with that for now, hmm? Makes it a whole lot easier. Now, I don't see anything wrong with that man down there. Why is he here?"

Simon scowled. He stared. Only after Ian failed to give him any attention whatsoever did Simon Peter answer: "Look again. Closer."

Now Ian once more found the man within the crowd. In that same moment the man lifted his head to the fifth story window, as surely as if he were beckoned. Though the distance muted the effect of his injuries, it was clear that his face was covered in scars. Thick ridges ran from chin to one ear. The other ear was missing or had become fused to his scalp in a way that made it imperceptible. Discolored flesh was pulled so taut over his features that his eyes were a permanent squint; his mouth a thin, lipless oval.

Ian's stomach pulled.

"He was burnt," Simon Peter attested. "Four years ago. One thousand, four hundred and nine days. To be exact. He still counts them. He just no longer includes the hours or minutes." There was no frivolity in the statement. "But he did. For more than two years, he counted each minute. And every brutal one of them was a choice."

"Nine-Eleven," Ian said aloud with somber recognition.

"A former Marine. Tower Two."

"Local boy?"

"Visitor, by the name of Greer Eliason. From a horsey little place in South Carolina, here on vacation for the week. He and his fiancée had tickets to a Broadway show that night."

"Why were a couple of tourists anywhere near the World Trade Center so early on a Tuesday morning? The elevators to the observation deck wouldn't even open until nine-thirty...."

"To surprise her brother who worked on the seventy-fifth floor. When the plane hit two floors above them, Greer insisted his fiancée and her brother make their way down the stairs to safety. But he couldn't just leave. He chose to go further up. He knew his military training could help. This was his chance to live his Purpose."

"Did he? Help anyone, I mean?"

"Seven souls are around today who wouldn't be, if Greer had put his own wellbeing first and simply headed for the stairwell. Like everyone else."

Silence laid heavy as Ian pictured that day in his mind, the horror as vivid as if it had been yesterday. He momentarily considered how Simon Peter could relay so much detail about this stranger, but then quelled the incredulity. For he understood only too well how Simon Peter knew.

"And Greer's fiancée?"

Simon Peter shook his head. "Never saw her again. He does not understand what happened that the love of his life is gone. He also cannot fathom why God, to whom that life has been devoted, would allow such an act of courage to destroy it, on every level."

"But you understand, don't you, Simon." It wasn't a question.

"I do."

"So, after today, Greer will also know...?"

"He will."

"And his scars, they'll be healed? Physically, I mean."

The silence was palpable as Simon Peter reflected upon Ian's question. Eventually he answered the way he thought best.

"That will be down to Greer ...."

II

The officers flanked either side of Simon Peter as he stepped out from the building with Ian in tow. Officer in Charge Roberts cleared a path before them, muscling aside the instant, violent surge of pressing bodies that attempted to flood the stone stairs; sweeping away flailing arms desperate to touch the child prophet. Several resisted, one man latching both hands onto Roberts' collar and using his momentum to twist and pivot around the policeman as he lunged for the boy. He was stunned to find himself on the ground a moment later, Roberts straddling him while adeptly expanding his metal baton with a swift flick of his wrist.

"Enough! Put your weapon away!" Simon Peter demanded, and Roberts, displaying some hesitance, stepped away from the prone man, a blend of frustration and indignity distorting the officer's face as the thrum of the crowd fell to near silence.

The nine-year-old approached the multitude and abruptly the throng separated, a sea of humanity parting before him.

"You come to me so that you may be restored. Yet you make it less appealing to do so by the day!"

His eyes were hard. His voice raspy, resounding with a commanding robustness which surely exceeded the capacity of the boy's immature vocal cords. He turned to an elderly woman in a wheelchair, oozing pustules covering her hands.

"You, old woman. Would you have me overtaken by this mob? Swamped by the very disease and rot which afflicts you?"

She shook her head nervously, shrinking from the boy.

"You! Would you have it so?" The question was brayed at a

middle-aged man whose sightless eyes had long ago clouded grey. Their faces but inches apart, he winced when Simon's bellowing voice erupted in his ears, the child's breath blowing hot upon his own cracked lips.

"Would *any* of you!" This Simon bellowed to the crowd as a whole. Rising above them by lighting upon a stone retaining wall which separated the city sidewalk from the building's private, neatly manicured entrance topiary, his voice had risen to a booming echo.

Heads mostly lowered, eyes averted, the crowd murmured its denial in unified humility. Inching slowly back.

"Yet *you*, sir," Simon turned slowly, his eyes hunting through the masses until they found the man who had been felled by Roberts. The perpetrator was unaware, for his own eyes were cast down, drilling a hole through his shoes. Yet, as if by cable, Simon Peter drew them up to meet his own and the offender's timorous gaze became a spellbound, unblinking stare. "Yet *you*, brother, would have it so. Come to me."

A handful of people in front of the man shifted, and he marched obediently toward Simon Peter, gripped in the boy's commanding glare. As though a great weight had then pressed upon his shoulders, an invisible force dropped the man to his knees at the base of the low retaining wall. Now his hands came forcibly together, an impetus external to his own will, and his palms met in a single, loud clap like two great magnets drawn to one another.

So manipulated into this prayerful pantomime, he became the caricature of the overeager Catholic genuflecting at the chancel rail as he awaited the communion wafer.

His lips visibly trembled, issuing a series of small sounds inaudible to all but the one before whom he knelt.

Simon Peter looked upon his servant. Arms wide, palms to the heavens. Merciful clemency in his eyes. "Speak up, speak up! Let all who have ears hear!"

With great effort the man unclasped his hands from the supplicant pose, peeling one finger from another as if freeing them from glue. Nerves fluttered the hands like birds' wings as he reached above him, aching for the boy prophet's touch.

"M-My name. I-I-I am—"

"—You are Clive Astor," Simon concluded. "I know who you are, brother. I have always known you." He bent down so that he may place his palm upon the crown of Clive's head. "When no other was with you, *I* was there. I have been with you through all of your days."

The tears were thick and sumptuous as they swelled over Clive's bottom lids to roll down his cheeks like drops of life-giving rain upon the thirsting leaf.

"See? Your soul recognizes me, Clive. Your heart aches for me. Your eyes proclaim this with the tears which form and fall. And yet, you would have me overtaken as I now come to you in the flesh?"

"No. I-I just.... No! I just needed to see you! I've waited days on this goddamn sidewalk, finding what little sleep I can in a child's tent as the rain drenches us all. I looked for you, weeks before this. And before that, years. Decades! I've waited so long. So long!"

Unable to go on, Clive buried his face in his hands and sobbed.

"Who among you is as Clive?" The congregation again lowered their gaze. "None, then." Simon confirmed. "None so eager to be made whole that they would put themselves before all others?"

The people shuffled in silence; most looked away in shame. All knew their desire was as intense as the man's who now cried at Simon Peter's feet. Then one in the crowd began to lift his hand above his waist. Decided against it. Raised it again in fits and starts...then lifted it high above his head, having decided there was nothing left to lose.

This man was Greer Eliason, and Simon Peter beckoned he join him and Clive at the wall.

"Come, come my brother! I have been awaiting your submission!"

III

"Look upon this man and tell me his affliction." The petition was directed at Clive who despite a sea of overt brokenness and deformity had still found it impossible not to notice Greer the moment he arrived at the cardboard congregation unremittingly spreading from the steps of West 93rd Street. Since that day Clive had obsessed in stealing repeated, furtive glimpses of the man in whom, other than walking upright, he recognized little other similarity to human.

Now invited to unabashedly stare upon Greer's scars at close proximity, he found himself incapable of doing so. The monstrous disfigurements twisting and tumbling his stomach, Clive could only turn away. You may think his doing so was cruel. Callous. But in fact, it was the result of Clive's empathy that his body felt the same searing pain Greer had felt as the jet-fueled flames had fed upon him. Empathy that drowned his heart in Greer's dire isolation within a society to which the man was now nothing but a freakish object of interest to be pitied or shunned, and then forgotten either way.

"He's been burnt," Clive answered as he faced not Greer or Simon Peter, but sought a point in the distance, high above the heads of the assembly who watched in riveted silence. His cheeks gleamed with moisture.

"His name is Greer," Simon Peter informed Clive and the crowd at once. "And though you cannot see past him as he is now, Greer was once, not very long ago, incomparably handsome. His fiancée, the woman who had stolen Greer's heart and to whom he was ready to dedicate his life, so enchanting that men and women alike would often do a doubletake as she'd pass them by."

Still, Clive stared into the park, far from here.

"Greer lost that woman he loved more than life itself. She is gone because he chose not to abandon seven strangers who today bask in lives which are bright and beautiful. Lives indebted to Greer's bravery and selflessness." He paused to allow this to sink in. "Now I ask you to open your eyes and look upon the life which is Greer's. The life bestowed upon him because of his act of courage."

Greer removed his baseball cap and turned to face the assembly. Though the rain stung his skin, he removed his raincoat, allowing it to fall to the damp concrete. One hand latched on to Simon Peter's and he mounted the low retaining wall in a slow, laborious struggle as the pain scoured his extremities like wire brushes scraping his flesh Clad only in jeans and a T-shirt, he stripped both from his body.

Greer now stood in his underwear before the assembly, trying hard to govern his shivering in the rain which had become cold.

"Go ahead!" Simon Peter commanded as the mass uttered a shared cry of dismay at the work of the flames which had licked across eighty percent of his body. "I tell you, look upon him!"

Gross discoloration. Sunken crevices where the unimaginable heat had melted skin, muscle and tendon like chicken fat on a skillet. Two fingers of his left hand had burnt away; two and his thumb had fused together into a thick, sinuous claw. Taut, hairless skin covered his head, chest and back in a patchwork of grafts whose pigment did not match, their texture and seams calling to mind the indescribable torment of Frankenstein's monster.

Despite their own abnormalities, the congregation looked away with a gasp that, if uttered by just one, would have been little more than a forgivable lapse in etiquette. Uttered by the group in unison, it was a tragic, indiscreet chorus.

Many began to sob.

A small handful screamed . . . and then were ashamed for their unconscious response.

"This is the life Greer's compassion has earned him!" Simon Peter's voice boomed so loud that the echo of his declaration came back twice: an ominous confirmation from the nearest building on the south side of narrow 93rd Street, then more faint but no less poignant as it replied from the high barrier wall and copse of trees lining the park opposite. "This is Greer's reward for helping his fellow man. The recompense of his God, to whom Greer has prayed every day. The same deity you have trusted your lives to. Believed in. Worshipped on a Sunday morning!"

Somewhere in the distance a lone crow called twice, shattering the uneasy quiet with its rasping judgment.

"Now look upon *this* man and tell me the disease from which he suffers." Simon nodded to Clive Astor who had remained kneeling at the base of the wall. Just as he had for Greer, Simon extended his hand and beckoned the man join them.

Rising, Clive rubbed the meat of his hand across his face, smudging away the tears and a thin, transparent line running from his nose. He swiped the back of his hand over his shirt then stepped effortlessly onto the landscaping wall to stand beside the other two.

"Greer," Simon Peter addressed the ex-Marine while gesturing toward the clothes he'd shed. "What suffering do you witness for the sins of *this* man's affliction?"

Struggling into his jeans as his entire body trembled, Greer stole sporadic glances at Clive Astor. He concealed his trembling claw within his pocket but left the other hand bare so that he might pull his T-shirt over his dripping wet skin, the nerves of his chest and back screaming as the cotton clung and pulled. Donning his baseball cap, Greer thrust his hands into his pockets. Now he studied more consciously this man who stood before him on the wall beside Simon Peter.

Mid-forties. Sheepish. Perhaps a little homely, but far from unpleasant to look at.

Unlike me, he thought, then brushed the self-pity aside,

Muscular enough. Bright blue eyes that probably glinted in the sunshine when not reddened by the salt of tears he'd shed.

Still, Greer found nothing to indicate that Clive suffered from any kind of affliction.

"There isn't one. I see no disease. No sickness. No disability. Nothing at all!" The more he spoke, the more Greer recognized that familiar anger roiling in his gut; the fury which had slowly engulfed his life until it threatened to consume him as assuredly as the flames had done. That was before his conscious decision to no longer give it his power, revoking permission for it to destroy what the fire could not. Now that pilot light of rage was flickering once more. "Why are you here? *Why* ... are *you* here!"

Clive Astor did not reply.

The crowd of infirm and immobile began to mutter.

"He is here," Simon Peter answered, speaking to the followers as one, "because Clive wants cured of his *invisible* affliction. For though it is a sickness we cannot see, it spreads and consumes all whom he touches. Lives are ruined. Lives are taken. Because of Clive's illness. Because of his ... *desires*."

Greer took a stuttering, half-step backward as the sight of Simon Peter and the makeshift congregation began to run like crayons forgotten on a dashboard in a treeless July parking lot. Only Clive Astor remained in crisp focus, the scene around him morphing into a nighttime scene illuminated by moonlight as it reflected off a gentle stream meandering beside a small, temporary camp.

The motion of this scene was eerily jittery; the picture grainy, underexposed. A cheap 8mm home movie.

Clive is crawling into one of the rudimentary tents. A pup tent. Inside a boy is weeping, curled into a ball in the corner. His knees pulled tight to his forehead.

"I just w-wanna go ho-ho-h-home!"

"Now, now," Clive assures him as he crouches lower, slithering deeper into the tent. "Are you homesick, there, my little pal?"

The boy nods without lifting his head from his knees.

"Oh, my. Yes, that's awful. I remember being homesick, too."

At this the boy peers over his knees with red, blurry eyes.

"Oh yes," the camp leader reassures. "I remember feeling so scared

on my first trip, too. So alone. So ... vulnerable."

Now the boy's eyes well. His mouth twists and his gentle sob becomes an audible cry.

"No-no!" Clive reassures with a warm smile, his tone soothing and soft. *"No more call for tears! 'Cause we're gonna make those yucky feelings all go away. You know how? You know what I did when I was your age ... to make them go away?"*

Curiosity—desperation—has stopped the tears in their tracks. *"Wh-wh-what. What did you d-d-do?"*

Clive Astor nestles closer, pulling the boy tight to his chest and wrapping his well-defined arm around him. He presents the ketamine laced gummy in the other palm, one-by-one his fingers slowly releasing from its miniature pop bottle shape like petals of a flower seductively opening to reveal the stiff, swollen pistil at their center. It wouldn't do for him to force the hypnotic sedative upon the boy. Oh, no. That just wouldn't be cricket, as the Brits say. Not at all. The boy must take it willingly. He *must* want it. There was no eroticism in the act for Clive otherwise. *"This will make it all go away. I promise, it really will!"*

Skeptical but trusting, the boy takes the gummy from Clive's hand and places it in his mouth. He bites down and smiles softly with the initial sugary-sweet explosion on his tongue. That smile twists down at the corners when the intensely bitter liquid inside the candy bursts from its center and is absorbed almost immediately into the soft tissue of the boy's tender gums.

It is not long before he begins to feel detached from his body—

"See! I told you!" the camp leader boasts as he unbuckles his belt.

—Numb to all pain.

"Not long now and you won't be homesick at all, little pal. Not even the tiniest, itsy-bitsiest bit!"

The boy is viewing himself as if he has died, looking down upon the unfolding scene from outside of his body.

But he is still very much alive.

He will not remember what happens next. And this is the smallest of mercies. For if his awareness were intact, he would surely wish for the death that does not come as the camp leader begins t—

Greer Eliason was extricated from the vision with such sudden and sharp loathing that before he'd made a conscious decision to do so, his fist was slamming into Clive Astor's face.

A mallet upon a hardboiled egg, the camp leader's nose spread wide as his top front tooth splintered in two. Propelled by Greer's fist, Clive's head jerked to the side at a violent angle. He bit his tongue . . . nearly in two. Hot blood sprayed in a red plume, coating Greer's fist. Speckling his face. It even dashed young Simon Peter's pale cheeks as Clive reeled and once again was on his knees.

Stunned, silent astonishment filled the eyes of the congregation as the boy prophet stepped forward to seek their judgment. For just like Greer, they too had experienced the hallucinatory vision he had planted in their minds.

"Now that you have witnessed the truth of these men, which of my two brothers would you have me cure?" he beseeched. "Shall I extinguish the flames of perversion in the repentant monster? Or eradicate the monster borne of flames in our unrepentant hero?"

The people barked out Greer's name without hesitation, their voices unifying into a single, hungry chant.

"Greer! Your brothers and sisters have spoken." Simon Peter beckoned the hero to him, taking Greer Eliason lovingly by his hands. "By the blood of the man who has become monster," he said as he glanced toward Clive Astor whimpering on the ground, "so the monster borne of flames shall become man once more, the scars enshrouding your body stripped away."

He examined Greer's bare hand which was still balled in a tight fist. The taut skin over its knuckles had split and already begun to swell. The twisted fingers and fibrous, desiccated flesh on the back of his hand were spotted red.

"For in his blood you are made clean again!"

Dabbing gently at the speckled pattern, Simon wiped Clive Astor's blood from Greer's hand. Wherever it had touched, the deep scar tissue simply sloughed away, peeling from the back of Greer's hand as readily as week-old scabs in warm bath water. Beneath it was revealed new, pink skin that glowed as healthy as a child's.

Unspeaking, Greer Eliason stared in disbelief.

The crowd pressed close, and Simon Peter held the man's hand out toward them. "Come! Let all who have eyes see!"

Before they could begin to grasp the miraculous renewal, the boy reached up and blotted a thick, coin-sized dab of Clive's blood from Greer's cheek. As the red came away, so a matching patch of unseemly cadaver graft also shed from Greer's face, exposing the man's own smooth, restored skin underneath.

Now Simon Peter painted Greer's twisted, colorless lips with this same congealing blood and their flesh became plump, supple and pink as his thumb swept across them.

Instantly sensing the transfiguration though it was impossible for him to see it, Greer licked an eager tongue across his lips, delighting in the moisture and softness he now found. It was an unassuming but uniquely satisfying tactile sensation he'd been unable to experience in more than four years; one he'd forced himself to forget, eventually accepting that such a simple joy so easily taken for granted was, for him, never to return.

Nervously lifting his hand to his face, Greer then oh-so-carefully ran a fingertip over his newly transformed lips. He tenderly stroked the small, clear patch of new skin on his cheek the way one might caress the soft underbelly of a newborn puppy.

"Behold," Simon Peter declared. "I come to make all things new!"

The assembly, watching the events unfold with a slack-jawed combination of incredulity and awe, began to emerge from their enchantment with growing exultation on the cusp of frenzy. While Greer Eliason openly wept before them, the congregation of the afflicted lifted their hearts in collective praise. Their pilgrimage had been validated, witnessed by their own eyes. Thus buoyed by the first real, palpable hope of their lives, they gushed and sang with unadulterated joy, relishing the sweet, sweet anticipation of redemption .... But mostly, of restoration.

For lo, their Savior had come.

IV

Bathe in his blood.

That's what The Prophet told him as Greer implored for renewal over the rest of his body. Blessed by such miraculous transformation over but a few small patches, he ached now more than ever for the absolute exorcism of the hideous, pain-ridden specter he'd become and the revival of the handsome, strong, agony-free man he once had been. He yearned to turn a woman's head, for the right reasons. To feel the sunshine on his face and not fear the stinging pain. To dress without the fear of unbearable suffering. To undress without the fear of unbearable rejection.

These he desired above any riches he could be promised in this life ... or any life hereafter.

Bathe in his blood.

It took Greer more than a moment for The Prophet's directive to sink in as Clive Astor writhed in pain beside him, the pedophile's jaw cocked at an unnatural angle.

Bathe in his blood.

V

That night as most slept, Greer lay awake in his tent and watched more rain slowly accumulate on the fabric above him, puddling until the glow of the streetlamps was dimmed and diffused. The soft light angled through the tent as the breeze fluttered the nylon ceiling gently this way and that, the puddle ever shifting. It would have been beautiful if it weren't for the muted wails and groans of anguish which inevitably rose each night from so many of the other tents and impromptu shelters jammed in such tight proximity all around him. Tonight, Greer was certain that the most incessant and pitiful of those affects of torment must surely be coming from the tent of Clive Astor.

Bathe in his blood.

How odd, Greer found it, that he had started to become accustomed to such cries of misery which at first only fueled his emotional turmoil. In fact, if he were being truthful about it, he'd have to admit that he was not only becoming used to it but had begun to derive a certain unlikely comfort from the haunting lullaby. Perhaps this was a product of its unerring reassurance that he was not alone in his misery.

After all, they say it does love company.

He did not know how much longer he would enjoy the benefit of this unconventional solace, however. Word had begun to filter through the congregation that the authorities were growing impatient and planning to move them out soon. And to be honest, with the city not having a reputation for being especially charitable when it came to allocating what it felt was unnecessary (and definitely unbudgeted) resources, Greer was surprised they'd even managed to hold out this long.

The overnight rotation of officers had already been eliminated. Now faced with even more followers arriving by the day, even three officers per shift would be insufficient to safely manage such a burgeoning multitude of zealots. And with no chance of the city upping their spend, it was logical that they'd simply choose to close the whole thing down instead, under the auspices of 'public safety' of course. It didn't help matters that the terminus of everyone's pilgrimage had now begun to spill across Central Park West, with followers setting up camp in the park as well. As a result, the line between busy thoroughfare and makeshift campus was becoming increasingly blurred. To the point that traffic was often unable to pass altogether, a chorus of honking horns and angry shouts from commuters late to work, or keen to be home, alerting everyone to the fact though achieving little in the process.

Greer was all too well aware that soon their hundreds would be thousands, perhaps even tens of thousands once the news of today's miracle spread.

News of *his* miracle.

He again inspected his hand and the new patches of smooth, fresh skin where Clive's blood had sprayed when he'd broken the disgusting excuse of a man's nose, one tooth, and probably—very likely—his jaw.

He deserved it. Sickening piece of shit.

No one among the followers thought otherwise. Indeed, they had chanted Greer's name after he'd decked the evil, vile thing that looked like a man on the outside but was really a monster within.

My opposite, Greer thought with no little sense of poignancy, the theatrical irony of Simon Peter pairing the two of them on the wall hard not to appreciate. *The monster hiding inside the man, versus the man shrouded by the monster.*

And when The Prophet had asked the congregation which of the two he should spare from further pain of their affliction, the people—his new brothers and sisters—had chosen him. But then, how could they possibly choose any other way?

How…? Greer's inner voice interjected in a sardonic tone. *I'll tell you how. Exactly the same way they chose Barrabás over Jesus.*

Immediately Greer found his soul immersed in that biblical scene as Pontius Pilate presented Jesus of Nazareth alongside the notorious murderer, beckoning the crowd to give voice to which of the two men they would have him pardon. Every time Greer's mind went to this place he became blanketed by the guilt of those ancestors and the terrible, cruel weight of the choice they had made so swiftly; so exuberantly.

But this is hardly the same. And I'm hardly Jesus.

Still, it was a startling realization that things could be very different in this moment. It made him wonder what The Prophet would have instructed of Clive had the crowd chosen differently; what he would have insinuated the sick bastard do in order for Clive to be exorcized of his disgusting, demonic desires.

Bathe in his blood.

Greer gently probed the new skin which had appeared on his cheek, captivated with the sensation as his index finger slowly circled the soft, smooth area about the size of a quarter until the uniqueness of the feeling ebbed. Now he touched his new (old) lips and closed his eyes, his mouth tingling as his fingertip caressed. As it did, the memory of Jennifer swelled in his mind, a reminder of how it felt when his fiancée would kiss his lips so gently that it tickled; her lips a feather barely making contact with his own.

She came back to find you, Greer...

The Prophet found no joy in sharing the truth he knew.

... She turned and went back up the stairs. Insisted her brother keep going. Against a current of panicked people she climbed to a floor filled with searing heat and smoke so thick it was as though she were wading through freshly poured concrete. She got turned around, Greer. Lost her bearing...

Greer's stomach pulled. Outwardly, he'd accepted that Jennifer was gone. But somewhere deep inside, locked away in a place he only allowed himself to go when absolutely necessary, he'd preserved the treacherous comfort of thinking that maybe, just maybe, Jennifer had walked right out of that tower and simply chose to keep on walking. He'd rather think of her as alive but no longer wanting him (and who would blame her?) than to think of her as still his, but gone forever.

... Jennifer is dead because of her unfailing love for you. Because she couldn't leave you behind...

It was beyond wrenching to hear, and Greer cried out with the anguish of losing her all over again.

... She is no longer with you because you *could not leave behind anyone you were still capable of helping. That courage and ultimate selflessness saved seven lives. But it did so at the cost of two.*

Two? Greer was only able to ask after a very long pause.

Jennifer's, The Prophet explained as he evaluated the man standing before him, the boy's piercing eyes slowly traveling from head to toe. *And yours, Greer. The years ahead of you stolen, as surely as if they had been curtailed that day.*

Thick and wet like a wool blanket in the rain, the silence weighed upon him until Greer found it hard to breathe.

There had always been the question of how her brother, Carlisle, managed to survive while Jennifer had been reduced to nothing but a statistic. Just one more added to the list of 'Missing Presumed Dead.' Not once did Carlisle come to the burn unit to check on Greer. Eight months later, he refused Greer's calls. He ignored his brother-in-law-to-be's manic pounding on his Jersey City home's front door at three in the morning. And he avoided the hangouts he had once frequented just in case Greer might show up there.

Which Greer often did.

Finally, Carlisle put a bullet in his brain. And any chance of knowing the truth about what happened to Jennifer died with him.

Until now.

In his tent Greer's sobs consumed him, the confirmed truth finally breaking his ability to bear the endless torment. The sound of his lament harmonized with the congregation's nighttime hymn of misery until he had no more tears left to cry.

Which is when Greer began slapping, then clawing at his face in disgust. Encrusted with week-old street grime, ragged fingernails tore into the skin which had once been someone else's. Numb to the acute, blistering pain, he stripped ribbons of flesh from his own cheeks with a sound like tearing fabric. A sour, metallic stench filled his deformed nostrils as deep red blood began to flow beneath his nails. Soon these became rivers of red that followed the path down his face which his tears had already primed.

He flicked the clinging strips of skin from his fingers and pressed the heel of his hand to the sinewy, exposed flesh until the flow eventually subsided. His face caked with clots of red drying to dark brown, Greer tentatively probed the raw, connective tissue which had been exposed beneath.

No new flesh materialized over it.

No smooth, renewed skin knitting in its place.

Greer screamed, his voice booming in the night as the realization he'd refused to believe ensconced itself in the torrent of excruciating, self-inflicted pain that suddenly came.

Bathe in his blood.

Was The Prophet really bidding what Greer thought he was? Surely, where his thoughts were leading could not be the same destination intended by the Savior's four poignant words. It had to be a metaphor. A matter of reflection. A charge possessing a deeper meaning yet to be revealed in time.

But time was a resource Greer no longer had.

He fully believed the word being passed down from the self-proclaimed elders (Antoine J. Washington being the principal of their number) that the cops were already planning how to disperse the encampment with the least amount of resistance.

Once they did this, Clive Astor would be gone. And with him, Greer's last chance.

As standing tears stung his lips—

those renewed, corpulent lips

—and planted the taste of tepid iron upon his tongue, Greer rose from his tent, shirtless and streaked in his own blood. The rain which had slowed was again threatening to come heavy as he strode with singular focus through the sleeping congregation. Adroitly weaving in and out of the hodgepodge shelters and tents his mind was fixed only upon three minutes in the future.

Three minutes till redemption … or eternal damnation.

Eyes on the prize, their toes to the skies.

The mantra he hadn't recited in over a dozen years bobbed so easily to the surface of his mind as rising adrenaline spiked epinephrine to his muscles, eyes, heart and lungs. He now chanted it silently over and again, the cadence bolstering his resolve just as it had done in Kuwait as pre-combat tension ignited through the squad like an electric current igniting one fire team to the next.

His dilated pupils darted back and forth, unconsciously studying the path ahead. His chest thudded so loud it must surely be audible to all around. The air in his lungs grew rich with oxygen, his warm muscles limber and ready.

As the followers slept and the wails of despair had settled into silence, Greer Eliason stood before Clive's tent.

Slowing his breaths to quiet the pulse coursing through his ears, Greer listened but discerned no sound from inside, aware that the tent's thin nylon was all that separated him from a monster so vile it issued acid to the back of his throat.

Bathe in his blood.

Carefully, silently, Greer unzipped the front flaps and slid inside unseen. There, lying on his back, Clive Astor had cocooned himself in a bedroll, his head the only part visible as he found merciful release from his pain in deep but troubled sleep. His breaths came soft and rasping, small saliva bubbles foaming from the corner of his mouth where his slack jaw had pulled his lips into a grotesque snarl as if unconsciously expecting his covert visitor.

Greer observed him this way in silence for a length of time he would not be capable of recounting later.

Then in a single, dexterous move he simply dropped to his knees.

The weight of his body pinned Clive's arms inside the sleeping bag as Greer simultaneously clamped his clawed hand over Clive's mouth, pinioning his head to the ground. In a single, effortless motion he dragged the carbon blade of his K-Bar combat knife across Clive Astor's throat. He swiped hard and deep with detached indifference, slicing the man's trachea in two.

Clive hissed through the instant swell of blood as the carotids either side of his neck jetted in two high arcs. They sprayed Greer in hot, viscous blood that pumped into the deep fissures and ridges of the ex-Marine's corrugated torso which ran in a helter-skelter web over his chest; up his neck; devouring his face.

Flaring wide, the white of Clive's eyes became fully visible around his irises. His legs kicked. His hands slapped inside the bedroll like fish out of water. His body quaked beneath Greer's weight until it could spasm no more.

Watching the last, clinging signs of life ebb away, Greer Eliason released his claw-like hand from Clive's mouth. Sheathed in thick, dark burgundy as if he'd dipped it in a vat of cork wax, Greer held the hand in front of him in fascinated reverence. He tilted his head, first this way, then the other, as he effortlessly spread wide the fingers and thumb which for the last four years had been fused together as one. As the digits pulled painlessly away from one another, Greer's ring and pinky fingers flexed alongside them, appearing upon his hand as if they were never gone.

When Clive's blood sluffed from his hand it was no longer a furrowed and jaundiced patchwork of grafts that covered it ... but seamless, healthy pink skin.

His skin. As it once had been.

Now he cupped both hands in the blood which had pooled beneath him, flowing around the pedophile's lifeless body like a macabre, demonic halo. Light wisps of steam rose from it in the cool night air. Greer splashed it on his face; cascaded it over his scalp; rubbed it across his chest and legs; lay in it and rolled until not an inch of him remained uncoated.

Thus painted, he emerged from Clive's tent to be lauded by a distant peal of rolling thunder. Raising his arms to the sky, he invited the rain of the Savior to wash away his scars.

Which it did.

And Greer Eliason became whole once more.

VI

Clive Astor's hollow-cheeked corpse was discovered the following morning in a puddle of blood as thick as molasses. Soon after, a swarm of police arrived to cordon off the area.

While no one had seen or heard anything of use, there *was* one observation which was noted by several of the congregation...

...A man by the name of Greer Eliason seemed to be gone.

When asked how they noticed a single individual's absence out of a crowd that numbered in the hundreds, each of the witnesses would sheepishly gesture in the general vicinity of their face. Some, their hands. A few gesticulated in a manner that incorporated their entire bodies.

"So," one of the detectives clarified, "what you're saying is, he won't be hard to miss." He smirked when he said this, then closed his pocket pad and chummed up much more closely than was professional to a female detective whose forced smile belied the feelings her body language could not deny.

Her discomfort was mercifully short-lived as one of the crowd interceded, a man in his thirties with thick dark hair and a rare smile borne of deep, genuine joy.

"He was burned—" here the man nodded awkwardly towards his groin. "All over. I mean *everywhere*. He told me even his junk was torched. Poor bastard." Failing to receive the response he had hoped for, he spoke up again, choosing to elucidate for whatever reason the detectives could not fathom. "Not that it really mattered. The way the guy looked, he wasn't getting any action any time soon. If y'know what I mean."

The male detective raised one eyebrow. The female detective,

Maggie Romano, shook her head at the sophomoric comment that added nothing to the observation, or even this case, for that matter. She didn't care if this man noticed the obvious contempt.

Truth be told, she'd rather hoped that he would.

"So, you know this guy? He got a name?" She glanced at her pad as if having to refresh her memory when in reality the name of the man to whom they were referring had never left her mind. "Oh yes, here it is. Greer—"

"—Eliason," the man finished for her. "Yep. Greer Eliason. Though I doubt that was his real name."

"Oh?" Detective Romano asked. "Why's that, exactly...?"

"Why? Just take a look around, lady." He spun a three-sixty and chuckled when he nearly lost his balance. "You think any of these freaks want to broadcast their names?"

"And what about you? I mean, seems like there's nothing wrong with you—" Here she swallowed hard. She hadn't intended it, but the impeccable timing resulted in a comical but scathing insult. "So why are *you* here, then?"

"Me? I'm just here for the show." He spun around and began walking, nearly skipping, away.

It was just so...*odd*, Romano thought. Something about the guy was off. He was way too exuberant. And far too eager to volunteer what little information he had. Irrelevant information at that. She'd come upon this kind of guy a hundred times before. Nothing of value to say, they just want to insert themselves in the investigation. To feel important. But then, on a few very rare occasions, there were those like this loser who actually did have something to say. Something incredibly valuable. Because *they* were the perpetrator. Such an occurrence wasn't as commonplace as the movies or those cheesy TV cop shows would have you think. But it did happen.

Sometimes.

"Hey!" she hailed after him, staring at his back as he continued to strut away. "You got a name that *you* don't want broadcast?"

"Sure!"

She waited.

He kept walking.

She kept watching.

In the last possible moment he turned back to face her. Still walking, only backwards now. "You can call me Simon Lepros!"

Then he blended into the crowd and was gone.

VII

Maggie Romano woke up that night just after three-thirty-three in the morning, the detective finding it impossible to shackle the sleep she grasped only in tentative spurts.

Lepros.

The oddity of the man's last name who had accosted them with such strange fervor earlier that morning had been in no small part responsible for her insomnia, running through her mind to the point of infiltrating her dreams.

In the most salient of these she was in a bright, glaring place.

An arid place.

From one mountain range to the next the heat rises from the horizon in translucent waves, blistering dirt stretching for as far as the eye can see. It conveys an air of the region being all but habitable, yet there are people all around, busying themselves with the things of everyday life. A man walks beside her along this dusty road, sharing stories which fill her with wonder. Like hers, the man's sandaled feet are chafed and encrusted with the path's powdery residue. This place is called Bethany, but she does not know how she knows this fact. They are to stop soon to break bread. It is no usual occasion, for the man they are meeting is an outcast, a pariah.

Now they are inside the mud brick home. Detective Magdalena Romano has no idea how or when they arrived. She is cleaning the feet of the man beside whom she has walked, caressing them so gingerly and massaging oil into the parched skin. She anoints the man with perfume from an alabaster jar when their host appears. She smiles with genuine warmth and appreciation as he enters, seeing only his generosity and care as opposed to his features which are riddled with bumps and open wounds. He announces himself as Simon and remains at an oddly impolite distance. But the man she has arrived with goes to Simon and embraces him.

"Teacher," the host speaks and instinctively shrinks from the affectionate embrace, for Simon is the man known far and wide not by his surname, but by his affliction. "Teacher, I am not worthy—"

The detective started from the dream, the transition from sleep to wakefulness so abrupt she had to concentrate to discern where she now was. Her breaths came fast as she rushed from her bed and began tearing through stacks of books piled in the most disorderly fashion in and upon the case in the corner. It was the bible she was looking for; the one she'd stashed there so long ago that she could no longer remember the last time she'd seen it. Yet its appearance was as clear in her mind as the day her mother had given it to her. Distressed black leather. Worn edges. Faded dye on the corners and crisp creases of the spine, the outcome of countless generations opening and closing, bending and dog-earing it each Sunday and every Christian holiday for over a hundred years.

Until it came into Maggie's possession. There the tradition stopped dead in its tracks.

Born and raised a Catholic like every other good Italian girl from Hell's Kitchen in the seventies, as soon as the decision was hers to make, Maggie Romano put away the idolatry and said goodbye to the rituals and chants, the kneeling and the standing and the sitting and every other damned thing the dogmatic rite demanded.

Especially the Eucharist. Pretending to accept the blood and body of Christ, and then ingest it, always felt particularly distasteful to her. Even from the earliest age.

Still, she had been what she always called 'fully indoctrinated,' having attended weekly catechism classes with the other kids after mass, then receiving her confirmation with the same at the age of thirteen. So, while she was no longer a believer (at least not in its orthodoxy or blind, unquestioning ritual) Magdalena did have a basis of knowledge enough to be considered dangerous, as they say.

Jammed in a corner and tucked behind her mother's old cooking book filled with stained pages and handwritten recipes, the family bible sat in the dark and damp, not seeing the light of day for more years than she could tally.

She brushed the dust from its cover and opened it to the scent of her childhood, taking a moment for the mix of nostalgia and anxiety to dissipate. Thumbing through section upon section, page upon page, she scoured the four gospels. Though scoffing at some of the more veiled and recondite parables, she found unexpected solace, even renewed traces of her wayward faith, in others.

Sipping coffee as she sat cross-legged on the floor, she had to remind herself more than once that the purpose of this theological exploration wasn't to reminisce but to find a specific passage that just might substantiate the theory percolating in the back of her mind. An idea so outlandish she couldn't even say it aloud.

She found the answer as the sun began to break through the choppy Brooklyn skyline. There it was, plain as day in the book of Matthew, chapter twenty-six. The story of Simon the Leper.

In Greek, Simon *Lepros.*

"I knew it. You son of a bitch!"

She threw the bible to the floor after reading the sixth verse three times over.

"God-*damn*-it! I knew it. I just *knew* there was something off about that fucking guy. Because it was you, wasn't it," Maggie asked the empty room aloud as if the man were still in front of her. "You little fucker. We had you standing right there and we didn't know it. *Nobody* knew it."

She stood in silence, playing a fingertip over her lip as she contemplated the insanity of what this meant. The unreality that had to have taken place in that absurd, self-proclaimed D.I.Y. holy place the vagrants and stragglers had declared for themselves on the sidewalks of the Upper West Side. It not only flew in the face of every instinct she had, but every finely tuned logical process she'd honed over her years as a detective. All of which had refuted the array of myths and nonsense the endless procession of austere nuns had crammed down her throat as a child from as early as she could remember.

And yet here she was, considering the very real possibility of an event that could prove all those fantastical concepts true.

"Fuck me."

It was many more moments of standing in silence with only the hypnotic ticking of the wall clock marking off each of her flurried thoughts before she allowed herself to fully concede to the idea.

"Good for you, Greer Eliason," she finally saluted and raised her mug of tepid coffee to the man who was not there—in more ways than one—a surprising smile creeping upon her face. "Good for you, dude. And . . . well . . . just . . . well, Jesus! Who'd've thunk it. Those crusty old nuns were actually onto something."

VIII

"Understand this," The Prophet declared, the boy making a vital appearance the day following the discovery of Astor's body. Accompanied by his uncle, Ian, as well as Antoine J. Washington and the elders, he spoke to the congregation with an intensity they had not yet witnessed. "Greer Eliason has served me. And for this, his wounds have been healed. I know you are confused. Frightened, even. But all who *believe* in me *will* be healed. All who *serve* me *will* be made whole again. I come to you not as one in search of glory, but to glorify you. In so doing, I glorify my Father."

Simon Peter waited for his words to hit home, bedding deep

within their hearts, minds and souls.

"And so now the time has come for you to go. Into the world. To share what you know to be true. For you are my disciples. You are the keystone of our new church."

"But what do we do? Where do we go?"

"—my daughter! She hasn't yet been healed—"

"Noooooo! Please!"

"—haven't blessed me yet—"

Myriad cries rose from all but the most unwavering until no individual plea was any longer intelligible within the clamor. It mattered little, as each was invariably an echo of the same petition.

"Yo! Everyone! Shut it!" Antoine J. Washington cupped his hands to amplify his voice. He did nothing to hide his outrage at the self-serving response to The Prophet, clapping at the crowd and waving their voices down. "I said, fucking SHUT UP!"

Simon Peter stepped in front of him, reassuring the elder with a pat on the shoulder. He regained control of the congregation not by speaking over them, but by saying nothing at all.

Eventually a revered hush fell over the crowd like a blanket.

"I ask you, has the god you worship healed as I have healed? Has he made new the skin of the courageous while raining down justice upon the head of another? Has he restored you? Your loved ones? Has he done any of these things as Jesus did?"

Silence. Only the everyday hum of the city replied.

"I ask you, has he? Because all of these, and more, Jesus Christ did. In Capernaum, Jesus cured the royal's son. Raised the mother's child from death in Nain. Made the paralyzed man to walk on the shores of Galilee. So, where has *your* savior been? Why has He forsaken you?"

Simon Peter slowly looked upon the many, engaging their souls as if each were the only one with him in this moment.

"I tell you, the one true God has forsaken you because *you* are no longer with Him! On Sundays you worship a plaster idol which hangs above an altar strewn with fine fabrics of purple and gold. You revere a man who wears a collar and self-proclaims his holiness in the Lord's eyes. You pray to a god that is not, and never was, the father of the Christ Savior! You call yourselves Christian, yet you act not, pray not, live not, love not as Christ did."

Here the sky began to darken as Simon Peter's voice grew to a crescendo, the breeze kicking up scraps of paper and street debris into the faces of the followers shielding their eyes against it.

"Your god has not healed you because it is a false god you seek. A false god you worship! Your true God you condemned two thousand years ago. Humiliated, beat and tortured Him. Nailed Him to a beam of leftover pine from the field horse's stable to die alongside the wicked. It was not *for* you that he died, as you so like to exalt . . . but *because* of you. Over the centuries you have then fashioned your many myths. Fabricated your intricate truths. Rationalized away the vile choice you made. Going so far as to self-absolve the unforgiveable."

As it had in the early hours the night Greer Eliason sought his redemption, the clouded sky again opened.

"Worst of these sins, you cite your scientific advancement—the very progress made possible by the intelligence He has blessed you with—to write Him off as fable; a tale for the feeble of mind. Yet I say to you that despite your hate and greed and ignorance, your Savior has again returned to you."

With a resonant crack, the sky bristled with lightning.

"What fate shall mankind choose for Him this hour?"

Now the hard rain became a torrent.

IX

"And yet there remains one among our number who would not choose anew!" Simon Peter warned. "One who does not believe in your redemption; one who would have me exiled, crucified even.

Her thirty pieces chosen above your salvation."

Pondering if the traitor could be amongst their peers, each follower silently examined those around them. But the rain sliced like razors, painful to the bone, and all soon bowed their heads to shield from its fury.

"You will know this modern-day Judas not by appearance, but by vibration. For she was once a sister of our inner sanctum."

A mounting energy sizzled electric from The Prophet and began pulsing through the congregation in a current that was palpable. As it coursed from one follower to the next it emitted a sharp, audible crackling .

"The one who would deny you the restoration I now ordain to be yours is known as Diane Cockerton. The disciple who delivers this wayward lamb shall know no boundary in this life ... or that which follows. Who among you is willing to prove their worthiness for this holy crusade?"

Across the congregation, dozens of hands shot into the air. Of these, one in particular stood out: an elderly man, bent over a walker, every limb shaking with the effort of standing. Like an age-stained handkerchief fluttering in the warm breeze, his pale hand quivered above him until he could hold it up no longer.

"This man," The Prophet instructed Antoine J. Washington, his words spoken with quiet authority. "Go to him."

As Washington jumped spryly from the low wall upon which they stood, Simon Peter eyed him with uncertainty.

"Antoine. Do you trust in your Lord?"

"With every fiber of my being, Savior. I trust in you with my entire life. It is yours. Do with it as you will."

"And so it shall be." Simon Peter now called loudly to the elderly follower and the crowd parted from the man as the Red Sea before Moses. "Old man! I see unwavering faith in you. Am I wrong?"

The man attempted to speak but his voice was too frail, even for the single syllable. Instead, he shook his head slowly from side to side. It bobbed loosely atop his neck as Antoine J. Washington came to tower in front of him.

"Antoine," Simon Peter catechized. "Are you now free from sin?"

"Yes, my Lord!"

"Are you a faithful servant of your new Messiah?"

"Yes, Savior!"

"Antoine, are you willing to do what is needed that these people, our desperate flock, shall be free of what afflicts them?"

Without hesitation, Washington assented. Again with the verve of the most devout.

"Then it is decided." As Antoine turned to face the old man, Simon Peter nodded to his uncle and several elders who stood nearest Washington. "Antoine. Your life shall be traded for the flock."

Before he could protest, the men grabbed Antoine's arms and restrained them. Standing in stunned silence, he did not think to resist as Ian Cockerton bound his wrists behind his back with two interconnected zip ties.

"Old man—" The Prophet declared as he strode through the corridor of people to the man trembling with age, hunched over his walker. Indicating Washington he continued: "—this is my body. Take it and eat, in honor of me. And renewal shall be yours."

The crowd was silence itself as the old man inched forward, the only sound that of his walker's aluminum feet as they scraped methodically across the gritty concrete.

Devoid of emotion, Antoine watched the man slowly approach until they were facing one another in the center of a rust-colored footprint of a tent...the sidewalk stain that was all that remained of the pedophile, Clive Astor.

Washington's blank expression transformed into a smirk when the old man immediately attempted to strike him with the walker. Losing his balance instead, the man's left ankle snapped beneath his weight, the sound prefacing a pitiful howl.

Now one of the elders kicked Antoine's legs out from under him and Washington's smirk widened to shock. His knees clapped hard against the pavement, his stupor contorting to a mien of disbelief as the elderly man—now appearing decades younger—stood upright, straight and tall. Possessing the strength of a man who had earned his living in manual labor, he swung the walker again in a smooth, sturdy arc.

This time it made contact and a long, ragged strip of skin flailed from Washington's cheek. Several teeth shattered.

The last expression ever to cross Antoine J. Washington's face was unequivocal horror as the man, now barely in his forties, thrust one of the walker's aluminum feet through Antoine's left eye socket. It struck with such force that it skewered the skull of the self-proclaimed leader of the elders, five inches of the leg disappearing into Antoine's brain where his ruptured eyeball was embedded.

A fountain of blood gushed from the hole as Antoine broke free of the others' restraining grips and ran through the congregation, thrashing and screaming as the walker swung from his face.

Standing alone and covered in blood, the elderly man was no more. In his place stood a vibrant, healthy young individual with rippling muscles and a pulse of electric energy running through him which the man had not felt in over sixty years.

He was too busy marveling at the transformation to notice that the congregation of more than seven hundred had descended upon Antoine, pinning him to the ground and tearing his skin from tendon and muscle and bone as his screams disappeared beneath the sounds of the attack.

"This is my blood," Simon Peter proclaimed above the thrum as the fervor of the congregation rose to a frenzy. "Take it and drink! Do this in honor of me …."

Slurping handfuls of thick, warm blood from the ground, afflictions were immediately diminished with each mouthful. Disability, disease and the ravages of age were erased as Antoine J.

Washington was torn limb from limb until all but a skinless, formless mass remained. Even this was rived apart by men's hands and women's nails so that the scraps of sinewy muscle and marrow of bone could be shared amongst the less able followers until they too were blessed with renewal.

A very small few refused to participate, watching first with unabashed horror, then incredulity, then amazement as they witnessed the undeniable results. As the blood of their peer stained the faces of all around, the blind now saw; the deaf heard once more; the crippled rose to walk and run; the elderly became young; the youthful, invulnerable. And with opportunity fast passing, even the few holdouts fell to their knees when nothing more of Antoine remained but a shallow pool of blood which they skittishly licked like hyenas outside of the clan until the pavement itself was clean.

So it was that each of the faithful were made whole again. Relegated to the realm of forgotten nightmare, every affliction was vanquished as surely as if it had never existed at all. Suffering became no more than the remnant of a bad memory, destined to fade slowly into the oblivion of the past ....

X

As the impassioned celebration of what would become known as the Great Healing diminished, the followers began to steadily drift from the nucleus of the congregation.

Exactly as Simon Peter had instructed.

The following day, the number had thinned to half. Another three days, and only a handful remained.

They began merging back into the everyday world. Not to return with seamless ease to the life they had known, but to spread the news far and wide of The Prophet's promise and joy.

Thus overflowing with inextinguishable passion, elders and lay-followers alike shared the news of His miraculous works to a people yearning for healing. Their words were wrapped in the testament of their own salvation, assuring all who would listen that any who came to The Prophet through them would also experience suffering no longer.

For their Savior had returned at last.

And so, like a virus spreading through its host from one cell to another, the movement of the New Apocrypha had begun ....

FOURTH
DISCIPLE

And God unleashed the demons,

that He may renew the soul of man.

—Dr. R. Bartholomew, *The New Apocrypha*

The Pale Shadow

4:23

I AWOKE THIS morning under a metal stairwell, deep in the bowels of the Port Authority terminal. Far from the coolness you would expect, the air here is stagnant with summer heat and stinks of stale urine. On top of this, the nighttime noises of troubled voices echo my years at Barrow Moor.

Still, in my little spot I feel safe.

Not because there are no other homeless wanderers down here. But precisely because there are.

Alone I'm vulnerable.

With the others, I'm part of a tribe ... of sorts.

I woke up with three words echoing through my mind. They were spoken in my ear by my father, Bryan. Words whispered so tenderly that they would not alarm me as they drew me from sleep.

Beware the woods.

Of course when I awoke, my father was not there. That goes without saying, really. What I'm not sure about is whether it was a dream, wishful thinking, or another one of my interruptions. It can't have been a real person speaking. There's barely a handful of people in the world who know that happened in the malignant place we used to call the Little Woods, and I haven't heard mention of it in more years than I can remember.

And yet those woods have remained with me always. I still don't know what happened that day. Try as I might (and Lord knows I had plenty of time during those inane, endless hours at Barrow

Moor) I just can't find a way for my mind to take me back to that place...and that awful day.

Your daddy took his own life to stop something unimaginable from happening to you, Deedee.

Now the voice in my head is my mother's: Rebecca. At least I think it is. It's been so long since I've actually heard it, it's hard for me to know for sure. The last words she ever spoke to me were Thanksgiving night in ninety-seven...the night Andrew was killed.

Or should I say, the night they still think I killed my brother.

You see, I thought when word got out—and boy, did it ever—about Simon Peter's abilities, my getting out of that hellhole was gonna be a slam dunk. Game over.

Yeah. No such luck, I'm afraid.

Barrow Moor: 7. Diane Cockerton: 0.

"What we've just witnessed is a miracle," Dr. Maddox explained to me in her most soothing condescension at my eval. The one where I was certain they were going to let me out: no harm, no foul.

How painfully naïve.

"Your brother, Simon, brought that man back from the dead, Diane. In front of the whole world. He *resurrected* someone."

I just sat there, this blank look on my face. Not even believing what I was hearing.

"And you've told me time and again how much he adored his older brother. Isn't that correct." Again Dr. M hits me with one of her questions that aren't really questions but much more of a statement. I think I probably rolled my eyes at this point. No, scratch that. I definitely did. "So. Diane. Blessed with such a special gift and known to use it for miraculous Good, why would Simon use that ability to hurt Andrew...let alone kill him."

There she went again with another of her 'questments.'

"Do you understand?" she asked, this time actually raising the pitch at the end of her sentence. At last, a real question. Praise be!

"No, I don't. I don't understand what the fuck you're saying, because it sounds like you still think *I* killed Andrew. Is that what you think, Dr. M? Is it!" Now I've gone and hit her with a questment of my own.

Dr. M said nothing in response to that. Instead, she just sort of looked at me with those eyes in a way that makes you wanna share everything. Guess that's part of why she's so good at this game.

"Jesus H. Christ, you *do* still think that," I ranted. "You really do. I don't believe what I'm getting from you right now. I really don't. God*damn*it, Doc."

I was out of my seat and pacing tight circles, scrunching my fingers through my hair—that clipped, dishwater-blonde nest that made me look a bit like a pixie. (And I don't mean those cute ones like Tinkerbell, either. I'm talking a crazed, cornered wood sprite.) Mind you, I still have that same 'do. Only now, it's hidden beneath this beautiful raven-black wig that trails all the way down my back, almost to my waist. Maybe it's a bit overkill, as far as disguises go, I mean, but I like it.

"Simon loved him? *Simon loved him?* Is that what you're really saying to me right now? *I* loved my brother!" After a pause in which I felt a rush of guilt almost swallow me whole I clarified, "I *love* Andrew. Present tense, not past. Got it?!" (There I go with another questment. Man, now I know I've been in here too long—this place, not this eval—'cause all these sessions I've had with Doc over the years have got me tossing out those questments of hers like they're jellybeans on Easter.) I hold my hands over my heart. "He's not gone. OK? He's still in here. I know he is."

Dr. M didn't reply to my outburst. Or the crying it turned into.

Needless to say, she didn't sign my competency, and none of the other psychs disagreed with her assessment. In a way it didn't matter, because Plan B was already waiting for me. Sure, I'd formulated all sorts of intricate ideas for escape during the seven-plus years I was in there. Doesn't every inmate?

Sorry ... doesn't every 'patient?'

But in the end, it was so simple I'm almost embarrassed to tell you. It just might ruin this whole image you have of me, y'know? The same way that magic tricks suck once you know the secret. There you are, all mystified and awestruck, then you go and spoil it by finding out how the trick is done. And the answer's always so simple, isn't it? Sure, you lie to yourself and say you'll enjoy the trick even better now that you know how it's done; that you'll appreciate the magician even more for her cleverness the next time you see her perform.

But you don't.

It just becomes this big anticlimax.

Well, my great escape was just like that. I know you've probably been imagining it as voraciously cunning. But…are you ready?… all I did was pull the fire alarm between shifts. The staff that was going out just kept on going. No way they were gonna stay another two hours to account for all us crazies, not when they had dinner and family waiting at home. And the staff coming in just turned right around and waited for us all to come filing out in dutiful little lines. They have to take us a hundred feet from the building for everyone's safety. And since there are no guard towers or barbed wire palisades (this is Barrow Moor, not Alcatraz!) I just slid away.

Now here I am. Sleeping rough in a subway.

Do I have the money for a hotel?

Yes. If I wanted to use it for that. And I guess I might share more about that later. Has something to do with a bank account my father set up for me, forever ago, that I'd managed to tap into at Barrow Moor using the online library computer. You already know that I had plenty of 'me time' there, so figuring out the password my mother had set (I'm guessing some time ago) become an entertaining game. Once I had my list, each guess written down in the order I figured was most likely, I actually got it on the fifth attempt. And yes, I made sure to only try once a day so I didn't set off any alarm bell algorithms. I then set up a reloadable pre-paid card from another vendor and began moving some of the money. Quite a bit, actually. That's all there was to it. Now I just use the card which is essentially untraceable.

Well, there you go. Guess I just went ahead and told you now rather than later.

Anyhoo, hotels aren't an option.

Number one reason: I'd have to show my I.D. for that, and I can't imagine it would be very long before the cops would be banging on my door.

Number two: I have enough money to get by, but the idea of blowing through a grand a week just to sleep somewhere has no appeal to me. I need as much cash as possible to get the hell out of here once I do what I promised Andrew I'd do.

And number three: whether some front desk clerk stitched me up or not, after that *New Day* interview I know there would be a dozen more people willing to rat me out, even if they weren't entirely sure it was me.

I just can't take that chance. I wish I could. 'Cause I could sure do with a friend like Lucia right now.

But that isn't an option.

So, no lodgings for me. Subway stations and parks are my best bet. Hiding with the others in plain sight, as it were.

II

Next to the bench where she sleeps, Sofia is making a snow angel on the floor. But it's July. We're indoors. Underground. And instead of snow, she's lying there sweeping her arms and legs over floor tile that's coated with layers of grease and debris. She gives me a shit-eating grin as I step over her on my way to get something to eat.

It's barely nine a.m. and the heat is already stifling. My scalp itches under this stupid wig. I nearly tug it from my head but pass a newsstand and see my picture yet again on the front of a stack of tabloid newspapers. It's not the main story of course, so it's down near the bottom. But it's there. God help me, it's been three weeks, but it's still there. My face is cropped inside a small box about the size of a passport photo next to a sub-headline that reads:

BARROW MOOR HUNT FOR SISTER OF PROPHET CONTINUES

The main headline is news about the Church of the Apocrypha. Something about them planning to leave the city to establish a permanent worldwide campus.

It's an update I need to know.

"Hey," I ask the man busying himself with boxes of cigs and candy bars inside the stand. "Can I use a card to get this?" I waggle the newspaper at him.

He looks at me with curiosity until I realize his English isn't the best. I mean, I'm sure it's a damn sight better than my grasp of Persian, which is basically none, so you won't get any judgment from me. So, as well as the newspaper, I now wave my card in the air. It's not aggressive, just me trying to communicate.

"No. No card! Cash!" he says more fiercely than warranted as he reaches out to point in the general vicinity of the sticker showing all the major credit cards he accepts.

"Ummm."

"NO CARD! LOOK!" He leans so far out of his little sanctuary I'm sure he's going to tumble out, spilling half of his product with him. "CASH!"

Oh. So, yeah. I see it now.

There's a hastily handwritten index card thumbtacked beneath the other one. It's informing people like me that all cards have a ten-dollar minimum. I hate when they do that. I mean, I get it. I'm trying to purchase a fifty-cent newspaper with a card that probably costs the guy thirty-two cents to process. Subtract the wholesale price of the paper in the first place and the guy's now paying me to take the rag off his hands. But still, I hate when they do that.

Who carries change any more?

I'm not spending ten bucks to get this paper, and that's a fact. So I just stand there and start reading the cover story. I'm not even into the second paragraph before he swipes it from my hands so fast my head spins. I'm sure I've got a paper cut on most of the fingers on my right hand.

"You read you buy! You BUY!"

Wow, dude. Okay then.

I wait a judicious moment before turning to walk away. He gives me the evil eye and now I wonder if he recognizes me. Then I remember I've got my wig on, so the look he's giving me is straight-up personal. This is confirmed when he slaps the air between us, accompanied by an audible sigh of exasperation.

He returns to opening his new stock of cigs and candy.

The moment he looks away I snag the paper. Walking briskly, I whip it in front of me so he can't see it.

A dozen strides in, I stop.

Ahhhhh .... Damn it!

I turn around and slip it back on top of the pile with all the others while his attention is still diverted. I give him a loud *harumph* and point at the overpriced box of menthol lights ... and again, the newspaper. I have more than half a pack of cigs in my bag already but figure, what difference does it make? I'd just end up buying another pack sometime later today anyway.

Sure, they'd be three bucks cheaper from anywhere else. But I just couldn't bring myself to steal from the guy.

III

So, apparently, the Church of the New Apocrypha is the real deal now. As a result of the 'Great Healing' *(the newspaper's words, not mine)* which took place on the apron of our old apartment building it has become the fastest-growing church in the world. Ever. It's now being called more influential than any ideology since the birth of Christianity, some comparing it to the days when Jesus Himself walked among us.

Converts and the curious alike are now traveling from all around the world in hopes of Simon Peter laying hands on them. Some just to be in his presence. At least three A-lister celebs have announced their defection from the controversial organization to which they've been loyal for years in order to become New Apocryphals.

The article also noted that for safety reasons the city has barred the church from any further gatherings at West Central.

Or any public place without the proper permits.

As a result, and with the financial backing and influence of one especially notable celebrity, the elders revealed that they've already begun 'the necessary steps' to secure a new campus. Though several locations are up for consideration, one in particular is of special interest. If successful, the new campus will not only be out of the city, but out of the state altogether.

While the elders would not reveal exact locations to the journalist, someone—and here feel free to join the finger-pointing at the headline-hungry celebrity—had leaked that it would be in Pennsylvania.

That means my piece-of-shit uncle and Simon, that little freak masquerading as my brother, could be far away from me sooner than I expected. You'd think I'd be happy about that, seeing as Simon (or Simon and my uncle) somehow influenced my baby brother, Andrew, to leap to his death from a fifth-story window.

I still can't wrap my head around that, even all these years later.

But their leaving also means my mother will be leaving, too.

Possibly forever this time.

And just like the mystery about Andrew, I can't believe such a concept of finality about our relationship is even forming in my mind. Having always been so close, I never imagined, not in a million years, that my mother would forsake me like she has.

All of this, plus the three words I heard my father whisper in my ear, keep stealing any relief I have.

Beware the woods.

I've been telling myself it's time to just move on. That I don't have to know exactly what happened in those woods when I was twelve; how I got there in the first place; what the unimaginable thing was that my daddy was saving me from.

Or who pulled the trigger that put a bullet through his brain.

I don't need to know any of those things because my father is dead whatever the answer. But *I'm* not dead. I'm still here, just trying to make a new life for myself.

And as for that promise, Andrew loved me as much as I loved him. Maybe more. He definitely showed it more than I did, if I'm being honest. I feel bad about that, a lot more than I'll admit. But then I remind myself that I was twelve years old at the time and, well, you know what that's like. Still, if anyone in the world would understand me not living up to that promise, Andrew would.

Because my baby brother would never want me to do something that could put me in harm's way. No matter how good the reason.

But the thing is, I'm lying to myself. Because I do have to know all those things. And I do have to live up to my promise.

Just when I think I've finally started to get my life under control, I feel that paralyzing anxiety starting to churn like a buzzsaw again.

So I take a deep breath and remind myself that I can handle this. I'm a 22-year-old woman in the city now, not a 12-year-old girl hauled off to the woods by something so dark and awful that I can't even imagine it.

Can't imagine it.

Unimaginable...

And now I realize what they've meant all these years when they say that my daddy did what he did to stop something unimaginable from happening to me. They weren't referring to the outcome.

They were referring to what had taken me....

IV

My spot under the stairs is gone, claimed by somebody else. I can smell them even before I turn the corner: that rare fragrance associated with thankfully few habitual city wanderers. An odor I can only describe as smacking of rubbing alcohol, layers of filth, and that retching odor your dog puts out when his glands need expressed.

Listen, I'm on the streets too. But I'll be dead before I ever give up on life like that. Even Snow-angel Sophia steers clear of this unpredictable lot. Their reputation for unprovoked violence is preceded only by their distinctive territorial scent. And if you think that sounds a tad judgy, then you haven't been to the bowels of a major metropolitan transit center at three a.m.

"Hey! I guess you just didn't see that bedroll and pillow?!" Before the last syllable has even fluttered from my lips, I realize that questments are now embedded in the way I speak. I can't stop them even if I wanted to.

Touché, Dr. M .... Touché.

I'm stepping toward this person to reclaim my little space when my stomach becomes instantly heavy. My ribs scratch as if they are wrapped in pink insulation. It's suddenly hard to breathe.

It's another of my interruptions. The first kind. The ones that try to get my attention about something I need to know, right here and right now. And it's not a good one.

The trespasser slowly turns to face me. They stare me down with eyes milky white. Leathery skin as old as dirt. Their mouth a thin snarl.

I stop dead in my tracks, sucking in air when the jarring squawk peals from out of nowhere, so loud and unexpected that my blood runs cold.

There, perched atop the roll of my sleeping bag, is a massive raven the size of a housecat. Its luminous black wings lift and extend, as magnificent as they are intimidating. Its head bobs up and down several times before cocking it back like a shooter tracking a clay pigeon. With extraordinary volume it discharges another caw. I flinch, instinctively squeezing my eyes tight as if the sound might forewarn of some kind of projectile. Amplified by the little cubby under the stairs, the screaming call resonates through the cavernous subway, echoing from wall to wall before returning to us in diminishing waves. As it does, the bird leaps to the person's arm, digging tremendous talons into their skin. Like an elderly seamstress's thumb and index finger, their forearm is riddled with puncture wounds of the same size and grouping as the claws. Many are older, scaly but healing over. Others are newer and still ooze light crimson and clear serous fluid. Several need attention as they seep thick, yellowing pus.

The raven lowers its head and thrusts its neck forward, its powerful black beak wide. Tongue darting as if tasting my presence.

Like its keeper's, the bird's eyes are a blind, ashen void.

"You make him uncomfortable!" A line of spittle stretches from top lip to bottom as the person speaks. "And that makes *me* uncomfortable!"

I don't know how to react to this, still processing everything I've been exposed to in the fifteen seconds since getting here.

Not liking my hesitation the person stands, the raven continuing to bob up and down on their arm while squawking.

There's a real possibility they could be of the mindset to kill me as soon as look at me, so I take a halting step backward. Thankfully, they do not close the distance I've opened. Instead, the person stands silent at the threshold of my cubby, evaluating me with that blank, cataract stare.

I'd swear they can actually see me, but you can tell there's nothing in those eyes but blindness. I take the moment's pause to calm my nerves and see this person not as a monster, but as a human being deserving of dignity. A person who might be as on edge in this situation as I am.

Starting to speak, I begin to ask them to forgive my initial brusqueness. See if we can't start again. I want to preface this with the respect of calling them 'sir' or 'ma'am.' But the funny thing is, no matter how hard I look, I can't tell which is appropriate. Beneath that tattered, crusty knit cap, their face is so filthy I can barely make out its features. Their hair is a long tangle of matted thatch. And their voice, from what little of it I've heard, sounds like it *could* be female. But there's also a gravelly, masculine baritone beneath it. This could be the byproduct of more years than their fair share of hardship and pain, most likely kept at arm's length (though not very successfully) by inhaling nicotine-laced tar until their lungs now rattle.

You see? I point out to myself, reminded that I just paid ten bucks for a pack of smokes. *You're looking at yourself in ten years. Time to quit!* But I know that's as much a lie as my attempts to convince myself that I don't have to go through with my promise to Andrew.

Regardless, whatever this poacher's gender, I sense they may be considerably younger than the weariness they carry in their countenance.

So now I *do* feel like I've been a judgy bitch.

I don't want to disrespect them any further by throwing out a gender designation that's embarrassingly wrong, so I simply decide to introduce myself. Their reply will take care of the rest.

"I'm..."

And now I realize that I haven't established an alias. At least not one I can grasp like it's second nature. I managed to hold an entire conversation with Lucia without having to surrender a name. And since that was the last one-on-one dialog I've had of any significance in the past few weeks—Persian newsstand dude excluded—coming up with one hasn't been much of a priority.

"I don't care who you are!" she shouts at me with frightening vehemence, the spittle line between her lips finally breaking free.

Yes, you caught that right. I said '*her*.'

With the husky, underlying rasp overpowered by the intensity of her rebuke, the naturally youthful quality of the woman's voice has become evident. There's even a hint of a soft, southern lilt. And far from elderly as I first thought, I'd be shocked if she were barely fifty years old. Maybe not even mid-forties yet.

"Hey, okay," I indulge as I slowly retreat, hands before me in visible nonresistance. Then I remember she can't see the gesture, so I drop them, feeling foolish. "I'm not here to harm you."

"You're touched!"

At first, I don't know what she's insinuating. *That I'm crazy? Gifted? Diseased?* It could be absolutely anything. But then that scratchy feeling like insulation prickles my lungs and I start to understand as the raven hops into the air. It executes two powerful flaps of its beautiful wings, so lustrous black I'm certain I can see purple in their reflection of the subway's harsh industrial light.

It glides to a cushioned landing at her feet.

"You've been touched, child," she repeats, her voice softening as she reaches for me. "Come here, child?"

Her face softens in equal proportion and something inside me shifts. The heaviness in my chest lifts. In a literal heartbeat, the interruption which pulsed distress now feels like a connection to a warm emotional memory. One my soul recognizes despite the blank my mind is drawing.

The woman shuffles closer, her mouth beginning to tremble as visibly as the fingers that are reaching for me, delicately probing the air in front of her as the space between us lessens.

Now I'm struck by a mix of sensations that are not borne of my surroundings. I see faded yellow; smell an oddly pleasant mix of grease and old leather. I hear the labored hum of an engine and the cyclical, meditative sound of tires on an old highway. But most of all, I hear six-year-old Andrew's voice proclaiming with unabashed delight that the woman said he's allowed to drive the car.

Oh my God.

My heart starts pounding. Every hair on my body stands proud, starting at the nape of my neck and flowing down my back. The follicles rise in a wave across my arms, my legs, until I'm swathed in a cocoon of goosebumps.

"*... Diane...?*" The woman's mouth lifts at the corners, melting her hardened appearance into vulnerability. "*... Could it... oh my dear... Diane...!*"

Thick tears swell in my eyes at her touch, those ragged nails and calloused fingertips easily the most precious to ever caress my face. Through her fingers she is seeing me. Skimming light as a feather over my features they brush my cheeks and tingle my lips.

Weeping and breathless, I embrace her as her name passes over my lips for the first time since I was a child:

"*Della...?!*"

4:24

I CAN'T BE *dreaming*, I tell the Universe. *You wouldn't dare be so cruel.* I nuzzle into Della's shoulder. Touch my head to hers. The filth and the stench and the trepidation have gone. All that exists is the beautiful light of the same woman who held me in her arms when I was a twelve-year-old girl battling with the unreality of what happened in the woods that day. My father was dead. My mother fighting for life in a faraway Pittsburgh hospital. Yet someone cradled me to their bosom that night.

It's only in this moment, ten years later, that I recognize the energy of that person. As the tears had surged like storm tide from my eyes and the tendrils of darkness closed in on me, it had been DeLaCroix Laveau who absorbed a broken girl's pain. Safely in her embrace, it was the meditative rise and fall of Della's chest that eventually lulled me to the mercy of sleep.

That is how my childhood came to an end.

Not as a gradual and undetectable journey to adulthood, but as a watershed moment in which oblivion followed. As if robbing my innocence weren't enough, this numbness stole another year more.

And the rest you have witnessed with your own eyes.

"Oh, my child," Della responds as if the memory has been spoken aloud and not the private cry of my soul's angst. "This is no dream. At least not in the sense you think. And you are so much stronger now than you were the day this all began."

Am I? I wonder as the weight of it impresses upon my heart.

Yes, sugar. You are. Very much so.

No words have passed our lips, yet each understands the other. I've experienced glimpses of this telepathy in the past. But it's been exactly that: brief snippets. And me as receptor, not transmitter.

Now I'm experiencing both. And it's effortless.

Yes. I knew from the first moment I ever met you that you were touched, Della reveals as she pulls gently free of our embrace to 'look' at me once more with hands that smooth my hair and tenderly explore my forehead, eyes and nose. *Do you remember?*

I do. The car—

—Yes, my car. Andrew's car, as I've always thought of it from that day forward. My quirky, boxy, ancient little VW Thing.

I'm smiling. She feels it in her touch.

I knew then that you had the gift. Almost immediately. So strong for such a young girl. I felt it as we followed your mom's ambulance to the hospital that day.

She pauses and I can tell she's considering whether or not she should broadcast her next thought. This contemplation is not expressed in a way that I can hear, for Della's gift is much more developed than mine. But I can feel it. She decides to go ahead and share it after all.

That's when I knew your uncle has it, too. Though he has to work at his a whole lot more than you do.

My energy shifts at the mention of Ian. We both feel it. Della's vibration rises to one of curiosity. Mine lowers, resonating discomfort. I shy from the place I sense she might be wanting to take me, unprepared to go there just yet. So instead, I steer the conversation back to our original subject. It's awkward and stiff, but I don't care. I'm just not ready for what she wants to reveal. I will be. But not today.

Do you still drive it? The car?

I'm already grimacing at the stupidity of the question I've just posed to a blind woman. But it's too late to reel it back in. Unlike audibly speaking where (most people) can decide if they want to express something or not, apparently the moment a thought pops into *my* mind I've already made it telepathically available. Floating out there in the psychic ether. Maybe people like Della and others blessed with this gift can control what they transmit and what they don't. But I'm learning that mine has come with no filter.

Now I'm transmitting discomfort *and* embarrassment.

This Della senses psychically as well as tangibly, her hands feeling the corners of my mouth pulling taut. She laughs, out loud, with an expression of joy that I realize I've kept from my life for far too long. I wonder if maybe she has, too.

"Oh yes, babygirl," Della answers without hesitation, having clearly heard what I meant to ask only of myself. "I have expressed too little joy and gratitude these past years. Most definitely. How wonderful it is to be in the company of it once again!"

It sounds awful to say, but I'm grateful to know I've not been alone in my austerity. I'm also grateful for her spoken reply.

'Cause this telepathy thing is kind of exhausting for me.

II

For the first time since my—*ahem*—'departure' from Barrow Moor, I've decided to get a bed for the night. It's only a cheap place where we can both lay our heads. I could use the break from sleeping with one eye open. And Della, well, she needs to get right. I mean, you know I love her 'n all, but that smell and those seeping sores on her arm are too much. Nothing a nice steaming shower with those cute little hotel soaps can't fix, though. That, and the antibacterial ointment I bought along with a box of little round Band-Aids.

To keep us incognito I paid for the room in cash that I got back from buying several packs of unsalted peanuts from (yes, you guessed it) Persian newsstand dude. He doesn't really offer cash-back as an option, but I said he could charge the card for a hundred-fifty and just give us a hundred-thirty change. Minus the cost of the peanuts, that gives him a pretty easy ten-dollar tip for his trouble. But it turns out the guy is a softy beneath that gruff exterior because he declined the gratuity after seeing Della and catching the gist of what I was needing the cash for.

We picked a place near the Queensboro Bridge that looked clean, but about as basic as you can get. Thankfully, the old gal working the front desk couldn't give a shit about my I.D. once I slide a Benjamin across the counter. More than enough to cover the seventy-five-dollar room. I don't argue when she slips the hundred into her pocket instead of the register. Especially as Della has just made an entrance with Poe.

Oh, and by the way, that's who the peanuts are for.

Poe, Della's Raven.

"I know it's hardly imaginative," Della half apologizes when I ask. "I did consider naming him Edgar. For a brief spell, anyway. But, oh, I don't know. It didn't seem to go with his temperament."

Poe caws as she says this.

I wonder if he knows we're talking about him?

"Anyway, sugar, don'tcha think that would've been a silly name for a raven?" The questment is so much more disarming than the type Dr. M has conditioned me to expect: the type that trap you.

Still, knowing that Della's not really looking for an answer I say nothing. Especially as I don't know if I wholeheartedly agree.

I think 'Edgar' would be a pretty badass name.

III

I'm startled awake in the dead of night by a repeating hissing sound that's so subtle it's barely audible. Especially above the endless noises of the street which so easily penetrate the cheap single-pane windows. Yet to me it's clear as a bell and I'm robbed of the first decent sleep I've had in weeks.

My waking is so abrupt that the transition to consciousness is razorblade thin, affording me no time to acclimate to my actual surroundings. I'm confused and instantly frightened because I don't know where I am, my mind all static and blurred reality. Then I remember I'm no longer alone. And that I'm not on the streets, but in a cheap hotel room. With Della … and Poe, who is beating his wings and begins doing so with such ferocity that dust and feathers fill the room like black snow.

I've been holding my breath without realizing it and allow myself to exhale. If there were a list of strange things you could have in your room to produce a bunch of sounds you're not used to, a raven would hafta be top of the pops.

So I settle back into my pillow and close my eyes, wondering what on earth I was thinking by coming here. *By bringing Della here.* After all, in very real terms, I barely know the woman. And what modest interaction we shared was itself a very, very long time ago.

But then I hear it again.

Syme-seh.

It's a voice. But the words are incoherent. I look toward Della on the bed nearest the window to see if she is dreaming, but the room is so dark it's difficult to tell. Only a sliver of light penetrates the edge of the blackout blinds. It casts a crisp, golden line across the floor, over Della's bed. Across her throat.

I sit in the dark, watching to see if the sliver of light shifts with her movement. But after a time I cannot account for she has remained utterly motionless.

Sime—sehhhh.

The sound is coming from the window, behind the blind, and my chest contracts; the hairs on my neck rise.

Siiiimmme—sssseeehhhhh.

And I see it.

The shadow climbing through the window.

It momentarily breaks the plane of light and I jolt backward, slamming against my headboard so hard and fast that it dents the cheap drywall with a report like a gunshot.

The noise does not stir DeLaCroix from sleep. Neither does it disturb the stranger in the room with us. The stranger who has crept in from the fire escape. The stranger now moving so slowly but surely toward Della's bed.

Except, it's not a person.

Not a fully formed one, anyway. More of a dark, flowing mist, a circulating void, in an instant it becomes more solid, taking on a physical shape. But the manifestation is fleeting as it shifts and morphs, becoming everything and nothing all at once, pulling energy from the very space it occupies.

"*Del...Dell...*" I call out but am unable to find my voice, my cry barely a hiss. Frozen to the headboard, my chest squeezes the blood from my heart until I fear there is none left. I inhale sharply but am unable to let the breath back out. As second-upon-second ticks by, my breast becomes a furnace. "*Della...Dellllaaaa...!*"

The shadow solidifies again. Longer, clearer. Now fully a person. And I feel the hollowness inside as it syphons its energy from mine.

Feeding off my fear.

Beneath it, Della remains motionless and I pray she is still asleep. But the window blind begins to flutter in a breeze that does not exist, and I can see from the wedge of waxing and waning light playing over her face that her mouth is frozen in an oval of hysteria. Her eyes are perversely wide. And though they are blind, her mind sees what they cannot: that it is my dead brother, Andrew, who is standing beside her.

In pajamas soiled with the dirt of his grave.

Chanting. Slowly. Over and over.

...Simonnn sehhhs...

...Simonnnn sehhhhhs...

...Simonn saysss....

4:25

HIS CRUSHED HEAD is misshapen and facing mostly backward. The end of his spine has protruded from his split-open neck, the splintered vertebrae twisting in a semi-helix with fibrous, bloodied ligaments torn away. In order to peer down into Della's blind eyes, Andrew has to stand with his pajama-clad back facing her and bend backwards farther than is natural.

"... *Simon says! Simon says! Simon says ...!*"

There are a thousand small, opaque things moving across his grey and bloodless face. Over his lips. Into his ears. Finding their way to his once beautiful eyes which are now wrinkled, half-filled pouches of opaque gelatin. In the dark of night it takes me a moment. But then the wedge of light passes over his face, and I realize they are maggots burrowing in and out of my nine-year-old brother's rotting flesh.

The acid rises in my throat as I begin to heave.

"*It should've been you, Deedee,*" he tells me, the condemnation at odds with his childlike grin and characteristically sweet chipmunk voice. Now he tilts his head, first one way, then slowly the other as he stares at me with those empty eyes. But his broken neck cannot support its weight on one side and his deformed skull lurches to a grotesque angle, his jaw jutting out. This small but jarring motion disturbs a hard, shiny black spider from the dark void beyond Andrew's oversized baby teeth that haven't dissolved, and now never will. Spilling out of his mouth and clinging there, the spider sinks its chelicerae into Andrew's bottom lip. But it cannot hang on and falls to the floor.

I hear every tiny click of its tarsal claws as it scuttles away in the dark before Poe drops from the dresser to devour it.

At last my breath looses from my fiery chest and I scream louder than I have in my life.

It only acts as a call to beckon Andrew nearer and he shuffles grotesquely around Della's bed to lean over the foot of mine.

My dead brother starts inching along the side.

Closer to me.

And closer yet.

"Simon sayyyys, Deedeeeeee...Simon saaayyss! You have to do it!"

I cannot speak, but my mind has instinctively responded against my will. I can't control it.

Do what? I reply telepathically, the vibration fierce and intense.

"Simon saysssss...slice your tongue, Deedee. Cut it like a snake's!"

Edging ever nearer, he hisses at me with his own black and swollen tongue, flicking it in a way that drops thick globules of dark mucous in a line up the bed. The white cotton cover sizzles and dissolves with each one and I'm aware of how close they fall to my legs just underneath. I move aside ... but my body does not obey the command of my brain. Now a drop strikes the sheet immediately over my thigh, and I watch it burn the bedspread before it begins eating my skin like acid. I scream and thrash as skin melts to muscle but my response to the pain is in my mind, for I am paralyzed; a mannequin with moving eyes.

"Slice it right up the middle, Deedeeeeee!"

The drawer in the small desk across the room flies open of its own accord and a pair of heavy-duty scissors fling out, along with a pad of branded notepaper, a pen and chain of paperclips.

"Better yet, kill the witch! She's here to hurt you, Deedee. I know you can feel *it. Save yourself and kill the witch!"*

Andrew's bouncing and clapping with bliss in the way I had seen him do a thousand times before. An expression of unadulterated joy, what I called his 'delighted dance' had brought *me* so much happiness that I often did whatever I could to elicit it. It's one of the sweetest memories I have of my baby brother who meant the world to me.

Now it's just a sickening hoax by a malignant facsimile as the Andrew thing's deformed head bobs around beyond his control, his clapping hands on the wrong side of his body. His vacant, maggot-riddled eyes are looking down at me as he giggles, almost singing:

"Kill the witch kill the witch kill the witch!"

I dry heave at the perverseness, a vibration as deep as a subwoofer oscillating through my core. Now I feel as though I'm going to full-on vomit, regurgitating my partially digested dinner that rises in a thick, chunky mass. But paralysis denies its expulsion and it fills my esophagus. I retch again. More comes, rising to the clod already bottlenecked there. Unable to release it, the mass fills my throat, covering my trachea, and I instinctively gasp.

The vomit sucks into my windpipe with a squealing sound—*like a discordant whistling*—and now I'm choking.

I cannot breathe. Heaving and filled with panic, I think I am throwing my head forward to clear the blockage . . . but I am motionless, my body failing to move despite the image in my mind.

More vomit now obstructs my trachea completely.

And the clock starts ticking as my lack of breath and hysteria is already beginning to starve the oxygen from my brain.

. . . One-one thousand . . .

Help me!

. . . Two-one thousand . . .

Someone!

. . . Three-one thousand . . .

God! Please! Help me!

II

Thrashing in bed, my eyes open to Della's, just inches away. She is stroking my hair and gently reassuring me.

"Shhh, it's okay, sugar. It was just a bad dream. Shhh, now."

I lunge forward in a single, convulsive reflex, wheezing and pulling in a lungful of air as I nearly headbutt Della. She avoids it by flexing to the side in a smooth, delicate motion I don't understand given her lack of sight.

"W-Wh—" The words stick in my throat still burning with the taste of bile, though the sensation can't be real. "W-Where is he!"

I toss the covers aside and leap from the bed, startling Poe.

We are the only ones here.

"But—" I pull the covers back and point to the burn holes which are no longer there. Amid a flurry of vocal rejection I inspect my thigh, probing for the acid burn which had eaten my leg to the muscle. It is not there. "—I don't underst—"

I am unable to finish the word before my tears explode and I am wrapped into Della's embrace. Through blurred and salted eyes I see Poe stepping from side to side in anxious concern, this nervous dance the only way he can express his empathy with me.

"Oh, child. I know you don't," Della consoles, her voice soft and soothing. "There's so much that must be revealed ...."

4:26

I
T'S THREE IN the morning and I feel safer on the streets of New York than I do my hotel room. I'm quiet. Still a little shaken. We're slowly making our way to a church on the East Side that Della knows has an open-door policy, twenty-four seven. There's something—*actually a lot of things, she clarified*—that she's feeling compelled to share with me. But she won't say, or even think, a word more until we're safely in the 'protection of its holy sanctuary.'

(Her words. Not mine. I think you've gathered by now that I'm not especially religious.)

So, I'm expecting an inner-city building with a neon cross and some plastic, lighted letters. But what I get is a beautiful, imposing building of gothic architectural magnificence, far more deserving of the term cathedral than church.

The entrance is comprised of two timber doors that tower at least twice my height. Every inch has been intricately carved, a labor of love which boasts twelve exquisite panels, the focal point of each being a relief of what I can only assume to be one of the apostles. The doors are framed by a series of stone arches of increasing size. They easily double the height, width and depth of the entrance, and as I draw closer the whole thing instills in me a humbling sense of being very—

"—Small," Della correctly finishes my thought out loud.

But it is not a feeling of insignificance or being reduced. Rather, as I stand here in the shadow of the grand entrance, my heart is filled with a warming sense that I'm part of something so much bigger than my mortal limitations. And while the casual observer may feel the building excessive or overly grand in its extravagance, from this intimate perspective it feels deferential and adulatory to the One for whom it has been built, for precisely the same reasons.

Della has not accompanied me up the short flight of stone steps but waits alone on the sidewalk. Poe has hopped from her arm and with a single flex of his wings is now perched atop the apex of the entrance arches. He squawks once, loud and crisp in the still night air as Della waves me on.

"The first step has to be taken by you, child," she instructs. "I will be along. Momentarily. But this part of the journey is yours alone."

I want to question why, but any seed of doubt has immediately evaporated like a fine mist. There's a warm vibration expanding from my belly. It assures me that Della is right, though I don't yet know why.

While the doors' vast and elaborate handles are brass that has long ago tarnished, the grips still boast a bright reddish-yellow gloss from a million hands polishing it time and again for nearly two centuries. An electric charge spikes through me as I wrap my hand around one, and I flinch with surprise. At first, I put it down to static shock. But the energy continues to course through me, up my arm, across my chest, then spreading throughout my body.

Far from painful, the sensation is akin to a shot of adrenaline as I pull the heavy door open with a creak.

The air inside is cool and dry, and the contrast to the humidity of the New York summer night is immediate. I have an inkling that the indoor environment remains pretty much the same regardless of time of day or season, which only reinforces the cathedral's steadfast aura of timeless continuity and stability.

My steps echo through the enormous, vacant space as I walk alone through the nave. Passing pew after pew, I find I'm naturally pacing in the reverent step-stop rhythm of a procession as I astonish at the vaulted heavens high above and the great stone columns that stretch up to meet them.

Remembering that every cathedral is built in the shape of the Messiah's cross, I quicken to see the transepts up ahead where left and right arm of the architecture branches off perpendicular to the nave. Shorter but no less spectacular, the central point of each offshoot is a magnificent stained-glass circular 'rose' window.

The window in the arm to the east is dedicated to the Virgin Mary, and I'm filled with golden warmth as I become lost in its beauty and softly diffused light. Even in the dead of night, it glows spectacular in the backlit illumination of the city.

In the west arm, the window is dark and menacing, and chills run down my spine as I decipher the story depicted is the Last Judgment ... also called the Second Coming of Christ. The figure at the center of this stained-glass wheel is adorned with several crowns and wears a white robe covered in blood. This person is surrounded by an army of angels and the truly faithful. Below them, demons guard the fiery gates of Hell, a stream of people descending toward them. Above, only a few transcend a sky eclipsed by gargoyles to float toward the golden gates of Heaven.

It's beyond chilling and I see no merit for its prominence in this sanctuary which is a glorious tribute to God and Love and Light.

Yet I cannot stop looking at it.

A moth drawn to its flame, I find myself lost in its iconography and the more I study it, the more I find. The more I find, the more I'm compelled to study it. It feels like a message unraveling before me, revealed through a secret code ... the key to which has been hiding in plain sight all along.

In particular, I'm mesmerized by the demonic figures portrayed near the bottom of the window. Two stand out more than the others, and although I don't yet know why, I'm beginning to feel that bowling ball in my stomach as I edge nearer.

As stylized, glass versions of what the artist felt a demon should look like, neither are especially frightening. But there's something about the first that's pulling me to it like a magnet.

And not in a good way.

The churning bowling ball is now so intense that I feel I might be in danger of passing out. I've also become suddenly and acutely aware of my isolation. In the middle of the night. Surrounded by limitless opportunities for someone—or some*thing*—to prowl undetected in this huge, gothic space filled with columns and pews and tombs and monuments, any one of which can obscure a handful of people.

Alone I'm vulnerable. With the others I'm part of a tribe...

The reminder of the self-preservation logic I've applied since I fled Barrow Moor plays clear and loud in my mind. And now I'm wondering how I've allowed myself to be in this situation which contradicts this edict in every conceivable way.

The hairs on the back of my neck stand proud.

...Just a stupid, sacrificial lamb, led so easily to its own slaughter.

Now it's Ian's voice, the words filling my head like poisonous gas. It's the revelation that broke my heart, the night he found me on my special boulder. The night he admitted to killing my father.

The night he and Simon took my sweet baby brother away.

I feel like I can't breathe. The blood is draining from my skin to leave me cold and clammy. It's a terrible onset of panic and I have to focus on something else or it will carry me away.

... Della ... Della ... Della ... I repeat over and over again in a soothing mantra. *Della would never forsake me. Della would never put me in harm's way...*

My legs weak and trembling, against every instinct I creep closer to the window that is drawing me in. My footsteps are tentative and light, but their sound still traverses the high, vaulted ceiling to return to me as echoes from the opposite side of the cathedral. Standing as close to the window as I can get, I study the first demon guarding the gates of hell.

Depicted as a surreal mix of serpent and mammal, its seven heads have a total of ten horns between them. The tangle of snakelike necks merge to a single, sleek, almost feline body. But instead of nimble, catlike paws it has imposing, powerful feet and claws like a Grizzly's.

I study it for no more than a matter of seconds before I double over from a pain so raw it's like a pair of rusty, serrated scissors tearing through my gut.

"IAN, I NEED THE GUN—"

My breath catches in my throat at the sound of my father's voice. My legs turn to rubber and I have to latch onto a nearby pew to stop myself from crumbling to the ground. I know it must be in my mind. But the acoustical echoes of his plea are still reverberating through the cathedral, bittersweet chords to my ears.

I spin to find their source but see only stone arches and grand design. Except the columns appear different from the way they looked just a moment ago.

They feel...*alive*...somehow.

Mesmerized, my vision blurs as I try to comprehend what I'm watching as each column transforms from cold, chiseled marble to living wood. I feel like I've been drugged, though I know I haven't, as they twist and curve, losing their straight lines and crisp edges in favor of the imperfect, beautiful chaos of nature.

They are transitioning into towering trees, the veins of marble that support the intricately engineered roof, their branches. They stretch and reach, intertwining with one another until the vaulted ceiling is a thick forest canopy.

Coming to life like Max's bedroom in *Where The Wild Things Are*, the cathedral is deconstructing before my eyes into a lush, dense wood. It is magical, beautiful; hypnotic. I'm awe-stricken as it saturates with color and light, the scent of fresh pine and the musk of oak and dewy moss tickling my nostr—

—BEWARE THE WOODS.

Like a well of ink dashed over a beautiful watercolor, my father's warning dispels the mystique and the trees instantly darken, leaves shriveling and trunks blackening as if burnt. The air grows thick with hot ash. The pews have become row after row of dense, strangling brush that flickers and snaps as flames within intensify, devouring their pulp from the inside out.

My reality is now an impossible hybrid of gothic cathedral and wooded enclave, the walls of each aglow with fierce, blistering light.

"I don't see it! God help me, Bryan, I can't find it!" Materializing three rows ahead of me, Uncle Ian, a decade younger, drops to his knees and scrabbles with mad panic around the floor. He disappears under one pew only to reappear from another, the cold taste of fear draining the color from his face.

I know I've suffered this moment many years before, but this is the first time I'm consciously experiencing it. Some of my interruptions can be like this: unveiling a memory my brain has repressed. The difference between those and what is happening now is that my interruptions will present it as a mix of feelings or triggers of one, maybe two, senses.

This is triggering all of them.

In three-dimensional space.

The proof of which lies in the burn that stings my palm as I press my hand to the charred but still glowing bark of one of the columns. Despite what my eyes are telling me, I expect cool, hard marble. Instead, I recoil with a curt shriek when the intense heat instantly renders a coin-sized area on the heel of my hand to a taut sheen.

Every muscle in my body tenses as my heart pulsing in my hand confirms this impossible reality. I take three slow steps backward, nervously turning my back to the demon window when Della's forewarning resounds to my mind.

... This part of the journey is yours, and yours alone.

There's no time for its cryptic meaning to sink in before my feet sail out to the side and up. For a moment they're level with my head. I crash down, my ribs making a loud cracking sound as the air blows from my chest. Searing pain swells in my side as my body goes slack. No longer on the floor, I'm a dozen feet in the air, bent unnaturally around the curve of a large limb.

Then I'm falling.

Plummeting through a tangle of smaller branches and vines, I'm shrieking as one hand clutches in vain at the air, the other at the loop I know is circled around my neck. When the rope reaches its full extent, the deadly cessation of momentum jerks me violently. My neck makes a snapping sound and I bite my tongue in two.

Thrashing as the blood pours from my mouth, I bungee up and down as a boy many years my junior looks on in horror.

A boy I recognize as my father in his teenage years.

Like a grotesque Yo-Yo, the noose constricts my throat tighter and tighter until my scream is reduced to a sickening, snake-like *hissss*. One of my eyes has begun to protrude from its socket as if the orb is attempting to escape my dying body. The mad thrashing of my legs lessens to small, jolting spasms above the bonfire raging beneath me.

"Heel-lp...meee...."

My final plea wheezes through a stream of air escaping my body like a punctured tire as my protruding eye bursts from its socket and hangs upon my muddied cheek by its optic nerve. No longer full or round, it's a collapsed and hollow dime-store Halloween prop. My other eye is glazed and filling with blood as it stares vacantly but directly at the boy who will one day become my father.

I do not feel the rusty, metal can as it strikes my chest. I do not smell the pungent odor of gasoline as its contents spiral in a corkscrew behind it. I do not see it when another boy I do not know, yet simultaneously understand to be Stu Klatz, kisses a flaming torch to my sneaker. I do not feel it as the flames instantly take and lick furiously up my body.

What I do experience is sound, and the rushing *whoosh* as my torso becomes engulfed in flames.

"Die, Matt Chauncey! You sad bastard! Die!" Stu triumphantly proclaims as fire runs up my neck and kisses my face. My mouth, frozen in an eternal scream, stretches twice before dissolving into a mask of red and yellow ribbons.

Klatz smirks as it does, joining five other boys who are prancing around the bonfire, ceremonially chanting and shrieking and rejoicing as their scapegoat is gifted to the ancient harbinger of evil they do not see or even understand. Around each, the naturally light aura of childhood has faded. Some have lost their brightness; others have muddied and spotted with black. Consciously choosing his submission, Stu Klatz's is the color of excrement.

These boys were dead before I ever existed, yet I know them all by name. One of them, the kid called Big Dan, is blowing into a primitive wooden flute as he dances. The shrill, inharmonious result becomes a harrowing score as I am devoured by flames that I am no longer able to feel.

Now I separate from that body and watch the sadistic ritual from the edge of the clearing.

The boy who will one day become my father is now my brother, and I'm rocking back and forth on the damp ground, my knees pulled tight to my chin as the horror seats itself deep inside. It skewers into a place all its own. A place where it can never be removed. A place where it will fester and spread.

As my best friend's body hangs from a rope and burns, I witness each of the other boys' deaths.

The first is my other close friend, Craig Dalton. I feel my throat tighten and my lungs burn. And for a reason I cannot fathom, the face of his father, Charley, is the last thing I see as the image of Craig parading around the bonfire fades into nothingness.

Next is the boy called Jimi, the younger of two brothers in our gang. I feel dizzy as though I'm falling, just before incredible pain spears through my gut. It exits from my back as Jimi's image slowly evaporates along with the untenable pain he suffers.

Then comes Woody. His parents are hippies that refuse to accept we're only a few years away from it being nineteen-eighty. Just as they refuse to accept that anyone other than Jack and Jimi Raker's father could have possibly killed their son. They have no idea it was actually two of their son's own friends who drowned him in a swamp. Just after Woody himself killed Jimi: tossing his friend from the Beechnut, three-stories high, to be impaled by a sapling spike. My mouth is tainted with a taste of sour mud, and my lungs burn without breath as the sunlight is muted and Woody's prancing avatar darkens, then disappears forever.

Big Dan Mercer, the psychotic flautist, fills me with sadness as I feel his longing for the mother he lost long ago. There's a rush of wind across my face as I hurtle at speed towards a cliff ... then indescribable agony as my head swings from a steel cable in concentric but decreasing ellipses. For twenty seconds that tick away as slowly as twenty years, I remain conscious and am aware that the rest of my body has plunged to the creek far below, twisting into the motorbike I rode to my death.

Only the presence of Stu Klatz and Jack Raker remain. Oblivious that the others are gone, they continue the ritual around the bonfire until Matt Chauncey's father swings his pickaxe.

I feel my ribs shatter with a hollow, splintering sound as dark blood bubbles through the gash in my side. What little breath I have left is vacuumed from me as I lurch high into the air on the opposite end of a rope that Mr. Chauncey has leveraged over a limb of the iconic tree we know as the Father Oak. When he releases it, I strike the ground where I am shredded from the inside out by an ancient, possessing entity.

And So, the maniacal grin of Stu Klatz is erased as the boy's image wisps away into the dark, empty sky.

Jack's is the last spirit I see, and alone, he paces endless circles around the raging fire as my brother—my father-yet-to-be—grabs my arm and yanks me up, wresting me from my stupor and dragging me from the burning woods.

"Come on, Ian! We hafta get outta here! NOW!"

I struggle to keep up, my knees loose and hurting and barely able to hold my weight, but my brother-father will not leave me behind. As we near the outer ring of the clearing we are somehow racing right back towards its center, as if running into a mirror.

There, at the base of the Father Oak, a twelve-year-old girl is prone on the ground, wheezing and clawing at the dirt. Looming over her is a thing so corrupt it is impossible to comprehend, let alone describe. But I know in every facet of my soul it is the fallen angel depicted in the cathedral's west window.

The same as I know that the girl is me, ten years ago.

To the eyes through which I look, however, it is not a demon towering over the girl-me, but Stu Klatz. He is the same age as the boy who danced around the fire, but yet my brother-father, Bryan, has aged many years to become the man, the daddy, I remember.

I look down at my own hands now and recognize that they are the adult male hands of my uncle, Ian.

The Stu thing sneers and presses his black-rimmed glasses up his nose before reaching down to lovingly stroke the hair of the girl that is also me.

"It really wanted you, Bryan. The Witness. You to become his greatest disciple." He leans close to the girl-me at his feet and whispers in my ear. "But now it wants the girl. Her power is so much greater than yours."

Stu licks his lips, the tongue long and reptilian, its fork darting out to taste the fear in the air.

"Why now, you repugnant fuck!" My brother-father takes one tentative step forward. "After eighteen years? Why now!"

"What is time to the timeless?" the Stu thing replies in magisterial authority, the voice a low rumble like distant thunder.

"All will be as it has been prophesied. Ask the Priestess. She knows."

The Stu thing looks directly at me in my uncle's form, and I feel the darkness buried deep inside me rising like black bile.

"You piece of shit!" Bryan raises the gun Della gave him and aims it directly at Stu's forehead. "Satan, the great deceiver!"

"Hey! That's not cool, man!" Stu winces, turning his head to the side while defensively covering his face with his hands. When the hands lower, it is no longer Stu but my uncle's creepy friend, Craig, staring back at Bryan. "And I'm flattered, and all. But Satan? Wow, dude." Leaning to one side and peering around Bryan, Craig nods at Ian-me. "Hey dude, how's it hanging?"

The words slice through me like dull, rusted razors. The thing looks like Craig and speaks like Craig. But its vibration is such a perverse facsimile that it's out of register. Like watching a 3-D movie without those red and green cellophane glasses that help merge all the lines together just right.

"I mean, I wish I were the Fallen One and all, but I'm not even close. Not even this . . . what did you called me . . . Azazel?" Craig snickers, snorting as he slaps his thigh. "Say, Ian. How is Rebecca, anyway? After that shower, I mean. Anything interesting going on there? Any new . . . *development* . . . shall we say, on the horizon? Talk in the underworld is that there's an Unchaste Conception already taking root in that tight, sweetass belly of hers."

Ian-me yanks the pistol from Bryan's grip and presses it to the Craig thing's temple.

Cringing, Dalton falls to his knees, whimpering.

"No! Please! I'm sorry. No, no, no—" Then he starts laughing. "Ahhh! Help me!" he cries out in mock agitation, rolling his eyes and waving his hands in the air. "Ha! I actually had you going there, Cockerton. Whoo! This is all too good! I just—I just couldn't keep up the act."

He leaps to his feet, casually knocking the gun from the hands of Ian-me. It skates across the ground and disappears somewhere under a cathedral pew covered in the thick brush as he snatches the girl-me by the hair and wrenches me violently into the air. A small clump rips from my scalp but I make no sound. Little more than a limp marionette, I dangle from the Craig thing's grip as his fingers lengthen and twist. Thick, ragged claws extend from each of their torn and bleeding tips. The talons become tangled in the strands of my hair.

You were right all along, Ian. You can't kill the dead!

Craig's mental projection reverberates across the cathedral. Echoing from tree to tree, it billows into the night sky as he grows to inhuman proportions. His features wrinkling as if behind a veil of rippling water, in an instant only his face remains as the rest of his body dissolves and is at once the disturbing feline creature from the stained glass. Protruding from his lower back, a long tail swishes back and forth, covered in a film of mucous as though a snake freshly hatching from its egg. Atop its torso, six other heads emerge and loll loosely alongside his own. Each wavering in and out, the sallow faces of the boys—Jimi, Big Dan, Woody, Stu and Matt—all bob alongside Craig's in a sickening dance.

On the seventh, only a faceless, incomprehensible void.

Suspended in the air by my hair, my twelve-year-old eyes flare wide and white, a sharp intake of breath cut short mid-draw. My young fingers scrabble futilely at my neck constricting as if by an invisible noose. My lungs pleading for air, stampeding panic freezes my diaphragm so that all I achieve is a shrill, wheezing screech—

the discordant whistling of the flute

—as the girl-me's face contorts in panic and terror. Steadily deflating, my lungs burn like glowing pokers within my chest. And on the Beast's seventh head, my face begins to materialize.

Daddy! I scream in my mind, but it is impossible for the cry to release. The skin of my neck burns as it stretches from the weight of my body. I can't breathe. No sound can pass through my constricted throat, muting my cries. My legs kick at empty air as

I'm raised higher. I fumble for the noose that is cutting into my throat…but my fingers find nothing.

I feel every bit of this intense, untenable pain and fear. And yet I am fully detached from the twelve-year-old's body to which it is happening, watching instead through the eyes of my uncle.

"IAN, I NEED THE GUN!"

Dropping to his knees, Ian-me rummages through the brush and thickets that were sturdy wood church pews only minutes earlier. "I don't see it! God help me, Bryan, I can't find it!"

Savoring two millennia of prophecy about to unfold, the demon roars in dark ecstasy, its ribboned tongue darting and licking the sulfurous air as the life in me begins to ebb away.

The color draining from my face, I twitch and reach for my father, eyes pleading as the oxygen in my brain depletes. With one last effort, I weakly extend my arm, fingers spread wide…

…And the gun skates out from under a church pew cloaked by vines and strangling scrub.

Drawn toward my open palm like a magnet, it spins from the clasp of tendrils and thorns and comes to a rest at uncle-me's feet.

In that same moment the girl-me's eyes slowly close, her chin dropping to her chest. A long hiss escapes her parted lips as her arm falls limply to her side.

My brother-father lunges for the pistol.

But so does Ian-me, who gets to it first.

"IAN, GIVE ME THE GUN," my brother-father screams.

"NO!" Ian-me's response is vehement, almost venomous. "I know what you're trying to do, Bry! It can't be the answer!"

My brother-father grabs hold of the semi-automatic in our hand but is unable to gain control of it. Our fingers are wrapped firmly around the textured handle.

Realizing what is about to happen, my father closes his eyes and cries out: "Lord, forgive my sins! And deliver my child from evil!"

I have separated from my uncle's energy and am now fully at

one with the twelve-year-old me. Instantly, I am consumed by the pain and fear of being a moment from death, my consciousness finally experiencing the reality my mind so long ago refused.

My eyes lock onto Uncle Ian's.

As the ticking of time slows to impossible measure, his are ablaze with a mix of disbelief and pleading.

Mine are filled with the will to survive.

So it is that I concentrate the last of my lifeforce's energy ... and telekinetically squeeze the guh's trigger.

The high caliber shot enters my father's cheek, opening a hole the size a pencil might make, and takes off the back of his head.

Its report explodes like a bomb, resonating from chamber to acoustic chamber throughout the cathedral-turned-woods.

The seven heads of the demon squeal in vindication, the sound like infinite dissonant flutes. Releasing me from death, the beast rises to merge once more into the stained-glass window above me. Shaking uncontrollably, I crumple to the cold, hard cathedral floor.

As waves of tears pour down my face ....

4:27

FOR THE SECOND time tonight it's Della's cloudy but no less benevolent eyes staring down at me as she condoles a decade of pain gushing out in a concentrated torrent. I want to tell myself that what just happened was another bad dream. Or some kind of recalcitrant interruption I have yet to learn how to control.

But I know both would be a lie.

And for the first time ever, I long to return to blissful ignorance.

I Killed him! God, Della. Noooo! Please, no!

My anguish is received by her with such acuteness that she winces the same as if she feels my pain as strongly as I do.

She casts nothing back to me in reply, only holding me tight and, unknown to me, absorbs as much of the umbra of my pain into her light as her spiritual balance can bear.

"What was all of that? God Della! *Please!* Tell me it wasn't real!"

Her absence of a reply is a reply in itself.

II

It's hours until the sobbing subsides enough that I can control my breath. Yet in some ways, I feel I'll never be able to breathe again. Shafts of morning sunlight are beginning to prise their way through the New York skyline, and the east rose window of the Virgin Mary is glowing with lustrous golden light. With every moment another niche or nook of the cathedral bursts into glorious radiance, and the events of the night are already fading into the realm of the absurd, fantastical, and just plain unbelievable.

"I never wanted to hurt you, babygirl," she comforts me with that soft southern lilt that feels like safety. "It was the only way for you to truly understand. And still, there is so much yet to tell."

My trembling has diminished to the point that I feel at least modestly in control of my motor functions once more, and I pull myself from her lap to sit upright in the pew. It's still too soon to speak. I don't know what to say, even if I could make sense of the thousand questions and concepts colliding in my mind. So I just sit and stare at the massive crucifix hanging by a series of heavy chains from the ceiling above the pulpit. The cross itself is hefty, aged and weathered wood. It's easily life-sized. And seeing it on display in its actual dimensions is both humbling and spine-chilling. Thankfully, the clergy have chosen to omit the figure of the dying Christ which, at life-size, would present an all too real depiction of such a gruesome and torturous ritual.

The idea of it prickles my skin in a wave of goosebumps and I'm grateful for the distraction as Della's words flow over me. "The last time you saw me was ten years ago. Your father had just killed himself, or so we thought."

... He did it to stop something unimaginable from happening ...

I hear the words of my mom and Ian in my mind for the first time in years. The same ones I used to hear, over and again, anytime I asked what happened that day in the woods. That day that, until now, I'd blocked from memory, in hopes that it would be blocked from ever having happened.

"And your mother had suffered carbon monoxide exposure in the garage of your old house in Pennsylvania. I couldn't be sure how much of the dark truth you had uncovered since then. So, can you imagine if I just started talking to you yesterday about demons and ritual childhood murder and an entity of evil so ancient and powerful it can only be the right hand of Satan himself?"

The last two words reflect back to us from the north end of the nave where the cross hangs. Their echo sounds crass and foreign in this place of Light, though I'm not sure where I get off thinking so. After all, it turns out I'm a dark-hearted killer myself. So hardly one to be judging what's evil when I'm clearly a vile, disgusting example of precisely everything that's wrong with humanity.

My thought has formed in that mental space where Della can hear it, though its projection was far from intended.

"Oh, child. You are the direct counterpart to evil. You are Light itself, incarnate."

"STOP IT, DELLA!" My rebuff blows through the cathedral in an amplified wave that feels almost physical. For a moment, I think I see the centuries-old rose windows at each end of the transepts visibly shake. "Light itself, Della? I killed my own father!"

"You were a baby, Diane. In the clutches of an evil this world has not seen since the start of time itself. You were scared."

"I was selfish!"

"You were dying."

"I killed my father! I extinguished my daddy's light—"

"—He *gave* it to you, child. Now yours will forever shine brighter, your two energies so much more powerful than one alone could ever be." Della lifts my chin, and in her eyes there lies a certainty I will never possess. They move as if studying my face. As if they actually see me. "You've heard that Simon Peter has raised from the dead. I'm not sure you believe it's true. But I can tell you, sugar, that it is. But what if I were to tell you that you have the same powers as Simon Peter? That yours, in fact, will one day, eclipse his."

III

It's too much to take in. More than too much.

I understand why Della did what she did. Because she's right.

Had she just spurted out yesterday, 'Oh, hey babygirl! Nice to see you again after all these years. And by the way, you know all those dreams and weird psychic disturbances you get? It's because you're a murderer and your dad and uncle were part of a group of boys that fed an archdemon?' I'm pretty sure I would've just turned and run the other way. So, no. I don't like her method. But I understand the reasoning behind it. What I still don't get is how she made it happen. 'Cause what I experienced wasn't just a series of images passing before me, or some uncomfortable sensations like I get with my interruptions. What happened was real.

I was actually there.

I'd always sensed a special power in Della, since the day I met her all those years ago. Just as she sensed it in me. Our reunion yesterday—and how easily we spoke to one another without saying a word—confirmed that.

But what I've just experienced? That wasn't some harmless little telepathic conversation. We're talkin' a whole 'nother level right there. An ability that, quite frankly, is beyond terrifying.

"I did nothing, child." She stares at me with those clouded eyes that you would expect to be blank. Instead, they are filled with insight and emotion. I find myself melting into them. Becoming one with her. A million strands of information passing between us.

Astral projection. Bilocation. Clairvoyance. Dream telepathy. Precognition. Remote viewing. Retrocognition. Telekinesis....

"You claim to have these abilities?" I ask. Again a questment, and not a very nice one. Its tone is dripping with sarcasm and disbelief. I'm starting to realize that my years at Barrow Moor have turned me into a mini-me of Dr. M.

"I possess some of those blessings, child. Yes. But far from all," she humbly answers, hesitating before adding, "Unlike you, Diane."

"Me?"

"I told you the journey was yours. I could open the door. But the steps had to be taken by you. And you alone."

"Hey, wait. Just wait a minute, Della."

This is going too far now.

She's basically saying I brought that whole malignant, mind-trip on myself. That *I* was the one who made it happen. Like I have some kind of supernatural powers that allow me to drop into the past, or something. In this case, a disturbingly sick and violent moment from my father's childhood. And that I was then able to inhabit my uncle's body—and mine—at the same time to re-experience the day my father died.

And then the whole sick hallucination trying to pin his death on me...like it's some kind of twisted, hyper-guilt trip or something.

Well, if there's one good thing I can say came out of my time at Barrow Moor, it's that I've been desensitized to these kind of tactics. So, I'm glad she's pushed it this far, 'cause I'm starting to feel a sense of relief in no longer buying whatever it is she's peddling. And now I'm literally on my feet and walking. Tired of whatever game this is that she thinks we're both playing.

She may be into it, but to me it's sadistic and cruel.

All I want is to fulfill the promise I made to Andrew, before Barrow Moor or those freaks with the New Apocrypha Church find me. Then I'm bouncing from this awful city and never looking back. Not on it, not on them, not on my past.

Not any of it.

I'm halfway gone when I blurt out: "I don't believe you, Della! I don't believe anything you're saying! First I'm a murderer. And then you make out like I'm some kind of spiritual power guru. But you aren't even supposed to be here! Ian said he killed you. So how do I know you're not in on this whole thing with him? He confessed, Della. Just like he confessed to killing my father. 'Just a stupid, sacrificial lamb led so easily to its own slaughter,' is what he said. Twelve words I'll never forget!"

Refuting nothing I've said, Della allows me to simply run out of steam and reflect, knowing I'll find the answer myself soon enough.

Which, unfortunately, I do.

"Oh, God. Della," I break the long, uncomfortable silence. "He meant me. Ian was talking about *me*, wasn't he? *I'm* the sacrificial lamb!"

Della does not confirm this. Neither does she deny it. Which, for the second time tonight, serves as an answer in itself.

IV

"You believed for years that Ian killed your father. You were certain of it. The hate festered inside you, day after day as you sat alone and schemed between those stark, Godless walls at Barrow Moor. It clouded your eyes, as surely as mine are now. More so. But this morning you have experienced the truth of what happened, no matter how unpalatable, and that cataract has begun to dissolve. It's frightening, I know. But how will you respond when your vision is fully cleared, I wonder? When I reveal that far from killing me, your uncle Ian actually *saved* me that day?"

Despite dark ribbons of pain and fear coiling around my energy, I open my mind as Della tries to help me make sense of my new world. It's impossible to sit though, so I pace from one end of the two transepts to the other as I listen.

"For you to truly understand who you are and the part your uncle has played, I have to share with you what you were not able to re-experience. Are you familiar with the Gnostic Gospel of Thomas and the Infancy Gospels that were discovered, among other ancient texts, in Nag Hammadi, Egypt?"

I've heard of Christian documents that were found in the forties and have since been proven to match the oldest known New Testament documents in material, age, and writing style. And that an increasing number of academics and theologians agree they are as authentic as the traditionally accepted gospels decreed by the Council of Hippo, over sixteen-hundred years ago.

"Make no mistake," Della warns. "They paint a very unorthodox picture of both Christianity and Christ and can be disturbing." With no dramatic intent she adds: "The Infancy Gospel makes at least three references to Jesus as a child taking another's life. In each case the life of another child, no less."

She lets that sink in for a minute, aware that any faith I currently have in my own inner light is now overshadowed by the stark new realization that it was me who telekinetically pulled that trigger.

"Many feel this is where the second century Greek priest, Arius, derived the Christian doctrine of Arianism in Alexandria, Egypt."

"Excuse me? *Arianism*?"

"Not the hateful Nazi ideology spelled with a 'Y'. Arianism with an 'I' is a spiritual doctrine set forth nearly two thousand years ago. In it, Arius proposed that Jesus was, indeed, the son of God ... but *created by* God, as opposed to being one with Him. This means that for Arius and those who flocked to his theory, the life of Christ was one of *attaining* enlightenment as opposed to it being divinely and inherently his. In many ways, it could be said that viewed through this lens, Jesus's life is even more beautiful."

"And this is what you believe?"

"Oh, child. There are so many ideas across so many cultures and religions that if I were to share with you how they all intersect to form my own personal belief set it would take as many years as I have lived. What I *can* tell you is that religious theory will never be a tangible like science. Everyone's journey to God is personal, and very much their own. There are no Absolutes here. Don't ever let anyone tell you otherwise. For ignorance and rigid dogma is not the keeper of Light but the enemy of it. If there's one thing I've learned, it's that spiritual Truth can usually be found at the point of intersection of commonly held belief, personal testimony ... and myth. Find where they all meet, and truth will be found close by."

It's a valid point, and one which I will ponder in time. But I still don't connect the dots with its relevance to the experience I've just had. So Della continues to draw the lines for me, revealing that one of the most important commonalities between Christianity and Judaism is found in the ancient Hebrew *Book of Enoch* and John the Apostle's New Testament *Book of Revelation.*

"The prophet Enoch wrote of a class of angels known as the Grigori, or Watchers. Sent to earth by God to watch over mankind, they were heralded as the most beautiful of angels. But their leader, Azazel, became envious of the prominence God bestowed upon his mortal children. He turned the Watchers away from God by seeding their own perversions of offspring with humans, called Nephilim. In doing so, they were forever denied God's grace."

"So, they were fallen angels ... or what we call demons?" I stare at the surreal, serpent-like beast in the west rose window high above, residual fear contracting my lungs.

Della nods.

"But not all of the Watchers forsook God, Diane. A small number resisted Azazel, condemning him and his followers. All of them, however, were fated to remain here on earth. And so, from this moment on, there became two factions. The majority who sought the Darkness were banished by God to molder within it. These fallen angels became known as the Shadows, by every sense of the word. The few that still embraced God's Light, however, were tasked with containing them. These earthbound angels became known as the Shadow Watchers, and over the millennia it has been their mission to protect mankind from the Darkness the Shadows wield. Until, that is, the time of Judgment. The time which the Apostle John foretold shall be—"

"—Now," I conclude.

"Yes. If by 'now' you mean the past twenty-eight years. And who knows how many years more to come."

"And my uncle. Supposedly saving your life. He fits into this whole ancient scenario how, exactly ... ?"

"There are some perceived by the Shadows as threats. Mortals who, if not able to fully derail their mission, have the faculty to at least throw a wrench in their plans, if you will. After years of me laying low, God and the Universe brought me to your uncle and your father. That encounter was not my choice. But helping them *was*. And in doing so, I put myself on the Shadows' radar. Your uncle saved me from their destruction that night. Or worse," she adds with an unconscious quiver in her voice, "the absorption of my Light."

"So if he helped you, Uncle Ian must be one of the Shadow *Watchers*? Surely."

"Oh my. No, child. Ian Cockerton is very much human. As am I." Della is focusing inward now, a faraway look in her eyes. For once, I am receiving the emotion she does not intend to cast. Either her psychic energy is depleting, or I'm getting better at this. "At first, I believed Bryan—your father—had killed himself. The ultimate sacrifice. Like Christ, I believed he had given his life for you. For there is no brighter Light than to put another before yourself. But then it became clear that your uncle had killed your father. All the signs pointed to that being true. It may have taken eighteen years, but your father became the seventh scapegoat to Azazel."

"But we but w-we k-know it w-wasn't Uncle Ian—" Drowning sorrow again rises, and I am incapable of finishing the admission of my new reality which Della has known for years.

"No, that's right, child. What you re-experienced tonight is the truth. It was you who pulled that trigger. This was revealed to me the morning I was nearly taken by the Shadows. It was the next-to-the-last thing I saw."

"And the *last* thing?"

"I saw your uncle's face. The anguish in it. The Light that had been so bright and now was stifled to nothing but a match glow. I saw that he had given it freely to the Shadows. Not by spiritual choice, but in exchange."

"Exchange? For what, exactly, Della. Riches? Immortality? What did that piece of shit get in exchange for selling his soul?"

"You still don't understand." The silence in the cathedral becomes deafening. So intense it is a sound in itself. "He got *you*, child. Now, do you see? What he got in exchange was your life. And your soul to remain bathed in the Light."

Disoriented and stunned, I'm roiling in spiritual upheaval as comprehension washes over me and my reality yet again changes forever. Past, present and future now viewed through this new lens.

Because I was the one the Darkness wanted all along.

"So, that day in the Little Woods—"

"—Was intended to be your baptism into the realm of the Shadows," Della confirms. "You were never a lure, child … but the catch. All along."

"And Uncle Ian willingly took my place? You're saying he is paying the price for me killing my daddy?"

"Yes, sugar. He has been paying that debt for years. And he will pay it forever more. It was a choice he made because he knows who you are. He did what he knew had to be done."

V

I don't understand the 'who you are' part, but deep inside I believe that what Della is telling me is true. I'm still processing it. Reconciling it. With the life I thought to be real … only to learn that so much has been upside down. Yet a part of me still tries to resist, and there's bitterness in my voice as I throw out the last possible challenge to maintain the walls I'd built around my old reality.

"And your sight, Della? If what you're saying is true and Ian is a hero, tell me what happened to your beautiful eyes!"

She's disappointed in my final attempt to reject what I know, deep down, is the truth. I feel it. Thick and heavy. The way my father's voice dispelled the enchantment of the cathedral as it turned into what I felt was a magical wood.

"I was lying unconscious at the bottom of the tavern's old wooden staircase when Ian poured acid into my eyes. He threw me in the back of your mother's Blazer. Then dropped me in the woods, far away from anyone or anything I knew."

She declares it with such casual resolve there's no way I've understood her properly.

"You have," she asserts.

And this is your hero? I cast the doubt so aggressively that she picks up on it as easily as if it had been spoken.

"The Shadows are fallen angels, Diane. Soldiers of God turned mercenaries of Satan. An army of Darkness who, from this point forward, are no longer required to be held in check by the Shadow Watchers. Though I could not see them, they saw me. They were beginning to consume me. Wrapping their dark energy around mine, dimming my light until it was all but extinguished. I had begun cursing God and the Universe. Doubting my faith. Fear and weakness causing me to recant a lifetime of enlightenment. Which was the most frightening of all—how easily I was yielding. If your uncle had not come, I ... I ...."

Della turns away from me, her voice but a whisper.

"That's enough now, Diane. I can't. I won't. I promised long ago that I will no longer allow myself to even entertain the thought of what could have happened. Not even if it helps expose the false safety you cling so tightly to."

"False safety? If anyone's deluding themselves here, Della ...." I stop short of finishing the verbal dressing-down, as if that makes a difference. "So, tell me, exactly. Ian's blinding you with acid saved you *how* ...?"

I expect her to turn with her voice sharpened and ready to lambast me. To treat me like the stubborn, insensitive child I am being. Instead, she remains with her back to me. Her voice sullen and withdrawn.

"Because they were able to see through my eyes, Diane. Find me through my sight. To see whatever I saw; recognize the people and places that I did. When your uncle blinded me, the Shadows were no longer able to find me—or anyone else close to me—because, when I woke up two days later? Even I didn't know where I was."

There's a stillness between us as I have no other argument to refute a single thing DeLaCroix's telling me, and I feel the barrier I've erected between her world and mine starting to dissolve.

Whether I like it or not.

"I failed him, Diane. And your father. I failed your mother...and Andrew. Now it appears that I am failing you, too."

Della claims she's as human as anyone. But in my world, only a saint can be blinded by a man, dumped alone in the woods injured and unconscious, then turn around to say it was *she* who failed *him*.

Her energy is shining less bright, but there's a warmth that builds as my wall comes fully down, removing the distance between us both literally and metaphorically.

"That's not true, Della. How could you think that?"

"I should have seen what was happening. If I'd only understood then what I do now, your father—and Andrew—might still be alive. And your uncle might still be walking in the Light."

"Maybe there's a chance we can still reach...that part of Ian...?"

Della shakes her head.

"Any Light that remained in your uncle has been extinguished a very, very long time ago now. When he hid me from the Shadows it had been only a few days after what happened in the woods; after offering himself to the Darkness in lieu of you. And yet even at such an early stage I could feel the tendrils which had begun to wrap so tightly around his soul. Stifling his Light."

Hearing the passion in Della's voice, I'm ashamed at how wrong I've been. About so much. Especially my uncle.

"I was sure he was going to kill me when he broke into the tavern that night, Diane. Not protect me." Della takes in a long, deep breath, and I sense there had once been affection between her and my uncle. It's not vibrations or one of my interruptions or psychic energy of any kind. Just, as my mom would say, good ol' fashioned women's intuition. "But that man doesn't exist any longer."

VI

I'm again studying the rose window in the west transept, keeping at bay the unease it elicits as I try to identify the last part of its message. The artist has portrayed the second demon above the gates of Hell as much more humanoid than the first. It possesses an air of innocence which he conveys through the visual metaphor of two small nibs poking from its soft curly hair. Much as you might see atop a lamb's head. But at the same time, a cone of fire is billowing from its mouth.

"The Dragon Lamb," Della explains, aware of where I'm looking, though it is not possible that she can see me or the window. "A very literal interpretation, but it achieves what the artist intended."

Something is beginning to feel odd as I gaze at the stained glass.

A disturbing sense of familiarity I can't describe…

"What most people don't understand," she continues, "is that it was not Satan who placed the demons among us…but God…when he banished all of the Watchers to remain forever earthbound. This is where the overlap between the Book of Enoch and the Book of Revelation provides the key to your new reality."

… I'm sure I've seen this second demon before. It has the same disturbing vibration as the memory of a nebulous monster in a recurring night terror from my childhood. Dreams I had long before that day in the woods that changed everything…

"Azazel, the leader of the Watchers prophesied by Enoch, and the seven-headed Beast prophesied by Saint John, are one in the same Presence of Evil. Banished to its place in the wilderness, upon the day of Judgment, the archdemon shall be unleashed with his army of Shadows. No longer governed by the Shadow Watchers, they will mock the seven archangels by feeding upon seven innocents. They will then fulfill the prophecy by propagating the most perverse Nephala of all: the Dragon Lamb of Satan."

...And the icy realization dawns.

"That face. Oh my God, Della. That *face* ... it looks just like—"

"—Simon Peter?" Della asks rhetorically and I feel my legs becoming weak. "I know you've had your suspicions about Simon. Also your doubts about those. But your vibrations, Diane, have always been right. Simon Peter is not your brother—or even your mother's son—but the unholy prophecy fulfilled. His very name is a mockery, being the same as the holy Apostle of Christ who was the brother of Andrew and leader of the twelve."

There's an instant, dramatic drop in temperature in the cathedral and I feel the chill deep in my bones.

"He is the one who has come to deceive and corrupt; to turn us from God and Love until the Universal Balance is irrevocably weighted toward Darkness ...."

VII

I don't know how long I've sat here processing this staggering web of information, any single thread of which the average person will never have to process in a lifetime. But the light has begun to dim and the air has grown damp and cold, my fingers icy to the touch.

Everything's coming to a head now, and I'm not sure it's a feeling I like. Let me rephrase that.

I know it's not.

Why does it feel like I'm being led ever closer to a situation that I should be running from, as far and fast as I can?

At the altar, Della has been kneeling in silent prayer. I've tried to eavesdrop on her meditation, but she has turned off that channel, forcing me to reflect on everything in my own way.

I'm trying the best I can, but keep coming back to my promise to

Andrew. It's time I tell Della that we have to get my mom away from Ian and Simon Peter. I've no idea how we're going to safely get her out of the apartment. But whatever we do, it has to be tonight.

I promised Andrew I wouldn't leave without her.

Blowing on my fingers to warm them achieves nothing, and I'm getting an urgent feeling that it's time for us to be going.

"Hey, Della?" I call out quietly enough that I don't startle her, but loud enough to inject myself into her meditative trance.

She hasn't heard me, so I call again. A little louder.

Nothing.

Now I'm on my feet and leaning awkwardly as I stumble out from the narrow pew to see her at the altar. Still in the same spot, she has not moved in what's been hours now. But then again, neither have I. But this feels wrong somehow. Our old friend, the bowling ball, has dropped into my stomach. Weighing on my gut so that my lungs feel burdened.

"Della?"

My walk has quickened to a trot.

"Hey. Della!"

Still nothing.

My trot becomes a run.

She's stiff and unmoving when I place my hand on her shoulder.

Oh my God. Pleaaaase....

"Hey...DeLaCroix...? You okay...?"

Her eyes are closed but I breathe a sigh of relief when a vapor of warm air flows from her unmoving lips. It suspends in the air as a visible mist before the cloud dissipates and wafts away.

Mine is doing the same but with more intensity as my quickened heartbeat produces brief, fast puffs. I lean close to listen to the sound of her breathing and see that her lips are dry and paling. Her cheeks, just like her fingers intertwined in prayer, are beginning to lighten to the same translucent shade of grey.

The temperature in the cathedral is falling dramatically.

To unnatural levels.

And fast.

"Della?" I whisper, cupping my trembling hands over hers to warm them. Woven tensely together, they're freezing cold and rigid. I reflexively jerk mine away, a shudder passing through me from the unexpected feel of them.

Another haze mists thinly from her lips, so I know she's still alive.

But for how long?

I'm wringing the blood back into my numbing fingers as the sun that shone so brilliantly fades from the nave. Its spectrum of golden light has inverted, daubing the ancient stone walls in cold cyans and violets. It deepens the shadows lurking in every nook.

The columns are blemished with more cracks than I noticed before, and I take a hesitant step backward as they come alive to a sound I can only describe as two hundred years of aging condensed into a handful of minutes.

I feel my pulse growing in my neck. A line of ants march down my spine when—

please, Della, wake up!

—the immense timber doors fly open as effortlessly as plywood. I spin around sharply, clutching my chest. What's left of the perishing daylight sweeps in to play its pale light across the tombs and columns and vaults, animating every shadow. I flinch again when the doors slam against the interior walls, a curtain of splintered wood and flakes of broken stone raining down.

A deafening, reverberating clap follows.

As my mother lurches through.

I stumble backward as her silhouette collapses to the floor amid a patchwork of broken tiles ....

4:28

HER WAIL OF pain splinters the rafters but I'm too much in shock for it to register. *Is this really happening right now, or is it more psychedelic hallucinations of yet another repressed event from my fucked-up past?*

I decide it doesn't matter either way and run to her.

"Mama?"

"Get away!"

The enmity in her voice is so profound it stops me in my tracks.

"Mama. It's me. Deedee."

"I said, get away, Diane! Get…AWAY FROM ME!"

She's thin. *So thin.* Her once beautiful, strawberry-blonde hair is matted straw. Her limbs pointed and bony where muscle once flexed. In my mind she's forever remained the beautiful, vibrant, thirty-four-year-old with the killer smile and enviable figure her teenage daughter hoped one day to boast.

But as if tripling the years since then, she looks every bit the frail old lady. Sixty rings more true than early forties. And even then, only if the sixty-year-old were unwell and idle.

Then I see the blood. So much blood.

It's saturated the bottom of the simple full-length gown she wears. To the casual observer she might be sporting a white blouse over a long skirt cut from a fabric of muddied reds and browns.

She begins clawing her way across the filthy, uneven floor that's layered thick with pigeon feces and crumbling stone. I'm still too stunned to notice that the cathedral is disintegrating by the minute before my very eyes.

"Mama! What happened?" I drop to my knees and grab her hand. It's caked in drying blood and rife with the scent of rusty iron. Her face is ashen. I dare to lower my gaze to the gown clinging to her inner thighs. It's sodden with dark red patches that continue to grow. "My God, Mama! You're bleeding so bad!"

"*Go. Babygirl,*" my mother pleads in my ear, her words staccato and thin between the sucking hiccups of a suppressed sob. "*Please, Deedee. Go. Now. Befor—*"

Her appeal is clipped as Simon Peter emerges in the cathedral's antechamber, the dusky backlight glowing in a wispy, flickering corona around the nine-year-old as he slowly climbs the stairs.

In his right hand, dangling by its legs like a skinned rabbit, the newborn baby screams.

Increasingly magnified the deeper Simon Peter moves through the cathedral, the baby's cries are a high-pitched peal that rings through the vaulted chambers to send shivers down my spine.

Still attached to the baby by the umbilical cord, the placenta drags behind them like a sack of wet sand through the grit and droppings to leave a trail of blood-smeared mucous. It periodically snags on the ragged corners of broken tile, forcing Simon to tug on the fleshy, twisted cord to yank the sack free.

"Thought I'd save you the hassle of coming to us. You know, seeing as I'm your half-brother, 'n all. Isn't that nice of me? So here she is—your disgusting sow of a mother."

He relishes the stunned horror on my face. Adds to it by lifting the newborn high above and in front of him, displaying it like a prized catch. Fighting for life, the baby boy is still covered in a white, gelatinous film mixed with the blood of my—his—*our*—mother.

"Oh, this?" Depraved glee lights across Simon's face, sickening every layer of my soul. "Yeah, look what we found!"

We?

I don't intend for Simon to hear it. But you know he does and thumbs the air behind him to indicate my uncle who appears in the massive doorway. Ian's forearms are painted red to his elbows. Behind him, dozens more begin filing into the cathedral in a parade of silence. Each in the same white gown as my mother.

As the baby's torment fills my ears.

He can't be anywhere close to full-term. Suspended upside-down and stretched thin, his body is still barely over a dozen inches long. His innocent little face is beet red as the blood drains to his head, his mouth and fingers curling in unison as he wails.

I've never seen a thing more vulnerable. Or innocent. And I feel sick to my stomach as Simon Peter bobs him up and down by ankles so small I'm sure they're about to snap. Maybe they already have, because his wails have risen so high in pitch they've become a jarring whistle.

"Seems your uncle and that whore of a mother made this pathetic half-breed example of a Nephala five months ago. Twenty-one weeks, to be precise. Here, do you want to see it?" He lowers the baby as if he's going to throw him, and I am paralyzed with terror. "No? Okay then. Well, anyway. I had your uncle rip this annoying bastard from your cunt mother. Or maybe I should say, from your mother's cunt. Haha. Not ten minutes ago. Seems the ginger slut went from not being able to *have* kids to not being able to *stop having* them. And, well, there's just no room for another. You see, as Della rightly explained, *I* am the Alpha and the Omega. And aside from being a bit of fun to yank this abomination out of her, I figured it might turn out to be a half-decent bargaining chip."

For?

Again my mental reply is reflex. Instinct. And I'm angry at myself for even thinking it, let alone allowing it to be cast from my mind. I couldn't care less what this malignant worm parading as a nine-year-old wants. My mother is bleeding to death, her unborn baby torn from her womb, and Della is paralyzed on her knees at the altar. All I want is to grab that baby, pull my mother off the floor ... and run like hell for help.

Almost exasperated, Simon Peter rolls his eyes.

Are you trying to be irksome, Deedee, or are you just that lacking in control of your abilities?

"Seriously," he adds out loud. "I hear everything you're thinking. You stupid, insignificant slit. And yes, I knew that was precisely how you'd react. Hence the trade. So ...."

He flicks his wrist so the baby is tossed right-side-up, gurgling exaggerated baby-talk at him as its little face begins to go purple.

Its cries weakening.

"...Whaddya say there, Deedee? I'll give you exactly what you want. Minus the part where *you* are running—ahem, interesting choice of words—'like hell.'"

My mother is now lifeless in the dirt of the stone floor, her skin greying. In a wide circle around me, the freaks in white gowns have managed to form a perimeter without me noticing.

The baby's cries are fading, his body turning blue.

And constant glances behind me prove that Della's breathing has slowed to a point that I don't know how long it's been since the last one wafted a wisp of condensation into the frigid air.

"What is it that you want!"

"Me?" Simon Peter looks insulted. It's a good show, because for a moment, I almost forget who he—*what it*—is. "I want nothing, child. It's what I've been commanded by my father to get." His voice has changed. Sounding a little like ... Della's. "Something he's been owed for quite some time."

"Stop playing games!" My uncle Ian pushes forward, grabbing the baby from Simon Peter. For a moment it stops crying, seeming to recognize him as its father, though I know that's not possible.

Ian tugs the placenta from the floor and pulls me by the arm. I don't know why I fail to resist as he marches me to an adjoining alcove in the shape of a hexagon where a short structure, only as high as my knee, matches the geometry. Filled with water, if it were in a different setting, you'd be forgiven for thinking it was a kind of spa or Turkish bath.

A tattered, leather-bound book rests on an ornate podium beside it. The paper is delicate and edged in gold but covered in black mold. Barely visible at the top of the open page, 'The Rite of Baptism' is written in beautiful calligraphy.

My uncle throws the baby into my arms and I barely feel its weight. Its blue eyes are dimming, his mouth puckering.

I tried, Diane. My uncle's vibration is weak. Filled with static and exhaustion. But it's a message I alone receive, Simon Peter unaware. *God help me, Deedee. I tried. But I can't any longe—*

"—Kill it," Uncle Ian demands with a complete absence of passion, talking over his own mental transmission as if it is coming from a different identity. His voice is grating and layered, the sound of a legion speaking as one. When my reply is nothing but stunned silence, he screams it at me. "KILL IT!"

A thick vapor of breath ushers his words into the ether.

I shrink away, clutching the baby tight to my breast in an effort to keep him safe and warm. He's barely moving now, his temperature so low that coolness penetrates my shirt as I pull him close. I'm shaking my head in disbelief.

"Kill the half-breed!" Ian demands, his face gnarled and wrong.

"I won't!"

Before I can dodge it, my uncle's fist fills with my hair, jerking me around to face the baptismal font. I pivot so sharply, the baby nearly falls from my grip.

"Kill the runt!"

"NO!"

Still gripping a tangled lock of my hair, Ian mentally broadcasts the last plea I'll ever receive: *Please, babygirl! It's the only way—I can't hold on much longer.*

Simon Peter is studying me closely. Probing my mind. He seems bewildered at his inability to read anything but compassion.

"If you're worried about the half-breed, I can tell you, sister, that it's but a hundred torturous heartbeats from death already. You'd be putting the runt out of its misery by drowning it."

He attempts a bearing of consolation, but the expression is repugnant and brimming with contempt.

"When you fill its lungs with water it won't feel a thing. It's far too young. Even the doctors say so . . . just before their scalpels and curettes slice those babies into nice little vacuum-sized pieces." His eyes are empty and black as night. "Why would I lie?"

Ian yanks my head aloft by the twisted plait of hair in his fist, stretching my neck so taut that my muscles bulge, my pulse visible beneath the skin. It's impossible to turn my head in any direction, but Simon catches my eyes straining to see my mother. They widen, flaring white as I find her slumped over and motionless, her face in the pool of blood growing darker. Thickening.

"Oh, yes. Forgive me. I spoke of an exchange. In return for your loyalty to me, I will ensure that your slag of a mother lives."

At the opposite end of the cathedral Della remains frozen in a pose of permanent prayerfulness.

"Yes, okay," he adds with a tinge of vexation. "The witch, too. In fact, I'll even return her sight. How 'bout that?"

I yank my head sharply, freeing my hair from Ian's grip so that I may gaze upon the baby boy embraced to my bosom. His bright blue eyes are slowly closing. His breaths sparse. I'm wavering on my feet, my eyes filling. I can't stop shaking as I find myself actually moving closer to the font, disbelief devouring me. My arms have gone weak, the baby a hundred pounds if he's an ounce.

Cruel anticipation brightens Simon Peter's face.

I know he's right. The baby hasn't much longer to live. As I lower his head toward the water, I can feel his life already ebbing away.

Decades of my mother's life. And Della's, plus her sight . . . in exchange for the last minute of this child's anguished existence.

It's an impossible choice, but one I must make before fate makes it for me. I've so often said I would do anything if it meant my mother were back in my life again. But did I truly mean *anything?*

As if aware of the sacrifice I am about to offer it, the water begins to roil and darken in response. Now it's swirling in a clockwise whorl. Faster and faster.

The baby has gone silent, his fingers barely twitching as I lower the crown of his head to the surface so black it's become a mirror. And I see myself in it, leaning over the font. The ugliness in a face I no longer recognize, the depravity and decay of a monster as repellant as those in the west window's stained glass.

And it finally dawns that it is not the water that has grown dark, but the air above me. Air that has become alive with sound.

Hissing.

Screeching.

Jangling.

The inharmonic shrieks of a thousand primitive flutes.

The sound of the Shadows.

Filling the air above me, they eclipse the last of the light. Bodies both ethereal and solid at once, they are vile gargoyles with wings of tar and faces the epitome of pain and suffering and hate.

I choke on the realization and pull the baby to me, frantically wiping the murky, viscous water from the back of his head. But he has gone still, his body limp.

Saving me from the impossible choice.

"Okay, well you had your chance," Simon Peter declares as he snatches the baby from my arms and tosses his lifeless body into the font where it momentarily floats as if swimming. "Now your mother will die. Della will die. And you, my dear sister, will die."

The Shadows shriek with such a repugnant sound that electric fear skewers through my body. My heart is tripping over its own rhythm as my muscles stiffen, my feet anchored to the ground. I'm frozen in a cocoon of dark horror as the circling Shadows descend.

Behind me, the grinding of heavy chain and creaking wood rings out from the pulpit.

"*Wait!* Take me. *Take me!*"

My uncle Ian's voice. The voice I remember. Warm and earnest, and so like my father's.

"Oh, dear Uncle," Simon Peter tuts as the sound of the chains quicken. "We've tried that once, remember ... ? You were a cheap likeness my father never wanted in the first place. And still, in ten years it seems you have yet to grant him your unfailing gratitude."

A deafening thud booms through the cathedral, a cloud of dust billowing like smoke.

"Tell you what. You finally prove that, and I'll honor the compact I offered the self-righteous neophyte. The sow Rebecca will live."

He follows Ian's eyes as they seek the statuesque figure kneeling at the communion rail.

"The harpy, too. Yes. Same deal. Eyesight and everything. In exchange for the testament of your absolute loyalty."

Simon Peter hands my uncle an archaic iron mallet as the Shadows wail and a dozen faceless people in white gowns pummel me to the ground. I cry out from pain I could never have conceived as they punch and kick, beating me until the snapping of my bones and ripping of my skin induces the vomit that fills my throat.

I fade into the numbing void as the cat o' nine tails fashioned from barbed wire shreds the flesh from my back and sides while the people spit and jeer. They dip their fingers into my wounds to savor the lifeforce in the blood that spatters and flows....

II

Its broad head peals in metallic, ear-splitting chimes as the mallet slams against a rusty nail as thick as a railway spike. It rips me unmercifully from the salve of unconsciousness as Ian again raises the hammer high above his shoulder. The others are holding me down, laughing and sneering as they pin my quaking forearm to rough-hewn timber I can feel but not see.

Recognition shocks me fully awake as I realize the sounds of the chains and deafening boom that had filled the cathedral are linked to the sensation of wood I now feel beneath my blood soaked arm.

They've lowered the life-size cross to the pulpit.

And I am stretched atop it.

Hulking and unwieldy, the cross pitches at an uneven incline upon the riser, it's long vertical post dropping at an awkward angle down the half-dozen stairs. I kick to free myself, but a multitude of hands squeeze my ankles together like a vice.

Ian brings down the hammer again and I scream in agony as the crude iron nail slams further through my wrist. Blood spritzes my uncle's face, the ferrous tang on his lips and in the air as the spike bores through muscle and tendon. Another strike and it embeds into the wood beneath as I shriek in unimaginable pain. One more hit and the bones in my wrist snap as the wide head of the thick stake burrows beneath my skin, pinning bone to bone.

My face and chest are covered in vomit. Blood pours over my eyes as someone loops the cat o' nine tails into a series of bands and presses it into my scalp. Wire barbs burrow under the skin of my forehead. Through an eyelid. They bite into the bone at the rear of my skull as my head is slammed against the timber to secure the torturous headdress in place.

I hear the sickening sound of the bones in my feet breaking as Ian pins them together to the wood, my knees bent at a forty-five-degree angle. I do not feel it, however, as my body has exceeded its faculty for a neurological response to pain. I sense only the reverberant shudder as each clout of the mallet travels through the wood in a wave up to my head. And the unnatural way my legs bend as Ian breaks them just above the knee.

Now the chains have begun to clatter and the cross dislodges from its tenuously balanced station on the pulpit. It slides down the half-dozen steps and pinwheels to a jarring thump as they yank hard on the chains. Fastened to the colossal timbers, I am spun upside-down. As the blood flows from my face and my sight clears, I find my mother's eyes fixed upon me in shock and inconceivable sorrow. She is on her knees, wailing and reaching as Della holds her tight. The tears also stream from DeLaCroix's eyes. They are no longer clouded but have been restored, once again the most beautiful pale grey I've always remembered.

The women spin in a half-circle as the cross is tugged upright and begins lurching toward the ceiling. Notch-by-notch the ponderous chains are hefted ever tighter until I am hoisted high above the altar. Swaying in the air as the chains are secured, the cross is a massive pendulum tracing slow, diminishing ovals until we are motionless.

My shoulders have wrested from their sockets. My elbows and wrists follow suit as my arms stretch longer than a human can bear. The weight of my body is now supported by my torso as my ribcage rises to pull my lungs in an endless cycle of rapid, shallow inhalations without the ability to exhale.

I know I am suffocating.

Blood and fluid fill my chest as I hang high above the ruin of the cathedral that sprawls before me in its prior glory. What was once an awe-inspiring monument to God and Light is revealed to me now as the dank and dilapidated tomb it has been since long before I was born. The floor I thought so elaborate boasts only an uneven collection of broken stone tiles littered with waste and debris. The marble walls are damp and darkened by mold; scribbled with graffiti. Half the columns have long ago crumbled, causing the skyscraping vaulted ceiling to collapse in more places than it hasn't. Beyond is a bleak afternoon sky filled with storm clouds that stifle the July sun as the sky crackles with distant lightning.

I take my last insufficient breath as Poe appears in one of the empty rose windows. Their beauty has shattered decades before, a thousand shards of light having fallen to the earth.

The last sound I hear is the raven's mournful cawing as my chin drops to my chest. Della is knelt before me, eyes glistening. Her arms outstretched in reverence as she mouths:

'Forgive me...'

FIFTH
DISCIPLE

I saw a new heaven and a new earth,

for the first had passed away.

—Revelation 21:1

The Shadow Watcher

5:29

DETECTIVE MAGGIE ROMANO approached the historic ruins of what had once been St. Martin's cathedral with an air of trepidation that slowed her steps. Holding the perimeter, two uniformed officers had primed her for what she was about to see. And as a result, the scene Maggie painted in her mind was abhorrent.

Despite the years behind her, Maggie's imagination still never could prepare her for the real thing. Which was always, horrendously, worse. So, the idea of what awaited her inside the crumbling church, in the middle of an eerie, rain-soaked night, made the detective feel sick to her stomach.

And with good reason.

She offered a thin, sympathetic smile as she passed the two women wrapped in blankets and huddled close together in the rear of the ambulance.

Picking her way through the rubble and careful not to stumble on the slicing edges of countless broken bottles—or worse, a discarded needle—Maggie swept her flashlight back and forth as she navigated through the decay. Every once in a while, the old walls would moan as the summer storm made itself known through the expansive building, occasional flights of wind gusting between the maze of columns. She couldn't help but wonder if the structure were sound enough to support the portion of roof that remained. After all, it had been condemned and fenced off for longer than she could remember, the only parishioners passing through here in recent decades being devotees of the street.

Approaching the hexagonal baptistery, she clapped a hand over her mouth to mute the natural reaction her heart had never permitted her to stifle. At the font, a crime scene officer was busy taking photographs. With each garish, strobing flash, the heartbreaking image of a baby, so small it must surely be a fetus, was exposed bobbing in the stagnant water. Still connected to its placenta by the umbilical cord, the sack laid in the droppings that spackled the cathedral floor.

Maggie remained several minutes, observing in silence as her investigatory eyes took in the scene. Only once this was done did she allow her empathetic eyes to fill with moisture. She cared little if the crime scene officer noticed, but must have reflexively glanced away when the woman turned to pack up her camera.

"It's okay, Detective," the officer assured Romano quietly. "I did more than that. I'm guessing you haven't seen the altar yet ...."

II

Maggie's chest tightened, a knot constricting her throat as she turned the corner for the nave to stretch out before her.

At its far end: an actual crucifixion.

Hoisted by rusted chains above what still remained of the pulpit, the body of a young woman was bathed in the warm, golden glow of a half dozen work lights that sizzled in the spritzing rain. Her head was drooped to the side, her facial features shrouded by the thick veil of blood that had flowed from the wounds in her scalp like wax from a red candle. From her hands and feet, more of the same. Her legs were clearly broken; her arms grotesquely long and deformed, thin as the skin and muscle that covered them at each joint where the bones had dislocated.

Detective Romano stood and wept, unashamed.

5:30

THIRTY HOURS LATER she sat in Rebecca Cockerton's hospital room with DeLaCroix Laveau. Having gone over both women's statements as much as she felt necessary, this morning she had come in the capacity of a friend (albeit a new one) to offer what support she could.

When the call came in, she was glad she made the choice to do so.

Diane's mother had been awake for some time, succumbing to episodes of guilt-soaked grief that shattered long periods of numb stillness. Occasionally, she offered a forced smile or self-conscious chortle in response to one of Romano's corny jokes. It was during one of the latter that Della returned, showing her I.D. to the officer at the door while balancing a tray of black coffee for the detective, Earl Grey for Rebecca, and an herbal tea for herself.

"What'd I miss?"

"Oh, I assure you, it's not worth repeating." Romano winked at Rebecca then mouthed 'thanks' to Della as she slid the coffee from the tray and savored the aroma rising in the steam. "Just another of my terrible Dad Jokes. I wouldn't dare make Rebecca endure it twice. And frankly, it's not even funny enough for you to hear once."

She excused herself moments later when her phone vibrated in her pocket. Stepping into the corridor, Maggie Romano was visibly shaken when she returned.

"I'm afraid we've had an incident." Unlike the woman who had spent the morning sharing their pain and passing the time by talking about everything and nothing at all, the person now speaking was *Detective* Maggie Romano. She closed the distance between them to stand at Rebecca's bedside. "You know we've not only posted a uniformed officer here for your protection, but also two at the morgue where your daughter's body awaits autopsy."

"No, I didn't know that." Rebecca's voice was a distant whisper. She raised the head of the hospital bed until it approximated a seated position. "Two officers?"

Romano nodded. "We know your stories line up with what happened to your daughter Friday. And I assure you we're doing everything we can to keep the Church of the New Apocrypha in our sites. But here's the hurdles we're facing. For a start, we have no way of pinning Clive Astor's murder on your husb—"

"—He's not my husband."

"I'm sorry, your brother-in-law. We have nothing to charge Ian with Astor's death. At best, we could grab him for incitement to riot, maybe. But even that's paper thin. Every piece of information we have tells us that a man called Greer Eliason is solely responsible. And he's managed to vanish into the woodwork."

"And?"

"And you're aware of rumors of a second murder. A ritual involving Antoine J. Washington so disturbing that, if it's true, is beyond comprehension. But there's no evidence. No body. And—if you'll excuse the dad pun—no-body associated with the church who will talk. So, until we learn otherwise, Mr. Washington is *officially* alive and well somewhere." Here Detective Romano's gaze lingered just a little longer on Rebecca's. "But I think you and I can agree, we both know that's not the truth."

"Darlin', I'm sorry to hail your trolley," Della interrupted, the anxiety in her voice evident despite the lightness she attempted to inject with the colloquialism. "But...only *one* officer here. And *two* at the mor—" She refused to give the word life. "—Where Diane is? I don't see how that makes any kind of sense."

"Well. For a start," Romano answered, "don't forget that as well as the officer outside, I'm here too. And we don't believe they'd be so bold as to come after Rebecca. Not now, at least. And not like this. But we feared they might try to come for Diane's body. Remove the only evidence we have that can stop their movement in its tracks. They're aware we have nothing on the other two deaths. So right now, your daughter is all we—"

"My *dead* daughter."

"Yes. Your deceased daughter is all we have to make sure these sickos, your brother-in-law included, are put away. And see that Simon Peter gets the help that deluded boy needs."

At the sound of his name Della bristled. "But you said there was an incident? You came back in looking pretty upset."

Romano perched at the edge of the bed after politely asking Rebecca's permission. She gestured for Della to have a seat as well, but the woman remained standing at Rebecca's side, taking her hand and gently weaving her fingers into the mother's.

"Yes." Romano's voice was unsteady despite the breath she carefully governed. "That call was my Lieutenant. At the morgue."

She stood back up, anxious energy preventing her from being stationary as she dug deep for a way to say what had to be said. Her voice quivered as she stared down at her own hands, watching them repeatedly clench and unclench.

"I'm very sorry to report that your daughter is no longer at the morgue, Mrs. Cockerton—"

"Noooo!" Rebecca burst into a flood of instant tears. "Please tell me that's wrong! Haven't they done enough to my poor baby! Please tell me they haven't taken Diane from me...a third time!"

"Apparently my two uniforms are pretty shook up about it and—"

"—*They're* shook up? How dare you! How do you think *I* feel!" Rebecca's seething anger submitted to her sorrow as quickly as it had overpowered it. "A-A-All I w-w-wanted was to say g-goodbye.

To be able to b-bury m-my b-b-babygirl!"

Maggie again sat on the edge of the bed, cupping her hand over Rebecca's. The mother rejected the touch and looked away as the tears ran in lines down her cheeks.

"The officers who were posted outside the door aren't upset because the Church of the New Apocrypha took your daughter's body, Rebecca. They're saying ...."

Romano paused; cleared her throat one last time. The only way forward was to report the facts clearly and dispassionately. Exactly as they had been presented to her.

She consciously softened her tone.

"There is no one at the facility today. But they heard a sound from inside. One officer remained at the door while the other investigated. That senior officer has been on the force longer than me. And what he saw—"

Neither woman made a sound as unease thickened the room.

"—What he saw was *Diane*, Rebecca. Not her dead body. Not horizontal in the mortuary cabinet. But Diane *standing* there. Alive and breathing, and as real as you or I."

Her head in her hands, Rebecca's sobbing filled the room as she wrestled the battery of conflicting emotions immersing her.

"Do you understand what I'm telling you, Mrs. Cockerton? Both officers, as respected and level-headed as any on the force, have made official and matching statements that claim Diane—that your daughter—stood up and walked away from that morgue."

For Della, the spillways were thrown open, the dam of guilt discharging its murky waters to relieve the unbearable pressure they had exerted on her soul.

Praise be, oh glorious child of light! Forgive my betrayal of your corporeal body....

She squeezed Rebecca's hand, allowing the warmth of her hope to flow into the blessed mother.

II

Miles away, a withdrawn young woman squirmed in her seat. The cyclical thrum of the bus tires on the old highway had begun to finally lull her to peaceful sleep when Della's intercession prised its way past her thin veil of consciousness. The woman turned her palm skyward to again regard the wound in her wrist and the way the skin was already knitting together.

She leaned her head against the window and closed her eyes as Della's prayer continued to wash over her.

... For your mortal limitations are no more. Behold! The true Disciple has come to us upon a horse of Light. And an army of Heavenly warriors rides behind Her....

∞

A.G. MOCK is a two-time American Fiction Awards winner and online horror charts international #1 bestseller. He currently lives in rural South Carolina with his incredibly supportive wife, two peculiarly challenging but adorable rescue pups, and at least one harmless but mischievous ghost. This he knows because it likes to clatter about in the upstairs bedrooms and occasionally fill the house with its distinctive scent of warm leather, vanilla and tobacco.

His wife and dogs he treasures wildly; the ghost he can take or leave.

DISCIPLE is his second novel.

EPOCH

EpochThrillers.com

AGMock.com

~ the story continues ~

SHADOW WATCHERS

BOOK 3 OF THE GOTHIC HORROR SERIES

~ Please Leave a Review ~

I hope you enjoyed *Disciple* and feel it deserves five stars! If so, I would be honored if you'd take a moment to post a comment on Goodreads, Amazon, or your favorite book site. Please keep the literary arts full of fresh and diverse ideas by posting a review today! Thank you for being a reader, and I'll meet you in the Darkness again soon ...

~ Join My Inner Sanctum! ~

Receive personal updates before anyone else, pre-release offers, free book swag and more! Sign up for free at

AGMock.com *OR* EpochThrillers.com

~ Strike Up a Conversation! ~

Instagram • Facebook • Twitter • YouTube

@AGMockAuthor

Printed in the USA
CPSIA information can be obtained
at www.ICGtesting.com
LVHW052305080124
768489LV00035B/268